"*Utopia* is a marvel. Vividly beguiling on art, love, and what it means to be alive, every page thrums with magic."
— SOPHIE MACKINTOSH, AUTHOR OF *THE WATER CURE*

"*Utopia* is a bird's eye view of the desires of the human heart ... through characters who feel and live deeply at the boundaries of art and life. Sopinka's luminescent prose tackles the danger and vitality of artistic and bodily desire under the politically charged structures of masculine power ... with rawness, deep awareness, and razor-sharp critique ... This is an urgent book."
— ANGÉLIQUE LALONDE, AUTHOR OF *GLORIOUS FRAZZLED BEINGS*

"These brilliant and bold artists explode off the page as they try to transcend the boundaries of the material world in their work. But the most dangerous waters they must navigate are those of the male-dominated world of the 1970s, which erases their art and identities. Sopinka explores the minefield that is loving men in an oppressively patriarchal world. And she captures the volatility and power of female friendships, and the uncharted maps of women's untameable artistic drives."
— HEATHER O'NEILL, AUTHOR OF *WHEN WE LOST OUR HEADS*

"*Utopia* is interested in life as performance, in the ways that we attempt to transcend our own bodies, and in what it means to be a woman artist in a world that is run by and for men. Set against the backdrop of the arid California desert, full of scalding cups of diner coffee and burning tarmac highways, this is a book as seething as its parts."
— SABA SAMS, AUTHOR OF *SEND NUDES*

"With tense and glittering writing, Heidi Sopinka's *Utopia* blasts the dry desert sun onto the lives and afterlives of a circle of Californian artists, the women they are and the women they love. This is a thrilling book about artistic inheritance, jealousies, and affinities."
— LEANNE SHAPTON, AUTHOR OF *GUESTBOOK*
AND *SWIMMING STUDIES*

"Tense, sexy, and uncanny. *Utopia* shimmers with desert heat and burns with atmosphere. It's *Rebecca* meets *Zabriskie Point*. Luminous."

"*Utopia* is a searing novel about art, ownership, and the entanglement of power and performance. Heidi Sopinka's sentences have a bluish-orange intensity, a captivating energy that conjures a desert at dusk."

"*Utopia* is a study in contrasts: tart and poetic; sensitive and wild; bright and spooky like the LA light. It drove me onward; it let me linger. It made me angry; it inspired me. Above all, it clinches what we all suspected from *The Dictionary of Animal Languages*—Heidi Sopinka is a crazy good writer. I'd follow her anywhere."

"I was transfixed by Heidi Sopinka's incandescent prose. It blazed through me and touched my heart in the deepest, most tender place. *Utopia* is about a powerful bond between mother and daughter; the collision of art, performance, and female friendships; and how grief shapes our ability to love and hope. Sexy, devastating, and wise—this novel will make you feel alive."

"Flames of female rage run hot in this shimmering art-world ghost story ... Sensual, mysterious, and provocative, *Utopia* raises essential questions about women's marginalisation in the art world, loss of self and search for artistic grounding, the maternal impulse, and the demands of a life in art."

Utopia

Heidi Sopinka is the author of *The Dictionary of Animal Languages*, which was shortlisted for the Kobo Writing Emerging Writer Prize, and longlisted for the Royal Society of Literature Ondaatje Prize. A former environment columnist at *The Globe and Mail*, she is co-founder and co-designer at Horses Atelier. Her writing has won a national magazine award and has appeared in *The Paris Review*, *The Believer*, *Brick*, and *Lit Hub*, and has been anthologized in *Art Essays*. She lives in Toronto.

Utopia

Heidi Sopinka

SCRIBE
Melbourne • London

Scribe Publications
2 John St, Clerkenwell, London, WC1N 2ES, United Kingdom
18–20 Edward St, Brunswick, Victoria 3056, Australia
3754 Pleasant Ave, Suite 100, Minneapolis, Minnesota 55409, USA

Published by Scribe 2022

Typeset in Portrait Text by the publishers

Printed and bound in the UK by CPI Group (UK) Ltd, Croydon CR0 4YY

Scribe is committed to the sustainable use of natural resources and the
use of paper products made responsibly from those resources.

978 1 957363 13 4 (US edition)
978 1 913348 53 3 (UK edition)
978 1 922310 45 3 (Australian edition)
978 1 922586 70 4 (ebook)

Catalogue records for this book are available from the
National Library of Australia and the British Library.

scribepublications.com
scribepublications.co.uk
scribepublications.com.au

The body is not a thing, it is a situation.

— SIMONE DE BEAUVOIR

THE NIGHT WAS HOT AS ever. I sat on the bed in Milt's room with the door closed, my back against the wall, but the party was still loud. It was the kind of party we tried to avoid. Billy had grown tired of them, and I'd been working alone in the desert, jangly and on edge, though it was the most cathartic thing I'd ever done. Keeping something this big away from everyone I knew felt something like safety. Then I had you. But Milt, Billy's gallerist, was throwing the party for him, so we went. We brought you because you were barely seven weeks old.

The building almost felt like New York — a 1920s enormously high-ceilinged corner apartment, with big windows on two sides, except that what we looked out on were the tops of tall skinny palms. Nixon had kept an apartment on the sixth floor of the building, which lent the whole place a slightly depraved aura. Milt's apartment was all neutral Scandinavian glass and metal, done over by his wife, Makiko, who didn't live there anymore. She'd left him so quickly she had to pack her things in plastic bags and hire a limo because she didn't drive. People thought she was a saint to put up with Milt, until she couldn't and left him for another gallerist, one who wasn't a speed addict.

I had once been told that I sparkled, sparkled so brightly, but right then I felt like I wasn't even that good at my own life. My head ached. I opened the night table drawer. It rattled. I swallowed some aspirin and washed them down with gin. Sitting on the bed with you, I put my face near the top of your head and inhaled. You settled into the crook of my arm. We were still getting to know each other. I was thinking about how far away I was from the clean truth I wanted to live. But I couldn't make a living from art. At least not the kind I made.

I'd left Billy in Milt's living room surrounded by women flirting with him as though I wasn't there. Entourages had always been good for his mystique. Everyone was gathered to celebrate him in a way I knew I could never be celebrated, even though my work was as good as his. It shouldn't have been a contest, though, because how could it be? I was in here feeding you, understanding that everything had somehow come down to me. It made my pulse surge. I slugged back my drink and looked at the crack of light coming from under the door. I couldn't help but think he'd won.

I had always been saving drinking for old age because it wasn't compatible with my ambition, or new motherhood, but tonight I made an exception. As I was feeding you, the door flew open and a woman in a pleated silk dress looked at me and said, 'Shit, sorry,' and shut it abruptly. Her face said it all. Alone, tits out, baby. It was disgusting.

When you finally fell asleep, I wasn't sure what to do. I felt a bit slurry from the gin, from sleeping in fragments. You were too new to be left on the bed. You could roll off. Could you roll off? You were so delicate and long. I decided on Milt's dresser. People do it, I thought. I pulled out the bottom drawer and placed you as carefully as I could on top of Milt's shirts. I lingered for a moment and then kissed your head. I did up the buttons on my velvet jacket and walked out dazed and blinking at the lights, a bit stunned by the change of frequency. There were two stereos playing, people talking, communication getting lost in a mix of machines and voices.

I sidestepped a low table crammed with plates heaped with shrimp shells and chicken bones, ashtrays, and martini glasses. 'Romy,' a woman I didn't know said, reaching for my arm. She was wearing a dark men's jacket and had tucked her long hair into the collar the way I often did.

I hadn't physically submitted to pregnancy. Even though I'd felt all womb, that my guts and vital organs were all exposed, I'd worn the same clothes. Women liked how unconcerned I was about what other people thought, my friend Fina had told me. Apparently, they were all sick of sucking into tight satin, lipglossed, feeling trapped. Fina said those women would never get what they wanted, though, because it was something only I could pull off. As if freedom was something to pull off.

'Billy says you are working on something big in the desert,' the woman said.

'He told you?' I said stiffly. It was unsettling looking at someone dressed like me.

'How did you think of it?'

I picked up a glass, glittering from a silver tray offered to me by a young woman — a girl, really. The light was burned out in the bathroom but there was someone serving expensive champagne off a silver tray. That was Milt.

'It went from the divine to feeling like something real,' I said.

'I didn't know people could decide to make that kind of thing happen,' the woman said.

'What do you mean, decide?'

Milt came toward me through layers of smoke, offered me a cigarette, and leaned over and lit it with his gold lighter. His expensive suit jacket looked a bit rumpled, as though he might have slept in it the night before. The woman clinked his glass, saying, 'Happy holidays.' Milt held it up and nodded. 'To the season of tinsel, depression, and alcohol.' The woman's face fell. She quickly made her way to a nearby group of artists.

Milt turned to me. 'You're looking good, Romy.'

'I am good, Milt. I'm an ox.' I took a drag of my cigarette. 'This is new,' I said, facing the giant, red word-piece of Juke's that said, ANGEL.

'Place needed some fucking color,' Milt said, exhaling. A slight, I presumed, to Makiko's monochromatic minimalism.

'So, when are you going to let me see this mysterious work of yours,' he said. 'You know, I could represent you instead of that alpha dog in a caftan you've been showing with.' He took a sip of his drink and swallowed. 'Get you really out there.'

I looked at Milt. I was an inch taller than him. I hated this vile angle of the business. 'The thing is, I want to make the kind of work that seems like no one made it.'

'Fantastic,' he said excitedly.

'I thought you only worked with men.'

'Listen. I don't want to be categorical, but there are two kinds of women.' He paused, looking at me. 'You're the other kind.'

I downed my drink, and Milt poured me another. The champagne was doing its job. I felt an almost perverse vitality, already a bit unsteady on my feet. Across the room, Billy was talking and smoking by the window with a woman who was looking up at him. They always wanted the part of him that was no good.

'Buck up,' Milt said, taking a pull on his cigarette. 'You know you could wipe the floor with him anytime you choose.' He said it teasingly, but it made me sullen. Milt was smart about art, but he was a lout. If I thought about it, I knew no one in the art business who acted with a proper adult response. I'd never told Billy, but often when he left the room, Milt put the moves on me.

'It's confusing for him,' Milt said leaning closer, 'that the coltish beautiful woman he married has turned out to be this spooky genius.'

Billy saw us. He wasn't a jealous person, but I knew he had a thing about Milt. He came over and took the glass of champagne out of my hand and banged it down on the table a little too loudly, then pulled me aside by my elbow. We squared off in lowered voices.

'I just want to have a conversation,' he said.

'This isn't a conversation,' I replied. 'It's warfare.'

I needed air, but there was no balcony and the windows in Milt's apartment only opened a few inches. I looked out at two pinprick stars high above the palm trees. That was my sign. I realized what my prevailing emotion was — had been for a long time. Rage. I was lit up by it. I'd had enough. Maybe even forever enough. I checked in on you, miraculously sleeping in all the noise, grabbed a bottle of gin, and walked out of the apartment. I heard the muffled sound of Otis Redding singing 'Merry Christmas Baby' behind someone's wreathed door as I walked to the end of the hall, swung open the heavy fire-escape door, and went up the metal steps, my heart going crazy in my chest.

The building's neon-green letters on the rooftop blurred and fluoresced against a hazy strip of dark sky, the party swelling below. I tried to focus my eyes. The gin was hitting fast, which was how I was drinking it. I wanted everything that had happened before to vanish into the night. I could only move forward. It was quiet up there, with only the thin buzz of electricity coming off the neon sign. The skyline was smudged and glittering through gradient smog, making the city look like a broken disco ball.

It was impossible to know how much time had passed. My head was having trouble hanging on to my thoughts. I was drunk but still drinking when I heard the door, a squeal as it opened. I'd worked myself up and was now so furious I felt vicious, like I could take out the whole goddamn sign, but there was nothing up here, just me, and now Billy, the warm air, this bottle. I put it between my knees and lit a cigarette, stumbling a little. It took four matches in the wind, my hands shaking, pacing wildly, hair blowing in my mouth and eyes.

'What are you doing up here?' Billy asked.

I thought of all the false faces performing themselves, champagne sloshing from their glasses, mounds of powder getting smaller on the low glass table. 'I'm sick of it.' I was wearing my velvet suit with nothing

under it. But it was the wrong weight for this dry wind that had blown
in a freakishly hot December. I was sweating in it. I told him it felt like
a prison. He said he wasn't sure if the prison was the suit, my body, this
party — us. It seemed devastating that he didn't know.

'We don't have to talk about this now,' he said. This is what he did.
He papered over.

Gravel crunched underfoot as he walked toward me, the green light
flickering across his face. I flinched. I took the bottle I was holding by
the neck and threw it at him. He ducked and it nicked the bottom of the
letter Y, the crystalline sound of glass shattering into glittering splinters.
Gin sprayed its Christmas-tree smell into the air. He told me to calm
down. At first, I kept my voice low and steady, but then I started to say
things, things with such bitterness he looked stunned. Anger climbed
in him too. We shouted at each other. Soon we were yelling insults, and
suddenly I seemed like a stranger to myself, so fully transformed by
hate. Though that was the wrong word. Unless hate was the other side
of white-hot love, which I suspected it was.

'We can figure it out,' he said.

I laughed and he didn't. It was almost funny how he continued
to humiliate me without acknowledging anything. Anger was already
gathering cleaner, sharper edges. 'I'm making my best work in this
darkness from you,' I said.

'Shh.' He came closer. 'No one has ever mattered to me except you,'
he said. 'That is the truth.'

I hit his face, hard. A bit of blood trickled from his mouth. He wiped
it with the sleeve of his jacket and grabbed my shoulder. I swayed a
little. My breathing slowed with his. He winced looking into my eyes,
as though they were too bright. The problem was, despite everything, I
found it hard not to look at him and see him the way I did when we first
met. Almost everything had been wrecked except that. He was about
to speak, and instead I put my hand over his mouth, wild animal in my

chest. I needed to keep the words from coming out. He leaned toward me and kissed me, or rather, we kissed each other.

We were lying on the roof. He'd taken off my jacket, my pants. Gravel had bitten into my back and legs. It wasn't that long ago when at parties we would lock the bathroom door, barricade it, oblivious to people banging. We had been wild with happiness. My eyes went to the two small stars that had led me out here. There was a tingling sensation in my legs and arms. I kept saying, 'Please, please,' but didn't know what I was asking for. I'd lost control and I couldn't decide how to feel about it, about what it even meant now. We lay there in silence after, a distant siren the only sound.

I felt woozy lying down, so I sat up, holding my head as if to steady it. Putting on my jacket and pants, I'd had to lean on him. I wanted to go downstairs to check on you sleeping, five stories below. Just thinking it made my breasts leak a little. The dry palms rattled in the wind, but the air was molten.

When we began talking, the fight crept up again. I felt the hard energy of resentment fill my body. I didn't want to know what he would say or how much it would hurt me. It was then that I reminded him of our agreement. He became very still, but his face twitched, like a fly landing on a horsehide. I was moving around wildly. Something stabbed my foot, dazzling me with pain. I'd stepped on the green glass from the gin bottle. There was a lot of blood, all that red like an alarm going off. He wanted to take me downstairs.

'Romy,' he said sharply, a kind of dark shadow moving behind his eyes. For a moment everything was quiet, things hanging unspoken. There was something different in his face when he looked at me. I was trying to work out what it was. My throat closed up. I felt the blood in my veins. But it was too late. My heart was not in the right place. My heart was a bruise. It was not so much a heart but a fist. He could see that there was something wrong with me. My body felt light as a feather.

I blinked back black. When the world came back into focus, I found myself near the edge of the building in a hot wind, my lips stung. Every experience and image I'd ever seen ticker-taped breakneck right up to you in a drawer and all the people at the party below. There were so many people, but now I couldn't think of a single person or conversation. I could see all the stars, all the molecules, every single thing. Even the circulation of my own invisible air through my lungs. Billy came toward me. 'No.' He moved closer. 'No.' I shook my head. 'No.'

Los Angeles, 1978

Friday

SHE SQUATS AWKWARDLY IN THE stall. Flea is heavy, hanging forward in the damp sling, warm and wriggling to get out. Paz's dress is tight under her arms. She is sweating. Her period had come that morning. She's never been lucky in life, at least not the kind of dumb luck that, in her opinion, usually ended up being the best kind. And now she's got pee on her dress, her wedding dress, and suddenly she feels overwhelmed by her situation. She is twenty-two, married, with a baby strapped around her neck. She straightens the dress as best she can, runs the tap cold, and splashes water on her face. She can't remember much, just a glimpse of the too-handsome, too-tall man beside her, two yeses, and then a wrong turn trying to find her own reception. She'd ended up in a hot empty room where a large man was polishing the floor with one of those machines that plugs into the wall and vibrates all around. He switched it off and said, 'What are you looking for, sister?' with such tenderness she thought she might cry. Wearing a baby usually made the world feel dangerous, but something about the man, and the way he said this, jumped her heart.

She is fighting a cold and has to carry Flea in a yellow patterned sling that ruins her outfit and makes her look malarial. The low-heeled sandals she bought for the occasion are pinching her feet. Her lipstick has worn off and the bouquet she holds, an after-thought of flowers picked from the lawn, itches her hands. (Ragweed? she wonders.) In the garden that morning, ripping out the dried-up flowers, the late-July sun had felt like a knife. He'd given her a ring before the wedding. It had been too tight, and when she'd had a jeweler resize it, it had shattered. She'd worn Billy's ring until Flea rolled it straight into a sewer grate. She is trying not to read into it.

Eventually she finds the conference room in the basement where someone has laid out cake with white frosting, and bowls of peanuts. A few people have come. Her only friend, Essa, and Billy's friends Maarten, Milt, Doug Cotton, Juke, and Juke's girlfriend — Wanda, or maybe it's Gloria. She is surprised anyone is here. A lot of people blame Billy for what happened to Romy, although they don't talk about it. Some of them blame Paz for taking her place, she knows. No one says much to her, though — she always has to hear everything from Essa. Paz finds it hard to keep up with everyone's alliances, especially with the fact that they all seem to be in various degrees of sexual contact with one another.

The only other person who is here for Paz is her Aunt May, whom she lived with in Ocean Park growing up. She had shown up in thick support hose, a chocolate ice-cream stain on the bosom of her floral polyester like a bullseye, already potted at 11.00 am. She is accompanied by a volunteer from assisted living who clearly isn't aware what the effects of alcohol look like. Aunt May, who has early-onset dementia, had pulled Paz aside before the ceremony. She felt tension with her. 'What are you doing?' she'd said so sharply it took Paz completely off guard. Her mind was already shot to pieces. 'You were destined for great things,' she'd hissed. 'Married. Baby. Anyone can do that.' There had been no rain, and the grass had been brown and spiky against her bare ankles as she walked up the steps to the registry office. What she couldn't tell Aunt May was that she'd always believed herself not fit to be loved by any person. She feels lucky because Billy has done what no one else has — looked right past everything to see her as she feels she is. Though, if she thinks about it, it was Romy who did this first.

'In some ways,' Paz had told Essa before the wedding, 'it was an arranged marriage, I swear to god.'

Monday
six weeks later

THE DREAM STARTED AFTER BILLY left. There was no time for a honeymoon and no one to leave the baby with even if there had been. He hadn't even said goodbye because he hated goodbyes. She'd heard nothing from him when he landed in Rome. A week had passed, then two. Not one thing.

What is the weight of light?

Romy had asked this in her artist statement for her last show. Paz can't ask that kind of question because right now, the baby is pulling a ficus apart. It's not even noon but it's so hot Paz's rear end is welded to the vinyl floor. She's not sure how long she's been lying here. The dog drops like lumber beside her, panting. She can't even imagine this kind of heat with fur. The house is unfamiliar, though god knows she's spent most of her time here since moving in. Lying at this angle, she notices that something is off about the coffee table. Maybe it's the fingerprints everywhere. She hoists herself up and goes under the sink to find the Pledge. Her eye catches the coffee can, the one she stuffs dollar bills into. She's not sure why, just that she likes knowing it's there. She starts polishing the table because she is a worker. But when she touches it, she feels the faintest vibrating, and then it stops. She jerks her hand back like it has an electric volt.

She turns around, opening the freezer and leaning in so she can feel the air, cool on her face. She digs her fingers in, and her wrists graze the frost. Her face is practically touching the baby's placenta, frozen in a Ralphs bag. They'd wanted to plant something with it, but nothing grows here because the weather is like a hoax where rain never falls. The land is sick right down to the flowers. Snakes warm themselves by moving across the pavement and are run over by cars, their bodies becoming rubber tires. Stop thinking of dead things.

Her eyes go to the small black-and-white photograph taken in Rome. It's Romy and Billy's wedding photo, though neither of them is in it. One long strand of Romy's hair has escaped and blows across the pale stone of the Campidoglio. It looks cold, the way photos can oddly reveal the temperature. The photo is sticking out, curled edges, from the bookshelf. She hadn't liked looking at that long strand of hair so she'd dropped it behind the shelf after Billy left. Now she crosses her arms over her chest studying it, back in the same spot, and shivers.

She runs her fingers over the books and artwork that now look a bit shabby without Romy there to give them shape. She still can't tell to what degree the house is hers, and to what degree it's Romy's. It's about as layered with unknown objects as Paz's life has become. Romy pushed the baby out on the bed Paz now sleeps on, undrugged and screaming red. The light is full of dust particles still made up of Romy's cells, including the pink soft embryo she carried around, now gumming Paz's arm. The house is down a long road you could never find unless you'd been here before. The views are beautiful, even on smoggy days, when everything looks fogged up.

Paz has to pee so badly, she stops polishing the table and sprints to the bathroom, plunking Flea in the crib on the way, even though she begins wailing. The telephone rings loudly, making her jump and the baby cry harder. She gets to the phone, but when she picks it up the line is dead, again. The calls started right after Billy left. Just like in *Klute*, a film that's been on her mind a lot.

Would Romy have done this — let the baby cry? When she goes to Flea, she is peering out from behind the bars like an animal in captivity.

Her cheeks are red, and her hair is damp and sticking to her forehead in a combover. It occurs to Paz that motherhood is also a form of captivity. Flea grins, and a stream of drool jets down her chin. Paz knew the cry had been a fake. She picks the baby up from the crib, heavy as a sandbag, and kisses her so loudly on her forehead it sounds cartoonish, making them both laugh. Paz is surprised that Flea can do this because her heart has been heavy, all her life.

She walks downstairs and just as she picks up the Pledge, the front door swings open. Her chest catches at the sudden sound. She thinks it could be Billy. It's so quiet here, and unfamiliar, so when sound does come, it startles her. She had grown used to living in New York, hearing someone yelling on the street, babies crying, couples fighting, people singing 'Happy Birthday' at the restaurant below — all that life coming in through the windows. Here there's the rustle of snakes, the creak of trees, crickets at night, the howling coyotes she often mistakes for sirens. One thin coyote had even come into the yard, eyes shining like headlights, her heart beating wildly as it looked at her in a way that unnerved her because it saw her like no one else had. It knew she was in the wrong territory too.

AS AN ART STUDENT, PAZ had idealized Romy and Billy from afar. The first time she saw them was at Maarten's opening three years ago, and she's never forgotten it. She'd heard about them so many times they already seemed remote and legendary. Paz was watching them as she shared a cigarette with Essa outside the gallery. She'd gone to high school with girls who dreamed of being singers and ended up secretaries. It was almost enough for her just to watch them. Romy and Billy were tall and beautiful in midnight blue with a kind of energy that made Paz feel she didn't experience the world as intensely as they did. Billy interested her, Romy obsessed her. Paz felt, looking at Romy, that she would never know someone this beautiful again. Her beauty was almost technical, all the angles with no shadows, a face entirely propelled forward with these antifreeze eyes that sparked. She noticed a blue ring Romy wore that she coveted. It amazed her that men could call her beautiful without remembering a single detail.

Romy leaned against the brick wall. She and Billy were deep in conversation. Billy tucked a piece of her hair behind her ear, which seemed so intimate, but Paz didn't look away. She saw him reach into his pocket and then he was drawing on the side of the wall. He'd drawn something for Romy, Paz couldn't see what. A star? Even though Paz was visiting from grad school in New York and had felt worldly having just seen *Play* by Samuel Beckett, now she felt like a dumb kid in jeans and a polyester blouse with a long dark braid that frizzed at her hairline.

She didn't love openings — she felt awkward — but she found they weren't so bad if you got plowed as fast as possible. At one point, Romy was standing there smoking on the steps alone, the blue velvet glinting so beautifully Paz asked if she could touch it. 'Is it a man's suit?' she said out loud. Instead of answering, Romy looked at her and said, 'Why do you like it?' Paz felt heat in her face. She felt full of all the shame she'd ever had about her terrible clothes, which was really shame about being poor. Here was this woman in a beautiful suit, but it was a man's and probably something she'd just found in a thrift shop, because shopping seemed far too meaningless an activity for Romy to engage in. It struck Paz that she'd always been focused on the wrong thing. And then she felt embarrassed because she didn't know what to tell this captivating person. 'It's lovely,' she said after a bit too much time had passed.

Later that night, Essa asked her, 'Are you in love with Romy Leigh?'

'Why?' she said defensively.

'Every time her name comes up your face goes maroon.'

Paz was devastated when she heard the news of Romy's death. Everyone was. She remembers getting off the phone with Essa, stunned, and walking right out into traffic. She was crying, heaving, so shaken she didn't notice anything going on around her, except that everything was too bright, too loud. Only the sound of cars honking shook her out of it. That someone who wasn't yet thirty, someone she'd known, could die so suddenly made everything feel flimsy to her.

That was before she was sleeping in Romy's bed and eating off her plates. Before she had a wedding photo of her own — a Polaroid that looked like a punchline. Billy had chosen to show up on crutches. *Crutches!* He was perfectly fine. He'd studied slapstick, going back to the *Commedia dell'Arte*, and liked the idea of approaching a serious occasion with humor, and, apparently, alcohol. The heat had wrecked her hair and her expectations. Because of the way his whole body leaned into her, and how her hand was on his face and her head was on an extreme angle upward because of his height, and because they were kissing with such intensity, it seemed a bit indecent for a wedding photo.

It was before she'd moved into Romy's house, crammed with old books and furniture she'd dragged in from god knows where. Before the noises that made Paz brush past the furniture to avoid the walls. Before she started to feel real panic and wanted to leave — but to go where? Before she became the mother of Romy's baby. Before the dream. Always the same dream. Fighting her way through a wall of flames so hot her skin burns when she wakes up. She tries not to think of it, hoping that it will lose its power over her. But she can't shake the feeling that she's made a terrible mistake.

'LOOK AT YOU,' ESSA SAYS, as she walks in and sees Paz with the baby in one arm and the Pledge in the other. The dog thumps his tail, lying down.

'I need something to be finished,' Paz says. 'You scared me. I thought you were Billy.'

'Why? When does Darkness get back?' Essa had at some point given Billy the name Darkness, which Paz doesn't like. But she knows that if she protests it will only make Essa's case stronger. Neither of them had ever liked nice boys. They liked filthy, sensitive loners who scared them a little.

'Four days,' she says.

'Have you heard from him?'

'He left me a message — he sounded excited about the show.' Paz doesn't know why she said that, it just came out. Billy hasn't mentioned the show. He hasn't called at all.

'God, I should hope so,' Essa says, flopping on the couch. 'You haven't called back?'

Paz tells her it's been hard with the time change, the reverse charges. And it's probably better if she gives him some space. Essa raises an eyebrow.

'Well, at least you're in a good mood.'

'Yeah, well, the bad moods start later. When the day starts getting to me,' Paz says.

Essa steps over the mess of papers, baby toys, clothes strewn on the floor, but at least the table is gleaming. Her jasmine perfume brings relief to all this dead air. A thin gold chain glitters on her chest. Essa's left her son, Teddy, with her mom. 'It smells weird in here,' she says.

'Weird how?' Paz asks.

'Like a crime.' Essa pauses. 'Like old hamburgers and doll hair.'

Paz sets Flea on the floor. She studies Essa, mesmerized by this new human.

'How is Teddy?' Paz asks.

'Remind me how I ended up with a boy again?' Essa says. 'I have to stop watching him, looking for signs that he's going to turn out like Old Sumbitch.'

They now exclusively refer to Essa's estranged husband, Ed, as Old Sumbitch. It is the only way Essa can handle mentioning him. He was like the whole entire patriarchy gathered in a man.

Old Sumbitch is in New York, where he'd landed one of the big blue-chip galleries. After he left, Essa threw out every single thing they had used together — sheets, towels, and plates — and moved back in with her mom, who asked if she might be being a bit impulsive. 'You make him sound like some kind of toxin,' her mom said. Essa said that her mom was right on the money, that's exactly what he was. A toxin that charmed women. An alcoholic toxin who'd left her with a baby and a bunch of lint from his pockets. Essa's mom asked if there was any chance she was going to try to 'patch things up'. Essa said, 'Mom, you know the song "Stand By Your Man"?' Her mom nodded hopefully. 'Yeah, well, it was written by a man.'

'Sondra is having a women's meeting tonight at her place,' Essa says. 'You should come.'

'Oh. I want to go,' Paz says, but feels dread as soon as the words leave her mouth. No one would ever invite her. A lot of women are loyal to Romy, which Paz hadn't expected given how in with the men

Romy had been. Though, as Ora, Romy's gallerist, had put it, 'It's not that she thought she was as good as men. She thought she was better than anybody.' As far as Paz can tell, the women had also been jealous of Romy's talent and how her work scared the hell out of most of the men they knew. Paz is now the recipient of a lot of judgment dressed up as concern, which oddly errs on the polite side, considering.

'Will Fina and those women be coming?'

'Probably. But you can't let a couple of women wreck everything.'

'I would need to take a shower,' Paz says, not sure if it's an excuse or a reason.

'You just need to brush your hair,' Essa says, shaking out two cigarettes. 'You look a bit like a mental patient.' She holds one out.

Paz shakes her head.

'Are you serious? You don't smoke anymore?'

'I am stopping smoking,' Paz tells her. 'And drinking,' she continues. 'Because women artists don't make it until they are old.' This is her bit. Her women artists bit.

* * *

Paz hasn't smoked in a very long time. She finds it too intense with a baby. She never was good at it — she always feels everything too deeply. When you're four foot ten, everything is intensified. Besides, she already feels too much in this house. The objects seem to bristle with opposition, though Paz knows enough not to talk about it.

Since Billy left for Rome, Paz has found herself lying on the couch a lot, the sun burning fiercely through the windows. She has tried to put the whole subject of Romy out of her mind, but the house won't let her.

'I saw Ora yesterday,' Essa says, wetting her fingers and extinguishing the joint.

Paz doesn't say anything. She picks up Flea, heat in her arms.

'She asked about you.'

Paz has owed Ora a piece since before she married Billy, and it hangs over her. The problem is, when she tries to start it, she feels overwhelmed and often has the sense that she wants to cry, and doesn't always reject the temptation. The productive anger that had fueled her art has now been leveled by a feeling of formlessness she can't make sense of.

'Uh huh,' Paz says, putting Flea down again. The baby immediately shrieks, so she lifts her back up and rests her on her hip. Paz knows that Billy slept with Ora in the past. Which kind of surprises her. Ora is loud and talks about cunt art and works really hard at being one of the boys. Which is funny because Billy isn't one. Of the boys. Billy's friend Maarten told Paz that when they were in high school together, girls wrote Billy's name on their eyelids and fluttered them at him. They followed him home to know where he slept. They tucked long pink letters into his mailbox. He never said a word about any of it, which just made him legendary.

Women brighten in his presence. Paz isn't surprised. She knows that light well. The phone rings loudly. Paz answers and immediately hangs up.

'Who was that?'

'Nobody,' Paz says. 'Ess, I know this sounds crazy, but I think there's something going on with the house.'

'Okay,' Essa says, slowly, like a kindergarten teacher. 'Like what?'

She considers telling Essa that sometimes she suddenly feels the air leave the room and the hairs on the back of her neck rise up like antennae. But when she turns around, she finds nothing but the same old dim lighting and cluttered rooms. It took her a couple of weeks before she could see it was having a physical effect on her. Her skin itches, her teeth ache, her left eye has twitched for four days straight.

'Well, the phone keeps ringing,' she finally says, 'but there's no one there. And then there's a photo, Romy and Billy's wedding photo, that keeps reappearing even though I keep putting it away. And the glasses sometimes shake a little, like there's going to be an earthquake, but then nothing happens. I went to pick one up, but it slipped out and shattered. And then today, the table was off.'

'Off?'

'It didn't feel right.'

'Are you getting enough sleep?'

'Last night I dreamed —'

'That you went to Manderley again.'

'Ha. Ha. Very funny,' Paz says. 'I dreamed, not for the first time, that I was in an apocalyptic wall of flames.' She motions to the table. 'Touch it.'

Essa leans over and touches it. 'Nothing is wrong with this table.'

Of course, Paz thinks. But she has an uneasy feeling that this does not feel like real life, exactly.

FLEA HAD TAKEN A LONG nap after Essa left, and now Paz needs to get outside. Wearing the sling is too hot, and pushing the stroller over the hard dirt in the lethal sun feels wrong, but she decides to do it anyway. She gets Flea's sun hat, sticks the bottle in the baby's mouth, shoves some dry things that won't turn to slime in her bag — graham crackers, bread — and carries the baby down the steps, plunks her in the stroller, and walks down the bumpy driveway. She's already covered in sweat when Flea begins to cry. The sunshine is itchy. *Shit, fuck.* She turns right around and wheels back up to the porch. Her arms are perspiring as she hoists Flea onto her lap and swears at the sun. They sit on the steps. A smooth pink rock glints, and she reaches for it and puts it in her pocket. She swats a bluebottle, closes her eyes for a moment, then tears a big hunk of bread for her and a little one for the baby, and they sit there in the sun, chewing.

Flea and Paz have their own wild animal language, and she knows Flea loves her, but it's the way all young children love their mothers — they love them like a chair. Paz sometimes finds herself studying Flea's eyes, big and oceanic, like Romy's, in disbelief that she now has this raw, open proximity to Romy. That Flea is made of her. Though this doesn't tell her much.

It started in May, right after she moved in. Billy drove out to CalArts to teach three times a week, leaving her in the house with the baby. She found herself in a lull, somehow feeling more alone than she ever had in

New York. She couldn't even bring herself to call Essa. From the porch, she watched the lawn losing its green, like a lens tightening. Bodies of flies piled at the windowscreens. She began to wander when Flea was sleeping, searching for what, she wasn't sure. She'd move through the rooms looking over her shoulder, with the methodical self-absorption of a thief, even though she knew Billy wouldn't be home for hours and that it wasn't possible to find the kind of truth she was looking for in a drawer.

Billy never talked about Romy's death. She'd heard that he had given some initial confused contradictory statements to the police. The only time she'd asked him about Romy, his voice had been measured, uninflected. He spoke neutrally about her work, saying things like, 'Light was her greatest influence,' which told Paz nothing. In the absence of his account, the story she told herself became the default. It had been sudden, a horrible accident. But still she wanted to find some sort of evidence — a letter, a photograph, anything that might tell her something. She found photographs in Billy's studio of them together in Rome, and studied them, trying to determine whether Romy looked happy. It was hard to tell. She'd rarely smiled.

Most of Romy's sketchbooks were in her studio. Once, when Billy had left to teach, Paz looked through an old banker's box. It was mostly filled with receipts and papers. She knelt on the floor and reached her hand in. An old California driver's license of Billy's. Height: 6'5", eyes: black, hair: dark brown, name: Xander Rijker. She froze, staring at the name. *Xander?*

The next time she opened it, she found a thin notebook with pale-blue lines, writing of Romy's detailing works in progress with a kind of murderous compression that verged on poetry. There was a scrap of paper wedged in as a bookmark that fell into her lap. Paz unfolded it. In Billy's writing, it said, ONLY YOU. Her stomach contracted. The words seemed to leap out at her, bringing a flush of jealousy, and then shame at herself for having looked at them. She was too in her head to properly register the car tires popping over gravel, or even the door slamming. When the front door swung open loudly, her hands started to get a pricking sensation. Billy was almost two hours early. Her heart fired rapidly in her chest. She didn't know what to do with the notebook. Should she tuck it into the bookshelf? Try to get it back into the box she'd taken it from? She ended up tossing it under the couch and stuffing the little piece of paper in her pocket, swearing to herself she would put it back. The room had an air of panic as Billy walked in. Her frantic eyes met his. She felt a pressure in her chest. Billy must have known, had known all along, what she was up to. His eyes remained unreadable, and she saw in them that she was wrong. 'They evacuated the school,' he said, dropping his keys. 'A gun was found on someone in the building. It turned out to be a fake, but by then everyone had already left campus.'

I have the whole sky bottled in my head.

Paz had tried stopping, she had, but the problem was that Romy's notebooks had the exact same pull she'd had.

SEPTEMBER 7, 1968. *Arriving at art college was such an alive moment that quickly felt dead. The 'boys' get to go out all night and the 'girls' have to sign in the dormitory by eight o'clock. The first day, freshman women were literally being grabbed and thrown on a scale. They called it 'the weigh-in'. I saw a pouty wide-faced blonde slouched under a men's Goodwill coat. One of the boys strummed a ukulele next to her, singing in falsetto, She's got, fat-girl potential. Fat-girl potential, she's got — I unsuccessfully tried to make eye contact with her. My feet were sweating in my shoes. When it was my turn, I stubbed out my cigarette and held out my arms like Christ and stepped on the scale. That was when I still thought there was some reward in valor.*

I couldn't remember the last time I'd been weighed. Probably back when I used to get the curve in my spine looked at. I remember standing there at the doctor's office in my underwear, which he yanked down to get a better look at my back. After I was dressed he sat at his desk toying with his pen and said to my grandmother, I see she has matured, referring to the blood in my underwear. He said it as though he was talking about some sort of animal, not a person sitting in the same room with them. I'd gotten my period two years before, when I was ten, but was too mortified to tell my grandmother, so I made my own supplies out of Kleenex and duct tape. On the way home from the doctor's, my grandmother, behind the wheel of her enormous Buick, said, You are a woman now, which, to a twelve-year-old, managed to be both disgusting and ridiculous. None of this was as devastating to me, though, as the fact that I'd somehow thought that I wasn't doomed to grow ovaries and breasts. That I was somehow going to escape biological destiny.

A LOUD NOISE IN THE house makes her jump, and the baby does too and lets out a hiccup. Paz runs up the stairs, thunders up. The sounds had started not long after she had moved in, back when she'd been folding Billy's shirts, still feeling like it was something forbidden she was touching. Houses tell you things. It could be a rat infestation, she tells herself, feeling the afternoon sun on her back. A slight scraping noise is coming from the bedroom, but when she investigates, it sounds like it's coming from outside. You aren't supposed to stay stuck here. You are supposed to be free, Paz thinks. She wonders if Romy somehow knows that she is roaming around her house like a cat, traceable and not. She can't be *gone*. Not when everything is so full of her. Not when Paz reads the sentence, *I know I'm dead but I haven't given up the possibility of living*, sending ice up her spine despite reading it in a sheen of sweat. Why is it that she has never been able to see herself without Romy here? She can't help but constantly be aware of Romy's presence. Was she a better mother? Had Billy been happier with her? Was she better in bed? Had he loved her more?

She's never been alone with Billy. Even when she came back from New York to be with him and they'd started taking trips inland toward the desert, the baby was always with them in the back seat of the car. Paz never knew where they were going — he wouldn't tell her. Just that he was heavy with longing to be elsewhere. He would drive to the end of the burning concrete, to where the ground was dry as lint. Things would start to seed up and become honkytonk. Lives full of broken old washing machines and car wrecks on the lawn. The air was at least twenty degrees hotter. There were no breezes there. Even their weather was poorer. Only later did she realize these small towns with their jackrabbit homesteads were ones he'd passed through with Romy. There is footage of them traveling through the desert scavenging an abandoned mining town for *Remainder*, one of the early short films they made together. In it, they drive past the Panamint Mountains and the salt flats of Death Valley. All that blazing sand and deep luminous blue. At one point, in an outtake, Billy rummages through a junk heap, holding up some mangled bit of world and bringing it over to Romy, who is smoking a cigarette in an army coat with the collar flipped up. 'Look,' he says, 'the vestiges of civilization.' Romy stares directly into the camera and says, 'Boom.'

Paz reaches the bedroom in a sweat. The door is shut, which is strange because the wood is swollen, and nothing fits into its frame. A bit like the rest of the house. Everything is at odd angles — mismatched sofas and chipped china plates, and cardboard boxes full of baby clothes from Essa. She wants to say, like some of the other women who have stopped doing dishes and making meals, that it is part of a process of personal liberation from the domestic, but in truth, she hasn't had the energy to unpack. It's how she grew up.

The house she'd lived in with Ma and Aunt May in Ocean Park was always heaped with dirty clothes and takeout containers, if there was food at all. The carpet was strewn with dirt and torn fingernails and cigarette ash. She'd read somewhere, in needlepoint, that people truly engaged with life had messy houses. She suspected that person, sitting there smugly needlepointing about life, would have been scared shitless by poverty. Mess was also how a person could give up on life too. But underneath it all, her true self was a cleaner. A bit like her Aunt May, a nurse who became a drunk like Ma. Before things got bad, Aunt May had cleaned with a terrifying thoroughness. She'd run a vacuum through the room violently. You could bounce a quarter off the beds she made. Aunt May knew how to get knife-clean hospital corners. She always made the bed by circling it like a shark. When Paz would have one of her stomach attacks, Aunt May would change the sheets like they did at the hospital, with the person still lying in the bed. She worked quickly without saying anything, just carefully moving Paz to one side, then another, and then she was out of the room and Paz would feel the cool sheets against her face. When she was older and Aunt May and Ma were drinking alone in their separate rooms, Paz would lie in sour sheets holding a hair dryer on high, running it over her stomach trying to find relief, remembering the hospital-sheet changing as the good times.

Paz hurries back downstairs. She passes by the mirror and sees her dark eyes staring back. Her long black hair is hip-length, knotted, and growing progressively more deranged. Her problem is that sometimes she finds herself in something wholly messed up without any idea of what has led her there. She's done what she often does, made a decision that is not a decision.

She needs to go to the women's gathering tonight. She gets strange on her own for too long. It makes her worry that she will become like Ma or Aunt May. She is too tired to think but too dedicated not to work. Usually it's just lists in her sketchbook. She's written out two columns, SELFISH and SELFLESS, because being a mother and still making art involve the absolute opposite parts of her brain. Is she still an artist? So far, no.

She changes Flea's diaper, grasping her ankles in one hand and lifting her legs in the air like a hunter holding a shot bird. She should bathe her — she's sticky, with grit in the creases of her plump knees and a penny stuck to her rear. But there's not enough time, so Paz puts her in a dress, which is better for the heat. The one that Flea hates because her knees get caught on it and it jerks her to a stop when she's trying to crawl. Sorry, baby. She runs around collecting diapers, a bottle, a change of clothes, and stuffs them in her bag. The litany of items a small baby requires has been one of the genuine surprises of motherhood. Actually, that's not quite right. The real surprise is how the baby can get you to submit to her will without even having to learn your language. Paz grabs a bottle of Cutty Sark and wipes the sweat from her face with the back of her hand. She changes into white painter-pants and a white tank top with a small stain that her hair thankfully covers, braids her hair down her shoulder, and fumbles with a necklace while Flea is crying to be picked up.

NOVEMBER 1977. *I was told by the tarot card reader to take off my necklace. There is a superstition I was not aware of that says a pregnant woman cannot wear necklaces or any other objects around her neck because this could cause her child to be born strangled by its umbilical cord. She also went on to say that a pregnant woman must not kill any animal or witness its being sacrificed because it could cause her baby to be born dead. And then on the way home, the sun in my eyes, I ran over a fucking dog. It came out of nowhere. The poor thing must have died instantly. A terrible bump. I didn't want to admit that's what had happened, so I kept going. I kept my eyes straight ahead. I drove straight to a shelter and brought home a dog about to be put down. And when the baby was born perfectly fine, I thought, okay, now who is going to die?*

Paz has met the tarot card reader before. She shows up to parties weighted in turquoise and has excessively frizzy hair a shade of red that exists nowhere in nature. She's shaped her life around the readings and sometimes calls them a performance. No one seems to know if they are. Paz figured she was harmless until a few months ago when she cornered her at a party and said, 'So when are we going to talk about this thing obsessed with you? The ghost on you.'

IT TAKES ALMOST AN HOUR to drive to Ocean Park. She rarely puts on music anymore because having a baby means there is a constant soundtrack. Essa says, *You just wait, babies are actually quiet.*

She winds down the window and feels the hot wind. The baby is watching the blur of tall skinny palm trees from her plastic seat. The sun has dropped and left a fakey pink sunset that glitters and fades to navy blue until it is all black sky and stars sweeping over the ocean. The windows become mirrors. She'd heard women talk of wild swings between devotion and despair, but has been surprised to find just how much of motherhood is genuinely boring to her. No husband on earth would be caught dead shopping or Windexing or collecting children from the babysitter in an ancient car covered in dog hair, for fear of being considered womanly, which is funny because all these tasks just make Paz feel like she has no sex at all. She often wonders how Romy would have dealt with motherhood. She has no idea. It's not like they were friends from way back. Or even friends at all, really. Paz had never thought about being a mother. Now that she has a baby, she is often flooded with a five-alarm panic that she understands is parental love. She's done everything, including clipping her own nails down to blood so she won't accidentally scratch her. 'I'll keep feeding and rocking her no matter how mad she makes me,' she'd told Essa after she first moved in with Billy.

'You sound like a real mother,' Essa said, which stung a little, coming from her. But then Paz has also had a feeling that burns into her after a long break from the baby, a nap, or the next morning, when seeing Flea's face again is like a kind of medicine that doesn't seem right to love that much.

'When I brought Teddy home, I was full of excitement for how radical everything felt,' Essa said. 'And then the first thing he did was pee in my face.' She told Paz that in the first few weeks he did nothing but deplete her body of all its resources, and shit all day. Paz remembers coming home from New York to see Essa and meet Teddy during reading week. The house Essa shared with Ed was messy, and there was a steady flow of people bringing gifts, which eventually turned into just gatherings of Old Sumbitch's friends who came over to drink and ended up smoking all the grass, twigs, and seeds in the house. Essa had looked pale and tired. She'd pulled Paz into the bedroom, which had an overwhelming human-milk smell, and said, 'I don't love him.' Paz had thought she meant Ed. But when she realized Essa meant Teddy, Paz said, 'Oh. No. I'm sure you're just tired. I'm sure it's normal.' Though what did she know? Essa lay on the bed staring up at the ceiling. 'I don't.' Paz wasn't sure what to say. 'I really don't,' she said again softly. Paz felt her stomach tighten. She'd always suspected this was how her own mother had felt. They never said a word about it. Not then and not later.

❖ ❖ ❖

A year after she'd first met Romy at Maarten's opening, Paz was invited to be in a group show with her back in LA. It had given her a way in. Romy had encouraged Paz's performance, which involved singing country songs in chiffon prairie dresses as an alter ego sad-sack country singer named Jolene Arkell. She developed the performance at school in New York, where her roommate did wardrobe for theater and would bring home wigs that they hairsprayed into country-singer hair. She glued on false eyelashes and put on big sparkly swaths of eyeshadow and hot-pink lipstick. On Paz, it looked less like stage makeup, and more the kind they put on dead bodies. At the beginning she sometimes sang with a bag over her head. Partly because she was mortified to be onstage and partly because she liked that it looked so jarring given what was coming out of her mouth.

Romy had walked into Ora's gallery in LA explaining how she wanted her pieces to hang in the group show. Ora commented on the size of Romy's works and space constraints. Romy was quiet for a moment and then said, 'I want to make things big enough so that no one can erase them.' This was the first free woman Paz had ever seen in real life and she wanted to be just like her. She immediately felt insecure about her age and inexperience, but Romy did something unexpected. She turned to her and said Paz's technical skill was far better than hers. A comment that changed everything between them. Paz said she had to be kidding. She could never take a compliment — she still can't, she always has to give it away. But she liked Romy, the way it's easy to like someone who likes you.

Later that week, as they were hanging the show, conversation turned to the male artists. 'What do they talk about?' Paz asked her, knowing that Romy was one of the only women who hung out with them.

'Pussy.'

'Really?'

'No,' Romy laughed. 'But one of them, I think it was Juke, turned to me when I was talking about my colored-light piece and cut me off by saying, "Weren't you all just in girdles with purses to match your shoes?" And he *likes* my work,' she said to Paz. 'And then he told a joke. "Riddle: why haven't women made great works of art? Answer: because they are great works of art."'

Paz thought of all the men she'd encountered who'd rendered the female nude as meat, a knot of heat in her throat. Romy looked at her with the quality she had of slight otherworldly detachment, maybe in part from her girl-in-the-forest upbringing, or maybe from having seen too much Bergman at a very young age. 'I don't know about you, but I'm inclined to find sexism by way of artistic infantilization a bummer.'

* * *

Paz loves driving through this city at night. The giant orange sunsets that go from fierce to soft. And the wind that picks up the palms. She rests her arm out of the truck and sees that her fingernails are filthy. The air is still warm. It's weird to be back near where she grew up, only forty minutes of driving, and have it feel so separate. Everything, every building, every person seems so done over, even her. She sees the old surf shop that she used to walk by after school before she was friends with Essa. She'd passed by every day, salt in the air from the Pacific, until a guy asked her name, which, stupidly, she told him. He was eating a giant bag of potato chips, and picking the crumbs that collected in the creases of his crotch and then licking his fingers, eyeing her. She wasn't even five feet tall but already her chest and ass were so pronounced men got to make her feel cheap about it.

'You know, little blondes named Buffy aren't my thing, but girls like you — hoo boy.'

She wanted to say, 'Listen, you big dumb animal, I'm twelve.' But she didn't say anything because she was chickenshit and because being mean doesn't get you anywhere. Being nice doesn't either, though they are a little less lousy to you.

She puts the car in park and walks around to the passenger side. These women's movement meetings stir up a lot of feelings in her. She's always been a bit mad at men, she thinks, as she takes the baby out of her seat, and now she has a reason.

PAZ STANDS IN FRONT OF Sondra's watermelon-pink building. She's late and not sure she wants to go in. There are at least three women in there who hate her. She takes a deep breath and rings the doorbell. After a moment, Sondra sticks her head out. 'Quit pacing out here, you look like a narc,' she says. A narc with a baby? That would actually be the single best cover, Paz thinks, except it's a cover that would blow itself.

Sondra's apartment is so packed you can't even see the orange shag. Her place is full of women and dogs and a dense curtain of cigarette smoke and Joni Mitchell singing on the record player. She's missed the part where everyone begins to gather, nervous and uncertain but pissed off. They are all so pissed off and this is good, because this is what gets things moving. And then you add some Chianti, and boom. But still it feels covert. They still understand that as women, dedication to anything can make you ridiculous.

Paz scans the room for Essa. She hears a woman talking about how her boyfriend said he thought women are more serious than men, and by nature enjoy life less. The woman next to her says, 'Yeah, well, he'd enjoy life less if he'd been the one cleaning your toilet all year.' She takes a sip of beer. 'When I stopped doing the dishes, making meals, and cleaning, my husband split. So, yeah, that was the end of my marriage.'

'Well, fuck him and the horse he rode up on,' says Red. Paz is surprised Red is here. She mostly hangs out with the men. She says she wants to talk to every single person in Los Angeles, have actual conversations that she will record for the rest of her life.

Red: I like to say everything.
Person 1: I don't like to say anything.
End of conversation.

Red: So I told him, if you're going to sleep with other women, you'd better become a better liar, so he did.
Person 2: Did what?

Paz always wonders how Red got her name because it's not like she has red hair or anything. But it suits her perfectly. It is without gender, like something you'd call your car or tractor.

The woman whose husband split tells Red about the nineteenth-century material feminists who were looking for social change through domestic revolution. 'They proposed that the wives charge their husbands for their domestic labor,' she says. Red lights a joint while the woman continues. 'They argued for taking the kitchen out of the house.'

'Where would it go?' Red asks, holding the smoke in her lungs.

'I don't know. Something communal. They wanted to hire cooks so that they would lessen the burden of women's work.'

'Well, isn't that shit truer than ever. Husbands should be goddamn charged. After all, they're the ones getting free labor *and* pussy,' she says, exhaling and then coughing. 'Though honestly, I just go to Hamburger Hamlet when I'm hungry. Also,' she says, taking another big pull on her joint, 'taking the kitchen out of the house.' The woman glares at her.

'Listen, I'm here for the same reason we all are,' Red says. 'I mean, how else will we ever get out of this, when the patriarchy insists on torturing us all in such a tragically slo-mo way?'

There are a few toddlers on the shag rug, fighting over a plastic rolling telephone with eyeballs. When Paz leans down to put Flea on the carpet with them, two girls in falling-off sundresses glare at her. The littler one gets brassy and snatches back the toy for herself. Flea clings to Paz like a koala with such force she knows she will cry if she lets go of her, so she doesn't. She sips the Cutty Sark out of a sweating wax cup and hears a friend of Sondra's who is eating a handful of Ritz crackers talking about her boyfriend who is 'crazy into' meditation. Paz realizes she has met the woman before. She's got two kids with cult haircuts, both hyperactive.

'Yeah,' Red says, 'well, behind every man who is meditating, is a woman not meditating.'

The woman whose husband split asks Red what she's reading. 'SCUM Manifesto,' Red tells her.

'Oh god. Don't tell me you really think the elimination of men and the money system is the answer. It gives us a bad name. As though we're all maniacs, going around shooting people.'

Red just stares back at her. 'Yeah, but look where the conventional candy-ass tools of resistance have gotten us,' she says. 'Women being all polite and shit. Look, I'm not saying I'd want to put Warhol in a surgical corset for life. But I believe something more radical is necessary if we don't want to spend the rest of eternity on the fucking margins.'

Sondra walks up and hands Red another beer. 'Somebody told me Andy kept his wig on during the entire operation,' she says. 'You don't hear much about Solanas anymore, though.'

'True, true. No one talks about her manifesto. Or, say, how her uterus was tampered with when she was in the nuthouse after shooting Warhol.'

'Jesus.'

'You know that in New York she used to ask male passers-by on the street for a dollar in exchange for a dirty word. She would smile and always say the same thing.' Red takes a slug of her Colt 45. '"Men."'

Paz spots Essa talking animatedly in the corner, drinking straight from a dewy bottle of gin. She's got hairsprayed long actressy hair, Lady Dangerous coral lipstick. She must have been out at a call. Her dad had known people in the industry — that's how she first started. Paz once asked if being in commercials was what she really wanted to do. Essa shrugged. 'It beats working at the Liquor Barn for minimum.' She's lighting a Salem, wearing her black gloves. Essa's lint works — literally lint she had collected for years from all the laundry she'd done for Old Sumbitch — end up in her fingernails.

Red emerges from the beaded curtains eating a bowl of oily nuts. She wipes her fingers on her T-shirt, leaving grease marks, and finds Sondra who is getting ready to speak.

'You didn't bring Teddy?' Paz says, walking up to Essa.

'My mom's got him. You know, when I told her where I was coming, she told me she and her friends were just focused on making it through high school unraped,' Essa says, taking another sip of her drink. 'Like that was an actual goal.'

Sondra whistles and suddenly the room quiets, but there are still some murmurings. 'Jesus, guys, shut the fuck up. Can we just stop the bullshit small-talk? We need to get right to the stuff that matters. The stakes are high.' She looks around the room. 'We are the fucking stakes.' And then she yells, 'The First Amendment was written by slave traders!'

She is the perfect leader, Paz thinks. If anyone starts out neutral, they wind up willing to give one of their kidneys by the time she's finished. Sondra launches into how, in the last big LA show, where there was a huge grid of a hundred faces of the next generation of 'greats', not a single one was a woman. She and Ora have already begun teaching feminist art history classes, and so far, there is a Disney-funded art college in Santa Clarita that's letting them. She told the students they would only learn about women artists from now on, because they'd learned more than enough about men. They had Romy guest lecture once. She was the only woman doing light and space work. At one point, one of the students put up her hand and suggested that things might have been easier for Romy, given that she looked like a model. Romy just said neutrally that this was the problem with the movement. We can't be attacking *each other*. And then she turned back to the next slide and began speaking again. Sondra had warned her to be patient. These women had only ever been called girls. They'd never once been asked what they thought.

'Most of us aren't even making objects for sale,' Sondra says. She has a point. None of them are making any money from their art. Which also means there is nothing to lose. They are told they aren't making universal art because they are trapped in the personal, so there is no choice but to make the personal universal. Though Paz doesn't have any interest in making things out of the domestic, given that it is exactly what has crept into her life just enough to ruin things a little.

Fina walks toward Paz, but mercifully Sondra, fired up from her speech, begins speaking to her, allowing Paz to escape with Flea to the bathroom. She has no idea how long it's been when she hears Essa knocking.

'Paz. Open up. I know you're in there,' Essa says. 'What are you doing?'

'Freaking out,' Paz answers, letting her in as the baby chews the corner of the gold bathmat.

Essa blows smoke, closes her eyes, and eventually says, 'Who was it?'

'Fina.'

'Her? She's just mad because you married Billy right out from under her.'

Essa calms her down and eventually leaves Paz sitting on the edge of the bathtub for a moment. When she finally gets the courage to leave the bathroom, Fina comes directly for her.

'Who invited you?' she says stonily.

'Sondra,' Paz says. Which isn't exactly true.

'This is a women's liberation meeting,' Fina says, lighting her cigarette, her face rigid and serious, 'and last I checked, you stole another woman's life, so —' She exhales. 'I don't think anyone could count that as solidarity.' She pauses. 'You know he's not over her.'

This is a new intensity, even for Fina, who has the ability to tell anyone anything as though she's been hit on the head. Is he supposed to be *over* her? 'Billy is free to choose who he wants to be with,' Paz says.

'It's interesting to me, how sure you are. But you should know that you can't do both — hold feminist ideals and subvert them. Despite what you may think, you aren't smarter than your own fantasy,' Fina says.

The words coming from Fina sound so nasty, Paz feels them physically, like stones. Fina brushes back her hair, the color of an expensive camel coat. 'Ora couldn't tell the difference,' she hears Fina saying.

'What?' Paz asks, shifting Flea to her other hip. She's started to feel very heavy in her arms.

'The sketches for the work you sent to the gallery. Ora thought they were Romy's. Nobody, actually, could tell the difference.'

Paz is watching Flea's eyes watch Fina's hoops swing as she gets more animated. The baby is like a dog the way she picks out meanness. Flea's hand darts out and grabs for a hoop, and Fina pulls back. 'After I moved back here,' Paz tells Fina, 'I had no idea what to do next, until I realized I didn't need to paint. It was totally freeing.'

'I think you've mixed things up,' she says.

'What do you mean?'

'That's exactly what Romy said.'

'Which part?'

'All of it,' Fina says, railroading her. 'You're even talking like her. Walking around with her baby like this.' She leans in closer. 'Is that *Romy's* necklace you're wearing?'

'You said you needed to talk to me?' Paz says flatly, a flush creeping up her neck.

Fina feels around in her bag and then pulls something out. 'Here,' she says, shoving it at her.

'A postcard?' Paz says, confused, studying the detailed pencil drawing of what looks like the surface of the moon on a thick cream cardstock. Her stomach drops. She knows these drawings. She flips it over. There are two words written on the back. Her face is alive with attention as she reads. DISAPPEARANCE PIECE. 'Who is it from?'

Fina looks at her, and in that moment Paz knows what she's going to say. 'Romy.'

SHE HITS ALL GREEN LIGHTS on the way home. The radio is on when she walks through the door, loudly playing classical music. Miraculously, Flea doesn't stir. She carefully transfers her into her crib with the precision of a jeweler so she won't wake, and then checks all the rooms holding a hammer, which feels like an invitation to get murdered. As she walks by, she catches a glimpse of herself in the window. Her face looks wrong. Her hair has come out of the braid, it hasn't been cut in forever. Since when has she become someone who has let herself go? When was the last time she read a book? Her jeans are coming apart at the crotch. She mostly eats frozen enchiladas alone at night. She sleeps on her face.

She sits down on the couch exhausted, her eyes going to the familiar photo, the one with Romy's hair blowing across the frame. She knows there is another wedding photo in Billy's studio, one where you can see her hipbones jutting through a lace dress, stomach flat as drawing paper. Why did she wear a dress? Paz thinks, almost offended by how feminine Romy had made herself, feeling an unexpected bristle of rivalry.

A light breeze comes through the window. Looking out at the dark porch, she's hit by how everything is moving around her, not letting her in, making her feel alone. She feels something sharp under her and pulls it out from the couch cushion. It's one of the baby's blocks. Technically, she thinks, she's not alone. She sees the journal on the coffee table, as though left open for her.

SEPTEMBER 16, 1968. *Sitting on the grass like every other day, about to go to the studio, reading before class, something came over me. When I looked up, I caught eyes with a man for a few seconds. I felt stars in my body. The feeling was so strong I was embarrassed by it and immediately looked back down at my book. When I looked back up, he wasn't there.*

SEPTEMBER 21, 1968. *It had been a humiliating few weeks. I had chosen this school because of its gallery, which showed avant-garde works of big-name artists. But it wasn't until I was actually here that I realized that not a single show had included a woman.*

What's with all this nineteenth-century bullshit? a woman in my ceramics class whispered to me, heavily accented. I liked this person, whose name was Fina. She looked like a film star with all that blue on her eyelids. My childhood was deeply unglamorous, and secretly, I'm interested in glamour. She invited me to a party thrown by a well-known performance artist named Doug Cotton, who lives right off the beach in La Jolla. He apparently once spent five days in a meat locker. His work seems too physical, without a sense of poetics, to me — like a jock who's found another way to get attention — but everyone seems to love it, especially the critics.

I felt nervous going to the party. Fina said she'd meet me there, so I went alone. I heard a dog barking as I walked up to the house, already full of people smoking on the lawn. I went in, past a guy in a T-shirt that said, MY FACE LEAVES AT TEN, BE ON IT, and lit a cigarette. I didn't know anyone there, except Fina, who I couldn't find. And then the man from campus walked through the door.

Paz feels suddenly hot, a sour heat that needles her skin. She sits up, brushing her damp hair off her face. She decides that before reading on she will make herself go outside for a moment. Slowly she gets up and walks out to the porch and then into the yard. The sky has just a few opaque stars because of the smog. She breathes out and turns back to the house, the living-room windows glowing out at her like eyes.

The man from campus came with a very slight woman — a writer, I heard someone say. Someone handed me gin with pink soda in a chipped mug. I accepted it because it was something solid to hold on to. I walked outside and almost immediately a guy in a tight white T-shirt with prison-yard muscles walked up to me.

Never get a snake as a pet, he said.

I took a sip of gin. Wasn't on my list.

Good, he said. See that woman there? He pointed to a woman in a blazer who looked like she was in charge of something. Collector, he said as though reading my thoughts. Milt told me that she used to have a little baby python until it grew into a big giant snake.

Wait, don't tell me, I said. It ate her lap dog.

Nope. Milt said she called him and said something was wrong with the snake. It wasn't eating and it was sleeping a lot. When she lay down, the snake lay down beside her all stretched out, which was odd because it was always coiled into a tight little fucking ball. She was wondering if the snake was sick or depressed. She finally took it in to some exotic animal vet off Melrose. It turns out the snake wasn't depressed, he said, taking a slug of beer. It was going to fucking kill her.

How did she know?

The vet said it was starving itself. The fucking thing was measuring her when it lay beside her. Sizing her up.

Someone was retching in the bushes right beside us and he turned to me. I don't know about you, but I always feel healthy when I puke in all this nice California air.

There's nothing wrong with throwing up, I said, which made him stop and look at me. Sometimes it's good to burn.

Good. A fucking weirdo. You'll fit in perfectly. Then he nodded and said, Cotton.

Just as I told him my name, another man walked up.

Juke's a weirdo too, Cotton said, by way of introduction.

The man whose name was apparently Juke began talking about a show he'd gone to in New York that had some towering sculptures.

I suddenly had to get the hell out of there, he said. I was thinking, fuck conceptual, this fucking shit could fall on me and kill me, man.

He took a sip of his beer and stared at me. He was acting at looking tough, like one of those guys who ask you to fuck in the street. He asked me if I'd seen Cocteau's Blood of a Poet.

You mean the one where Lee Miller plays the statue? I said.

You remind me of her, he said lighting a cigarette.

Great, I thought. He sees me as a statue.

The collector came up and started talking to Cotton and Juke, allowing me to wander off. I sat, drinking the gin alone. It was good. It tasted like flowers and medicine. And then I saw the man from campus. He walked right up to me. I'd never felt small next to a man before. He was the only one there that could possibly have done that to me. He was standing so close I could feel heat coming off his body. He said he was teaching while preparing for shows in Europe. He'd just come back from working with a famous artist in Germany. He asked me about my degree, and we were suddenly both yelling over the stereo that had been turned up, deafening even outside. It's not what I thought it would be, I yelled.

He looked at me. What did you think it would be?

I thought of the weigh-in, the curfew, the macho sculpture-studio instructor. Different.

He told me he was making work that wasn't a commodity, that wouldn't wind up in a gallery. Something that isn't representing something, but something that is something, he said. The music was so loud I just saw his lips moving. And then he looked me hard in the eyes and kissed me.

I've spent this whole week since in the studio trying not to think about him. But everything I make keeps breaking. At the party, Billy said my name. He put his fingers in my belt loops and pulled me closer. A slow current passing from his body to mine. He smelled like the ocean. I suddenly felt very drunk and told him what I'd told no one. That I had wanted to erase myself. As far as I could see, my identity existed only in the eyes of other people, and I hated that. I had wanted to disappear but starving myself was the most alienating thing I had done. He told me he'd taught himself English by watching High Noon over and over again while Bill, an old war buddy of his uncle's who'd billeted him in high school, was at work. At first he'd thought this was how all Americans spoke. Like cowboys. I couldn't take my eyes off his eyes, dark lakes I wanted to drown in.

Paz pictures those eyes. She has stared into them too. She's also watched them go out, everything going black, a flatness in them that chills her.

SHE GOES INTO THE KITCHEN and there's almost no food, so she empties a box of crackers onto a plate and eats them dry until she sees a small cracker-colored insect racing across the plate. *Shit*, she thinks. She looks around in the freezer and finds a chocolate Sara Lee cake, bringing it to the living room. She peels off the cardboard top, licks it, and chisels at the cake with a large knife. She's trying not to think about the postcard so she turns on the TV and flips through. *Modern Times* is on, and she sits back on the couch to watch it. She has always felt a secret bond with Chaplin. He was one of the few people of power who was very short and famous, and not Charles Manson or Napoleon. The knife slips on the cake, and she just misses cutting her finger. The thought of Romy somewhere out in the desert scares her. Things could never go back to what they were. Her body is full of tense anticipation as she rifles around and opens a bottle of wine. She drinks it, and most of another, and feels a bit calmer and warm from the inside. The sugary cake makes all the wine in her stomach stop rolling around.

❃ ❃ ❃

She wakes up a few hours later sweating like crazy on the couch with a kink in her neck, her heart beating very fast, her throat as dry as a stick. The house is different at night. Every single noise turns to harm. Something brushed her arm, she's sure of it. Maybe the dog. She pulls

out the postcard, places it on the table, and looks at it. It's bent and a
bit damp on one corner from Flea's bottle that has leaked a little in her
bag. She studies the drawing. It is definitely one of Romy's, she knows
those studies well. She flips it over. The postmark is slightly smudged.
SEPT 07 1978, four days ago. She feels her heart sharp in her chest. In
the postcard she sees everything that is wrong with her situation. Is this
supposed to be from Romy? It could just be Fina trying to put her in her
place. She hated that about people, always trying to put people in their
places. She has heard some of the artists talking about Romy's death as
a possible performance. But who would leave their life, their work, their
own baby, for a piece of art that no one even understood to be art? She
does not want to expose herself to the answer. It feels like poison. She
studies the postcard, lying face up on the table.

Paz can't go back to sleep. She tucks her feet up on the couch. She
feels as if someone's hand might dart out and grab her ankles. It's a new
feeling. She was brought up to be cynical, not fear the beyond. She's
seized with a kind of panic and wants to tell someone. She'd made up
her mind not to call Billy, but it's hard work. She finds herself dialing. As
soon as she hears the Italian operator, she immediately slams down the
receiver and sees the notebook right in front of her.

SEPTEMBER 29, 1968. *I woke in the middle of the night to a tapping sound, stones, at my window. When I looked out, Billy was standing below, saying my name. I met him behind the dorm, which I had to sneak out of. If I'd gone to Berkeley, where free love was practically invented, it would've been different, but Pomona is still uptight. I saw him watching me as I crossed the lawn. I stopped in front of him and he didn't say anything. He continued to look at me with total attention. I knew he would kiss me, and he did. The same kiss, brutal and intense. I hadn't been with anyone yet. Sleeping around was going on, but I saw how it took away women's power. His body was on mine and I felt his weight on me. It was prolonged and astonishing and almost unbearably erotic. After, at some point that night, I remember lying in the grass looking up at the moon, asking him, Do you ever think about light? All the time, he said. Which is when I fell in love with him.*

Paz feels a strange unease at the thought that Billy loves her not with his heart, or his brain, but with his skin. Her longing for their time together makes her body ache. She lies back on the couch, suddenly feeling deeply tired. She's been living on nerves and adrenaline for the five months she's been out here. The night just keeps on going when you can't sleep, like how Cotton said that when you make a performance you can't say how long it's going to be, you just have to pick something to make it about, and *that* is what determines how long it will be. Like when he lay on a gallery floor for three days. Everyone was freaking out and consulting doctors about how long a person could go without water. They really honored his work, though, and didn't want to interrupt it, so they waited. The piece was full of oversights, he said later. He'd figured the night guard would tell him to leave when the gallery closed on the first night. But he didn't. Cotton, who liked to eat Manwich from a can because he actually *liked* that it tasted a bit like dog food, didn't eat or drink for a few days before so he wouldn't have to take a piss. He ended up shitting himself, which possibly was worse than death for him. Three days later, when they were worried that he might go into some sort of coma, the gallery assistant placed a pitcher of water and a glass beside him. That's when the piece ended.

She'd had her own version of that in grad school, after reading a lot of Thoreau. She had never read in the normal way. She got into his obsessive lists and simplicity of vision, even if it turned out his cabin in the woods was only a few feet from railway tracks that led straight to his mother's house, where she did his laundry every Sunday. She decided she would wear the same clothes for a pre-determined time. At first it was just her shirt that got some oil stains on it from the donut job. It started to smell a bit like old frying grease. A button popped off, revealing a part of her bra that had turned gray. Her pants became too thin for late-November wind and eventually got a rip in the seat. She felt dirty and a bit crazy but realized that oddly no one had really noticed, which made her feel alone. Who would have noticed? She hadn't yet met Romy, who noticed everything in the deepest way.

Tuesday

THERE IS A RINGING IN the distance and Paz wakes feeling sick. The light is so strong she has to close her eyes. She can't believe the baby isn't up yet. She doesn't want her to wake, so she shoots up off the couch, tripping before she gets to the phone. Let it be him. She has been rehearsing things to say. She wishes she was the kind of person who could get dirty right away, but she's not that kind of person.

'Hello,' Paz says, like a question mark.

'Have you gotten a hold of Billy yet?' he says curtly. She lets out her breath. It's Milt, who is normally more charming.

'No.'

'I haven't been able to get in touch with him in Rome. Did he happen to mention to you anything about a Bob Stevens?'

'A Bob?' Paz says distractedly, popping the cap off a warm Coca-Cola and bringing it to her mouth too fast, the bottle hitting her teeth as she takes a long sip, fizz pelting her throat and then disappearing. 'Sorry, Milt. I keep missing him. Can it wait?'

'It's a bit urgent. Can you have him call me when you next speak with him?'

'Sure,' she says. 'Milt?'

'Yes?'

'Is there anything I can do?'

'I'm afraid not.'

As she hangs up, her eye catches the box she'd taken out of Romy's studio to make room for the resin discs, but for some reason hasn't opened. The lid is slightly bent, and she pulls on it with a bit of force, jamming it up with her palms. It is full of papers and a tiny midnight-blue notebook, which she immediately knows is Romy's because she said that small books helped her get to the point. She sees a journal with articles and a photocopied image of Rimbaud in Africa during the third year of his disappearance sticking out. Paz had thought of him only as a famous French poet, not as a teen rebel who had written SHIT ON GOD all over buildings in his hometown, who by twenty had given up writing for good. Everyone in Paris had thought he was dead but he had apparently disappeared to Africa, where he spent the rest of his life as an arms dealer. Paz has to admit she knows very little about France, except for fondue, Godard, and that there is no word in the French language for cheerleader. When she turns over the journal she sees its title, HOW TO DISAPPEAR. A feeling of nausea runs over her. She'd sworn she would quit, but this is what Romy's writing does. She feels real air from Romy's real words. They manage to pull her in — reading them with her wrong clothes, wrong hair, wrong mind — and always, a little bit, humiliate her.

She hears a noise upstairs that sounds like a large rock hitting hollow metal. She runs so fast she trips on a step and stubs her toe. When she gets to Flea's room, she can't see her anywhere. The crib is empty. She's gone. A high hammering begins in her chest. Flea can't even walk yet. She flips up the crib mattress, pulls back the curtains, looks in the closet, and starts sprinting down the hall. Paz is crazy with worry, running through all the rooms, her body unreliable, moving in jerky patterns like a caged animal let out. A fierce panic burns her chest because, of course, it is her greatest fear. The baby isn't even hers to lose.

She hears the toilet flush and runs to the bathroom. Flea is sweaty and triumphant and has a look of total concentration. She has hoisted herself up and is grasping the toilet seat with one tiny fist, rocking back and forth with delight. She must have hurled herself out of her crib and somehow inchwormed all the way down the hall. She's got a big grin as she flushes Romy's gold necklace down the toilet. Paz manages to put her arm in far enough to grab it and pull it out, which makes the baby laugh hysterically.

'How did you get out of your crib, she-baby?' She swoops her up and tries to hug her but Flea squirms and whines to get back to her game. She only likes real things. Toys don't interest her. Already she's a realist. Paz looks at her determined little face. She sees nothing of Billy. But Flea's face changes constantly, like weather. She often wonders about the time before, a great biblical unknown. Birth and feedings. The soft spot on the baby's head. It terrifies Paz that we all start out with dents in our heads like pieces of bruised fruit. She wonders if they spent long days lying in bed together, the three of them. She wonders if the baby was fed in a state of devotional meditation, or if she had siphoned Romy's nipples like a furious little animal and choked on the milk until becoming a dead weight, the way Essa described it. Essa has told her about women who adopt babies and manage to get themselves to lactate. The idea seems perverse to her. Though, in an exhausted moment, she once put Flea on her to see if she'd feed, but she just clamped down and bit her nipple, hard.

Her mind goes back to the postcard. She has to work very hard at ignoring the thought, like something crouched on top of her, making it hard to breathe — the thought that Romy is out there. Standing in the light of her own disappearance, seeing Paz as an imposter. She is not sure what to do with this image. It's too disturbing to consider. She wants it gone.

IT'S ALMOST AN HOUR'S DRIVE in traffic to Essa's house, a white stucco Mediterranean with big beams and wood floors and a huge fireplace. French doors open to a pool in the back fanned by palms and thick jasmine vines that grow all over the verandah. At night, the house fills with their scent coming through the open windows. Essa grew up here, falling asleep to parties downstairs, clinking ice cubes, the warm velvet of jazz records, to the *click click click* of her mom's kitten heels on deck tile.

Essa's mom answers the door in full makeup and a very long pale-denim dress with a zipper up the front, an armful of silver bracelets. 'Hi, doll. Come in,' she says, taking the baby from her. Paz unclips the leash, and the dog runs in and sniffs Essa's mom's toy poodle's rear. She's praying he doesn't lift his leg on any of the designer furniture. Essa's son, Teddy, is in pajamas and a toy holster, eating a bowl of Cheerios. He looks up at his newest little rival, points a make-believe gun at her, and pulls the trigger. He then goes back to the TV with a dead look on his face, tranquilized by cartoons — which speaks to the power of television, because the other day when he saw Flea, he literally tore off his underpants in joy.

'Essa's in her studio.'

'God, thank you, Mrs Kirvan.'

'I'm happy to help. And, honey, you've got to start calling me Georgette,' she says, giving Paz's hand a squeeze. 'Teddy loves when the baby's here. He has someone new to boss around. And he is crazy about that dog.'

'You have no idea how grateful I am,' Paz says.

'Any time. I know what it's like mothering on your own,' she says. Essa's dad had traveled all the time when she was growing up and then had a heart attack when she was seventeen. 'It's like being a Shaker. Or Quaker. Or whatever the one is where there's no sex and you're expected to work until you drop.'

Paz puts down the bag with the bottles and diapers and snacks. The baby is so interested in the blinking television she barely notices her leaving. Paz knows this house well — she spent most of high school here. She could never have invited anyone normal over to her own house.

❊ ❊ ❊

Every recess Paz would sit alone on the cement under the overhang and read or draw in her sketchbook. The sight of kids playing in groups crushed her, but over time she took pride in being alone, though she understood that from the outside her loneliness was laid bare. She wasn't certain yet that there was anything that exceptional about her, except drawing. Coming from her mother, who used the word 'artist' as a euphemism for someone lazy — that's not work! — art had seemed impossible. Everything had changed when Aunt May brought home a sketchbook, even though she didn't understand the quote unquote small and insignificant things Paz chose to draw. Something had gone off inside her.

One day in seventh grade, she was sitting sketching by the concrete wall on the north side of the schoolyard. Someone had spray-painted, HOPE YOU DIE. Essa, who was walking by, stopped in front of it. They had never spoken. She thought Essa was going to say something but then she turned to leave, and Paz said, 'I mean, safe bet.' There was a pause and then Essa turned around to face her and they both started laughing like crazy. After that, they were inseparable. It was like an illness. People were confused at first to see them together at school, huddled together talking, painting their nails with Wite-Out in class. Paz had been picked on. They said she didn't smell right. Aunt May had said that when people tease you it's because something about you scares them. She'd realized what they were scared of was her poverty.

They would walk back to Essa's house to avoid the bus driver who had a crush on Essa, arms looped through each other's, the dry cement glittering in the sun. Men were already leering out of long cars at them. Paz would give them the death stare and Essa would say, Heard it before, fellas. The heat got so crazy they would move in slow motion like old people. When they got to Essa's house, they would lift up their shirts and press their nipples against the refrigerator. Paz had never seen such a hygienic kitchen. They used to make avocado-and-tomato sandwiches and wash them down with Tab, sipping and swinging their feet in the pool. When Essa's mom told them they needed to eat fruit, they ate maraschino cherries from a jar, red dye number four radioactive in their stomachs. They practiced French-kissing the wall. They used Essa's dad's pool-cue chalk as eyeshadow and wore Cherry Bomb lipgloss that was sticky and tasted like sugar. Paz had immediately loved Essa's mom, who served them Jell-O with Cool Whip on top. She was Texan, a former state beauty queen runner-up with a smile that could stop trucks.

Essa's dad was a studio musician under contract at Fox. He'd studied classical violin in Moscow. He told Essa once that the quarter-note is closest to the duration of the human heartbeat. He had her playing the violin, which she had done reluctantly since she was four. He would shout poetic instructions that often confounded her, like, 'Vanessa! Play it like you are skating *under* the ice.' When she was fifteen, he offered her a yellow Sting Ray once she got her license if she learned a Paganini violin concerto, which motivated her for a few months because it would have been a lot better than the wood-paneled station wagon her mom drove around. They called it the Corvette concerto. Right around that time, Essa wrote in one of Paz's sketchbooks, FIVE-FINGER DISCOUNT, placing a question mark at the end. They both got a little jolt from it. A tube of lipstick, a magazine, and then, once, silk underpants from Saks. They didn't realize how expensive they were, though, and it was the first time they were caught. A cop car rolled up outside of Essa's house to her father's great shame. After that he took back the Corvette offer, which was especially tragic given that after all those hours she'd spent hacking through the piece, it was the exact point in time she'd finally learned it.

❊ ❊ ❊

Essa is in a large men's shirt covered in paint with the sleeves rolled up, and no pants. She is leaning over the table making meticulous little movements. 'I had three hours to work this morning, whole as pie,' Essa says. 'And I can't seem to get these damn concentric circles to work.'

Paz watches Essa bent over, working on her silkscreen. 'Do you need me to go?' she asks.

'No. Stay.' She glances over at Paz. 'What's wrong?'

Paz hesitates. She doesn't know how to casually tell her that Romy might not be dead. Everything has been replaced by question mark after question mark. Her heart is leaping everywhere. Instead she says, 'Everyone thinks the sketch for the piece I'm making for Ora's show looks exactly like Romy's.'

'Is that what Fina said when she cornered you last night?'

'Yeah.' Paz sits down rigidly, which is hard to do on a beanbag chair. She immediately slouches into an awkward starfish position. She feels her mouth opening but decides against telling Essa. She tries to adjust herself to this new reality. Normally she'd say everything she thinks to Essa, but her whole body feels like a record slowed down.

'So, guess what I got today?' Essa says, not looking up. 'Divorce papers. His lawyer sent them. They had a note on them from Old Sumbitch — a *Post-it*.'

'Uh oh.'

'He asked me to send out his dumbbells.'

'I mean —'

'I know,' Essa says. 'Don't worry. I'm not upset anymore. There was a time that I would have taken him out with a baseball bat if he'd been remotely near me, but I think I dodged a bullet.' She stops. 'I can't believe I just said, "I think I dodged a bullet." I sound like an idiot. I must be finally getting over him.'

Outside, the dog is chasing a bunch of birds that have flown up into the jacaranda tree in the yard, and then examining the various smells around its trunk. Georgette's little dog starts to sniff him feverishly. She's hyper but with the sad boozy eyes of a loner.

'Any sign of Darkness yet?'

Paz doesn't say anything. Billy had been acting so strange before he left for Rome.

SHE LOOKS OVER AT ESSA, intensely working. Paz hasn't been able to concentrate on anything since Billy left. It feels like parenthesis, all this waiting for things to start.

She'd gotten together with Billy first in New York, the spring after Romy died. He'd told her how much he needed her help, that he needed to feel good again, fast, but then she wondered if she would ever hear from him again. He'd left so quickly in the morning it was awkward. But a week later she received a postcard. It had an Apollo 8 stamp and only one word. BOURBON. (Good: he thought of her. Bad: he thought of her not enough.) Another followed. CIGARETTES, COFFEE, SUGAR, TOOTHPASTE, HASH, TOILET PAPER, WHISKY, CHICKEN, LIGHTBULBS, MOTOR OIL. Then another. PENCILS, SOAP, FOOD, SALT, VODKA, MATCHES, ORANGES. Paz sent a postcard back. It was easy enough to write to him but she felt her heart beating too quickly in her body as she did it. INCENSE, BALLPOINT PENS, CHAPSTICK, PEPSI, SUGAR, WITCH HAZEL, WATER, TOOTHPASTE, VITAMINS, NIVEA, COTTON, ELECTRICITY, RENT, DIAPHRAGM, PAPER. They referred to them as CONSUMPTION PIECE, sending each other what they used in a day. It was something between just them. Only a few ever came, but she could be patient, she could play a long game. She studied a photo of him in an art magazine she'd found on campus to remind herself what he looked like. He was incredibly good-looking in it, though he was even better in real life. Something in the way he talked to her and looked at her made her want to do anything for him.

But by April, when she moved back to LA, there was something automated about him. He seemed incapable of uppercase emotion. She was becoming used to knowing less and less about him, which was a bit like coming off a drug. Sex was her center of gravity with him, and because sex can't resemble anything other than itself, it meant there was almost nothing when they were apart. As if she'd invented him. He'd given her something outside herself, only to have it flow back into a kind of nothingness. It made her doubt the most basic things. When she heard rumors, she had no choice but to be affected by them. Supposedly Billy hadn't identified the body. He wasn't in any shape to. It was some random distant cousin no one had heard of. Paz couldn't bring herself to believe the things people said — that Romy was out in the desert working on the moon-shot project no one had seen but everyone had heard about. Or worse, that she was with Billy in Rome, where they had married. Would Billy stay in Rome? For everyone who talked, it was just a few minutes of gossip, but to her, every word was permanent dynamite.

'Are you going to the pyros right now?' Essa asks, not looking up.

'I told them I'd be there for ten.'

'It's nice to have an adult in the room for a change,' she says, scraping the excess lint carefully off the paper with her fingernail. 'Wait,' she says as Paz moves toward the door. 'Before you go, let's go out tonight. Maarten is having a party.'

'Oh. I don't know.' Paz hesitates. 'I really need to get that piece for Ora done.'

'Come on. Just one drink. My mom already said she'd look after Flea. You can sleep here. Besides, I need someone to celebrate with now that I'm officially no longer Mrs Old Sumbitch.'

'Okay, one drink,' Paz says, aware how rare it is for Essa to ask for anything. 'Two drinks max.' She lingers at the door, again considering telling Essa about the postcard, but she doesn't want her to see how broken everything is.

Before he'd left, Billy had said to Paz, 'A part of me wants this, more than anything,' as though they weren't already married. And now she wonders how many parts he has. Especially when he drinks. Sometimes she could smell alcohol on him, even when they'd been with the baby all day. It didn't make any sense, so she let it go. She had that splintering feeling at a party in June. Cotton was cutting lines and Paz and Billy did some too. It made her body feel like it was on an ice floe. After a certain point, she looked at Billy and the phrase mysterious jumble of fragments got into her head and wouldn't leave. At one point he leaned over to her and called her a little monster and she felt completely gutted. And then he said, 'The only good monster I know.' Why monster? she wanted to know and then thought, a woman always wants to know why, a man wouldn't need to know. Then she got incredibly paranoid and was unsure whether she'd imagined the whole thing.

No one would use the word happy to describe him, but he has his moments. She needs to remind herself. Like when she told him about new work she wanted to make and he listened to her intently, noticing that the whole time he had been lightly rocking the baby in her chair with his foot. 'To change your art, you have to change yourself,' he said, something he'd learned from the famous German artist he'd studied with. She could listen about that time with the artist nonstop. She liked that nothing was weird to him. Like the time she submitted a sketch to Ora when she'd first come back and was so full of nerves she made him lie on top of her to squash out her anxiety with his weight, and he did, until he had to get up and do something in the kitchen. Or the night after she'd had to put Aunt May in the home and couldn't stop crying. He scaled a fence and cut an armful of lilacs with a knife for her because she'd once told him she liked the smell of them. He was made up of gestures, but they spilled out beyond. When she watched his performances she was always a little shocked. There was something about the person in them she had no access to.

When she leaves Essa's house, she sits in the car for a moment without starting the engine. She notices the windshield is so covered in purple blossoms she has to turn the wipers on. Even all the flowers are dropping to earth.

ON THE I-10, PAZ SQUINTS — she's forgotten her sunglasses. The sun arrows brightly in her eyes. She's supposed to go to the pyros, it's the whole reason she arranged to bring Flea to Georgette, but now that she's in the truck alone, she just feels like driving. Driving feels weighted and strange ever since she got her pilot's license. It's flatly two-dimensional being on a road, like a drawing of a car on a piece of paper. The flight instructors call everyone down here 'ground pounders', running around in their mazes, learning to memorize turns so they don't even have to be awake. It makes a person different spending time up in the air — everything feels vital. It's the same way Romy felt. At least, it's the way Paz imagines she did. Romy had written about how clear she got when flying, about how ideas came to her in the air.

AUGUST 1970. *I had to adjust my flight patterns because there were constant Navy jets running practice drills over Wonder Valley. I flew at such a high altitude I saw the distant stacks of clouds a hundred miles out, flying so high I could see exactly where I was. I've never felt so totally oriented. Being up there flying, you have to learn to use your eyes all over again. Not like when I had to stare long and hard at bowls of fruit in art school. You have to pay attention in a way you've never had to your whole life. On my way back, flying much lower, I saw a glinting shape, an odd dome. I found out that it was built by a Howard Hughes test pilot who said aliens had*

64

instructed him to build a reverse-aging machine, so he constructed the dome
without nails that used some sort of electromagnetism of Tesla's. When I
told this to Red, she just shook her head and said, fucking desert. Makes
everyone a nutcase.

❊ ❊ ❊

The owner of the flight school wore a complicated zip flight-suit tight around his crotch and had a face like a hit man. Even his non-flight clothing had a surfeit of zippers. The first time Paz met him, he held out his hand, and when she shook it, he put his other hand over hers and held it there a little too long, like a sandwich. Somehow, he made it feel dirty. His hands were hot and big and damp. He was always making sandwiches of her hands. He'd eyed her and said, 'God, you're tiny,' in a way that made her feel like a dog treat. In the middle of her training, he asked her if she wanted to see a movie. She really did not, but felt she had to because he'd offered a bunch of night hours in one of his Cessnas so she could complete the instruments portion of her license, and it wasn't clear if they would be free if she said no.

They met outside the Pacific Theater in West Hollywood. She didn't recognize him out of his flight suit. He was wearing a leather jacket, white tube socks with black dress shoes, and looked a bit like a pimp. He looked her up and down like he had expected her to show up in something else. He said he wanted to give her some advice. Just like a man to have an opinion on everything, she thought. He said she would be more attractive if she dressed better and did something with her hair. He clearly did something with his, using something resembling shoe polish. She didn't say anything to him, though she wanted to. The movie was a quasi-film noir that had a lot of sex in it, which made sitting next to him in the dark even more awkward. She could see him out the corner of her eye trying to make eye contact with her.

But after that, he took her out flying at night and it was the most beautiful thing she'd ever seen. The black velvet night and a sweep of colorful lights, like an inverse galaxy glittering way below. Everything looked so organized, so simple from up there. Houses were just lights going out. She started to get this glazed-eye way of looking at it where every single thing was equal because there was no exact focus, something she knew she would use in her light works. The flight school owner could see that she was mesmerized and said, 'Some people pay a lot of money for this view.' And then looked at her funny because maybe he realized she too was paying for it. She landed precisely, one of her best yet. 'Not bad,' he said, and then added, 'for a girl.'

* * *

The wind is hot on the freeway and there is a hard pressure firmly on Paz's chest. She keeps thinking she's hearing the baby crying, and glances back, reminding herself she's alone. Her brain is playing tricks, the way you sometimes can still hear the ocean when you are in the desert. She looks up and realizes she's tailgating a Trans Am with a bumper sticker that says, HONK IF YOU EXIST. She turns up the radio very loud because music stops everything. Cheap Trick's 'Surrender' plays, followed by 'Baby's on Fire', and then Emmylou Harris and Gram Parsons singing 'Love Hurts', and she wonders if God is communicating with her through the radio. She feels so teenage, this much living in her head. She is going to cry, she might be freaking out, something is welling, but instead she bursts out laughing and can't stop. She's heaving over the wheel, laughing like a maniac, which makes driving difficult, so she pulls over. She is dangerously on the edge of the freeway. A car speeds by honking at her. *I exist*, she thinks and then starts laughing again. She turns off the car engine, and immediately the arm resting on the window starts to burn with heat. She is thinking, not for the first time, about where her body stops and where the air begins and what it would mean to obliterate whatever that space or point in time is and find some metaphysical dimension that would make everything connect so there would be no barriers.

APRIL 1977. *The event horizon is a term that physicists use for the boundary beyond which we cannot know what happens.*

She rests her forehead on the steering wheel. She doesn't know what this is. Anxiety weighs on her like a stone. She starts the car and accelerates off the shoulder, oncoming cars missing her by a hair, and is so in her head she blows right past her exit. Why hasn't Billy called? She suddenly sees the whole imagined spectrum of Romy joining him at the apartment in Rome. She pictures them huddled conspiratorially, low whispers, bodies touching, the gratifying solidity of what Romy has just pulled off. They could start again there. Who hasn't thought about altering radically and beyond recognition the conditions of their existence? Trading one old self for a new one. Paz has done it too. It panics her that he hasn't called at all, because then she has to acknowledge that something between them isn't working.

OCTOBER 15, 1969. I had my bare feet up on the dash. Wind whipping through the truck. The backs of my thighs stuck to the shiny surface of the seat. We didn't know where we were going. I drank big gulps of water from a flask that made it taste like iron.

We drove out along the Old Spanish Trail Highway. A ramshackle town with only a gas station came into focus. It was so hot the air was shimmering. I watched Billy as he filled up the gas tank, squinting into the sun. He went in to pay and came out with two ice creams, one in each hand, already melting in white lines down his knuckles. I didn't want ice cream but I ate it for the sake of the moment. We walked out into the sand, in the sun, drowsy with heat. The heat burned everything away, and there was only feeling left, of happiness at being here on the sand with him. No one else was on the road, at least that's how it felt. The light was so strong we had to shield our eyes. It seemed like we were in a race with the horizon, sharp and radiant.

After a while he said, do you want to tell me about why you don't eat?

There was a long silence. He was worried he'd offended me. He told me about how Milt had once been out for dinner in New York with Warhol and all he ordered was Jack Daniel's. Milt said Andy ate like a woman, always on war rations because he believed that eating was like pissing and shitting. He felt it was something shameful that couldn't be done in front of others, so he was always starving himself.

I wasn't sure why he was asking me this now. It might have been the cake he'd baked me for my birthday. It came out tilted from the heat. Confession:

I threw it up, I told him later. I liked having one bad thing a day, but the cake had been too much.

We drove a while longer and then I tried to explain to him that I hated that I was material. I said what I've always felt, that I wasn't attached to this body, it didn't at all house who I was. My body belonged to me, but it had never been my own. We didn't speak for a long time. I moved closer to him. I had never felt so good next to someone. I could have just kept driving forever like that through the desert with him. A hot rectangle of sunlight stayed on his hand while he drove. I kissed his neck and unbuckled his belt and when we couldn't bear it any longer, he pulled over. His body on mine, the sun white hot and shimmering outside. There was sand everywhere. He said my skin tasted like sugar. Nothing had ever felt so right as being with him. I felt insane with pleasure.

Back on the highway, I told him about the psychiatrist visits when I was younger. He'd said my eating issues stemmed from a desire to rid myself of the female form amplified by the 'utopian moral extremism' in which I'd been raised. Diagnosis: disassociated. On the drive home, I'd written the word UTOPIA *on my arm in black pen and then covered it with my sleeve. I'd felt utterly alone, with no territory of my own. I'd rejected being a 'girl' for a masculinity I would never be able to have. The psychiatrist had said one person alone is a utopia, but two people thinking the same thing is a reality. So I'm not in reality? I asked him. He seemed annoyed. What you are living in is almost a reality. I sensed he felt I was wasting his time. Almost is the longest word in the English language with all the letters in alphabetical order, I said.*

I told Billy that I'm always worried I'm going to have one of those grim periods again. I tried to explain them to him as these big dark oceanic states of mind that I felt completely lost in. I said it felt like I was flickering on and off.

The next time you feel yourself going dark, just don't. Use it in your work, he said. See what happens.

I laughed and shook my head — he didn't understand. Okay, now I've told you my humiliating things.

I've got nothing to tell.

Really?

No, he said, staring straight ahead. *Everyone has something to tell. If they don't, they're not human.*

He told me about the time his mother went to Antwerp when he was ten, because her own mother was dying. While she was away, Billy had come home from school early with a fever. He went to his bedroom so he could lie down and thought he heard a faint sound from the hallway. His father wasn't usually back from work until dinnertime. He slipped through the hall and followed the sound to a crack in the door. He saw a line of white, which he soon understood was his father's buttocks thrusting vigorously into a woman who was not his mother.

He said that growing up he'd been brutalized by his father, a very big man, also 6'5". He wasn't able to stand up for himself. His father bullied him until he had no will of his own. He had to get as far away as he could — the kind of far that involved crossing an ocean, learning another language, changing his name.

He passed me the flask, which was almost empty, and I took a sip. We decided we might just be saving each other. I wondered if it was fate.

I don't believe in fate, Billy said.

Of course he doesn't, I thought. He's a man. It's okay for men to make bad art. There's no price on their head for doing it. They aren't fixed in anything the way women are. They aren't born with all the eggs they'll ever get. Nothing for men is pre-determined, except their chance at great success.

Later, we got out of the truck to watch the sun go down. It was dropping, and the sky went pink as a sleeping pill. We could hear the screeching of some desert animal sluicing the soft air. He stared at the sand and then into my eyes. I'd already told him more about myself than anyone else I'd ever met. He put his arms around me and kissed my neck. He told me he loved me. It just came out. The moment was unbearably intense. I will always remember it, the origin of that feeling. The day the desert married us whether we knew it or not.

* * *

The sign blinks neon when Paz eventually pulls in. She switches off the engine and takes out the key, noticing how Ka-Boom is really just a trailer butted up against some of the driest land she's ever seen that isn't desert. Paz had gone straight from flight school to apprenticing to get her pyrotechnic license. It's the same place Romy had gone, but Romy had only picked up some comets and mortar tubes and got them to demonstrate. They also have all kinds of high-hazard special effects and don't seem to care about legalities or licensing. In fact, they have zero interest in women making art, which makes it simpler. Flyers for pizza, guns, and Jesus are tacked to the wall. For some reason they have a receptionist, even though Paz has never seen anyone in there. A large teenager in jeans and pancake makeup stares at Paz blankly, a face full of television static, cracking her gum. It makes her think of Fina's art. She makes what everyone calls cunt art, literally vaginas made out of clay and often chewing gum, because she says that's exactly what men do to women. They take them in, chew them up, and spit them out. If Fina had been remotely nicer, Paz would have wanted to get to know her. With women she finds threatening, there is always a kind of heat to it, the feeling that on some level what she really wants is to be friends with them.

The teenager motions to Paz to go out back where the two men who own the place, Kevin Anderson and Kevin Hill, are. They don't find having the same name funny but have to wait it out each time someone does. They are both in an arrested state of turbo-puberty but are very easy to distinguish. Kevin Anderson, or Kevin One as she refers to him, has an enormous paunch hanging over his belt buckle but is otherwise regular-sized. It always amazes her that men can have a huge stomach but go right on wearing the same size jeans. He's got big sweat marks on his shirt that go down his back like the boot of Italy, and is always splashing his face and neck with water from the bathroom sink, calling it his hoor bath. Kevin Two is a skinny little guy with baby hair who wears shorts no matter what. He has a dark beard covering up some rough-looking red skin. He's the kind of man who always keeps facial hair because he wants to remind you that he's a man, otherwise he's too small to get the sort of respect he's looking for. Though even if he got it, he wouldn't be any different.

Kevin Two had got weird with Paz like she suspected he must have done with Romy. Whenever they were hunched over some sort of firework, he'd suddenly wrap his arms around her from behind like he was showing her a golf swing, pressing his body so close against hers that she could feel his equipment. She wanted to knee him in the *holy jewels* as he called them, but she needed to know how to work with these pyrotechnics, which as it turns out, were quite complicated. Kevin Two said out of the blue, 'I like me a girl with good haunches. Not like your husband's first wife.' Kevin One said, 'What are you talking about, *hombre*. She was hot.' Kevin Two backpedaled. 'I mean don't get me wrong, she was hot. But not like, *hot* hot.' Kevin One piped up, 'In my experience, women without asses aren't good at fucking.' Paz wanted to say, And what experience is that? But she'd rather die than draw out this conversation further. She'd once walked up on them discussing Romy and her and Billy. They'd wanted to know who 'the husband' was. Kevin Two had somehow dug up a photo of Billy from an opening. 'Fuck me,' Kevin One had said in disbelief. 'That fruitcake?'

When they walk back around the trailer, Paz sees a snake move under a rock from the corner of her eye, and some kind of large lizard eating a ripped slice of Wonder Bread, blinking in the sun, robotically moving his arms and legs slowly across the dusty ground, hard as a bone.

PEOPLE ARE SITTING ON THE stoop and smoking outside Maarten's studio when they arrive. A bunch of the men, including formerly Old Sumbitch, have these big dirty studios all on the same block near Hill and Main. It's where they drink and do whatever they do in there. Essa says that if a meteor ever hit this block, it would be the end of the male gaze. Paz is aware that Essa has already had three sloe-gin fizzes and rolled a joint between her knees while driving here. Juke walks by them as they go in and nods. 'The feminists,' he says, and keeps walking toward Sam and Cotton.

'Is it me or does that seem like an accusation?' Paz says, mixing drinks and handing one to Essa.

'I told Juke to cut it out,' Essa says. 'But he just said, "You know I love women." I told him that's not what I meant and he said, "Listen, anyone that can jerk themselves off by crossing their legs a certain way has my total respect."'

Paz takes a sip of her drink. 'They hate it when we are up to something without them,' she says. 'They prefer fur flying, some blood on the floor. Anyway, he's not worth it, Ess. He's that kind of man.'

'What kind?'

'The kind that can't even hear a woman talking.'

'Maybe he'll get bored and leave,' Paz says.

'We'll never get that lucky.'

'Can I just tell you that your attitude toward men s-u-x.' They turn their heads and see Ora, who has magicked her way between them. 'The

73

original *homme fatale*,' she says, gesturing toward Sam. He is legendary for keeping to himself in the desert, talking to no one except Ora, who's been his gallerist for so long she's basically omniscient. Essa wants the latest story. 'Come on,' she coaxes her. 'Tell us.'

'Holy fuckoly. Okay, so I get this panicked call from a girl named Anna, an editor who is high up at *Art Forum*. She met Sam when they shot over the Mojave Desert. His family comes from out there, wherethefuckever in the desert, so he feels it's his. I'm always telling him, 'You can't own the desert, Sam, you little bitch.' Anyway, pretty soon Anna moved out there and brought her dog, a big Great Dane named Jonesy. Sam hated the dog.' She takes a slug of her Jim Beam.

'She soon realized that anything, any little thing that took away even a minute from Sam's work made him crazy. He woke up at the crack of dawn, got dressed in the dark, didn't even eat, and went out to the machinery. He'd stay out until dark and then do it over again. At first, she thought it was exotic, how filthy he was. The rare time she'd seen him in a clean shirt, she thought he looked like an ex-con trying to make a new start in life. He just looked better dirty. The equipment he used made this high-pitched squealing sound that made Jonesy go ballistic, barking and leaping at it like crazy. They tried to keep him outside, but it was too hot. Inside he began clawing everything to shreds. He tore up the floor, broke a window, ripped the screen door. Sam had to keep replacing it and they started fighting about all the damage the dog was causing. She would try to take Jonesy for walks, but it was impossible in all that heat. And outside he would just start barking and charging the equipment. Sam had this kind of farm-kid mentality and would pick up a rock and hurl it at him, saying, "Don't destroy it, for fuck's sake." One morning, after she came back from getting supplies in town, Jonesy was gone. She started calling for him and walking everywhere to find him but there was no trace of him. She looked frantically for him but started giving up hope after a few weeks. There was one small little creek that occasionally had water in it after a rain, and she went out to it and that's when she saw him. There was dust in his fur and his eyes were tightly closed. His body was oddly intact, though one thing was clear. There was a bullet hole clean between his eyes.

'When Sam got back that night, she confronted him. She had drunk several water glasses full of Scotch, so angry her hands were shaking so badly she had to sit on them. He drank his beer and stared at her with his goddamn blue eyes and said coldly, "Yeah, I shot him."

'She lost her mind. He'd said nothing. For weeks. Never once stopped her from looking for the dog. He'd shot the bloody thing and then after, he came back and slept with her. She said, "I mean, what kind of psychopath does that?"'

'What I wanted to say to Anna was how stupid it all was,' Ora says. 'Followed that man out there because of his goddamn looks and shacked up with him. And look what happened. The shit people'll do for sex. All for rubbing their dumb skin up to someone else's.'

'Jesus, Ora, I hope you didn't say that to her,' Essa says.

'Why do you think she called me? I drove out there and picked her up. She was crying and yelling at him, saying he was going to kill her. I exchanged a look with Sam. We both knew what this was. The elimination of distraction.'

'I mean,' Paz says after a long silence, 'he's not *that* good-looking.'

'My advice, sisters, is that maybe it's time we talk about turning this sausage party into a clambake,' Ora says, taking a big sip of her drink. 'You might want to consider coming over to the pink side.'

'Yeah, not sure I can deal with other women's parts,' Essa says. 'All those vaginas needing something.'

Ora puts her arm around Essa. 'Tell me, you given blowjobs before?'

'What does that have to do with it?'

'I'm just saying. There's a reason they put the word "job" in it.'

Wanda and Juke are arguing near them. She and her sister Gloria had grown up in Malibu, put fresh gardenias in their hair and painted their nails grape, and went out every night of the week. They were both like leading ladies out of an old movie, the kind where the men and women throw one-liners back and forth like darts.

Ora shakes her head toward Wanda. 'Poor kid tried to kill herself when she found out that Juke was sleeping with Gloria. People were saying that Gloria was pregnant, which I guess was true because I heard Juke say, "Hell, might've been mine, I was pretty gone, you know?"'

'Jesus Christ,' Paz says.

'Wanda apparently cried off all her makeup and then took eighty-nine Tylenols, counting them out on her bed. She said they looked like little footballs on her bedspread. When she got out of the hospital they got right back together.'

Gloria walks over, her gold bracelets sparkling as she lights her Salem. 'What do you say we take this bottle of Wild Turkey and ditch these fuckwits?'

An art student named Tammy joins them. She starts talking up her work to Ora, not yet aware that the kind of blunt-force self-promotion she is using never ever works. When eventually she notices Ora's face fixed in a kind of death mask, Tammy gives up, and then out of the blue says, 'I think I like Steve.'

Gloria blows a smoke ring. 'Which one is Steve?'

'You know, messy hair, tall. A bit of a drinking problem.'

'That's basically all of them, honey.'

PAZ TURNS ON THE FAUCET and fills a glass with water. The sink is littered with melting ice cubes, old olive pits, and a broken beer bottle. She feels a bit drunk, which always makes her try to act more sober. Ma and Aunt May changed when they drank, the sign of a problem drinker, she knows. Drinking like they want to get somewhere else. It happens to Billy too. He gets dark and remote. She hears Red talking to Maarten as she walks by. 'I've started documenting everything because I fucking love all of my ideas.'

'You don't weed them out at all? I would find that too much,' Maarten says, rolling a joint.

'I think it's criminal to come up with an idea and not see it through.'

Maarten says, 'Like what?'

Red looks at him. 'Are you kidding? I'm not going to tell you and then wait to see if you boost one.' She holds up a smooth egg-like ceramic sculpture and says, 'Where did you get this piece of garbage?'

'Careful with that. It's by a famous Japanese sculptor. We traded art when he was here.' Maarten turns to Essa. 'Red has perfect taste,' he says. 'She hates everything.'

'Ha fucking ha,' she says, standing back. 'Now, this' — she motions to a large light-panel of Romy's — 'this I can get behind. Because it's bitch work. And it rules.'

Paz's drink gets knocked by Luanne, the only woman in the room who's never judged her. 'Oh god, sorry,' she says. Luanne has heavily made-up eyes and is a bit hard to get to know, but she's taken mushrooms and is uncharacteristically chatty tonight. 'Did I finance my college education by stripping? You bet I did,' she says to Paz, her voice high but sultry. Her lipstick is a bit outside of her lips. 'Some guy told me I should dance, and I thought about it and decided I would make a good stripper, so I auditioned for him and the club's owner. I realized a bit too late that Brian Eno's "Here Come the Warm Jets" was actually a bit repetitive and esoteric to dance to.' She takes a sip of her drink. 'But I managed to pass with flying colors.' She stops to adjust her halter top, which stays surprisingly stationary. 'Damn it,' she says. 'Who the hell invented halter tops anyway? Must've been a man. Who else would design something that makes you carry the weight of your boobs around your neck.'

'How did it feel' — Paz is curious — 'to strip?'

Luanne shrugs. 'I'd rather sell my ass than my soul,' she says, looking directly at Paz with her beautiful hazel eyes. 'I mean, I sold a few minutes and a couple parts of my body.' She takes a long sip of her drink. The party has grown and they are getting crushed into a corner by the back door. She studies Paz for a moment and then says, 'I think you've got a secret,' which shocks Paz into a sudden alertness. 'Jesus, don't look so worried, you look like you're being murdered. It's just — I have a read on people.'

Paz doesn't have time to respond because Maarten is telling them all to move. He's making space around Doug Cotton, who is sitting on a red vinyl chair. Paula, a woman who had been with the Black Panthers and now makes films with a lot of muff and guns, is pointing her 16mm camera at Cotton's face while Keith, in a pair of aviators, bends over him with pliers. He holds them up to the light. There is an energy running through the room like water. Paz can feel a kind of quiet electricity sparking off Cotton. And then, in a few violent movements, Keith rips Cotton's lower incisor right out. Blood sprays and hits Keith's aviators. It drips down Cotton's chin. Paula holds the camera for a second longer and then stops it and says, 'Okay. Got that,' robotically, like she's reading off a teleprompter. Cotton pulls off his T-shirt, balls it up, and stuffs it in his mouth, and then punches a hole clean through the wall.

'One of these pills gotta work,' a guy in a T-shirt that reads, NOBODY'S HOME, says, offering them to Cotton who palms the entire handful. 'I'm going to call it *Tonight Beauty is Dead*,' Cotton says, gritting his teeth. Tammy, the art student, is holding Cotton's T-shirt up to his mouth, which is still trickling blood. They aren't doing anything about it because they are both so stoned they think the blood on the shirt looks beautiful.

Out in the yard, Paz sits on the back steps. She feels a bit nauseated. She can't see the moon. She's always felt grounded by its light, and the light of elusive planets. There is the thinnest breeze that makes the dry leaves rattle slightly.

'It's dark out here,' Fina says, standing on the steps. She sits down beside Paz who barely glances in Fina's direction. She's not up for another confrontation. She rests her forehead against her palm.

'I need to tell you something,' Fina says while she fumbles and lights her cigarette, and then exhales a stream of smoke. She seems nervous. She's wearing an iridescent dress that flashes in the dark like a fish in an aquarium. It hisses when she moves. Paz feels like her entire body is floating up, away from her, and if she says one word it will disappear for good. She sees that Fina is staring at her.

'I got another one today.' She clears her throat. Fina's skin is so smooth it looks like it's been polished. 'Here,' she says, passing her the postcard. Another cream-colored A6, with an intricate pencil drawing of star fields. Paz squints her eyes and turns it over. IIO DEGREES. She feels a bolt of nausea that suddenly comes right up out of her, and she grips the side of the concrete steps and throws up in the burned-out grass. Her eyes are watering, and her throat and stomach burn. Fina hands her a tissue from her bag and Paz uses it to wipe her mouth, which might be Fina's first truly generous act.

'I could let the first one go,' Fina says. 'But a second one? It's her handwriting.'

'Fina,' Paz says, 'she fell — off a thirteen-story building. It's got to be someone's idea of a joke.'

'Maybe you're right,' she says. 'But Romy had a different frequency when she was preparing for a performance. I could feel it. Even though she never liked talking about anything in progress. I felt it from her that night at Milt's.' She blows out smoke. 'No one was actually there when it happened. Everyone had already left that night.' Paz feels little pricks on her skin with these words. 'Billy was so gone, some cousin of hers I've never heard of was called to supposedly identify her body.'

Paz had heard people say things like this before but it had always washed over her. Has she just seen what she wanted to see, all this time? There are different accounts of the accident. Jumped or pushed hangs in the air. Her heart catches as the door swings open and an artist named Larry steps out carrying a fan of color swatches.

'Which color is heavier?' Larry says, shoving the swatches at them.

'Not now, Larry,' Fina says, irritated.

'I'm conducting a poll,' he says, 'it's for my color survey.' Larry strikes a match and holds it up to the strips. Fina begrudgingly points to a dark blue. 'Why blue?'

'I thought we just needed to choose the color, Larry,' Fina says flatly.

'I'm looking for your judgments,' he says. 'The results will indicate the truth.'

'Well,' Fina says, 'Yves Klein said blue has no dimensions.'

'You're quoting that colonizer?' he says. 'How can an artist *own* a color, man.' He then turns toward Paz and says, 'I can feel energy radiating off you, like, whoa.' The flame is getting close to his fingers.

'Red,' she says.

Cotton comes out and looks at Larry. 'The hell is that?' he asks, referencing Larry's eyeliner and piratey-looking shirt.

'I don't know, trying something out,' he says, a bit embarrassed.

More people are out on the stoop, and when Paz looks up Fina is gone and there are just bodies and stars and heat.

THEY SEE THE BLINKING SQUARE of light from the backyard before they go in, surprised to find Georgette still up, watching *Bonnie and Clyde* with Flea, whose face is red from crying. 'People who look that good would never need to resort to crime,' Georgette says, passing Paz the baby, who looks pissed, hot, and sticky in her too-warm sleeper. Paz remembers watching it with Georgette the year she threw out Essa's dad until he 'came to his senses'. Georgette had kicked the kitchen door so hard it came off its hinges. Eighteen years of commitment went into the force of that kick. Paz understood that coming to his senses meant ditching the woman he'd been sleeping with, some dancer he'd met at Fox. When Georgette started dating an actor, he came right back. Long before her dad, Essa's mom had briefly dated a very tall man named Marion, who later became the actor known as John Wayne. Supposedly Katharine Hepburn had confessed how thrilling it was to lean against him. She'd said it was like leaning against a great tree, a notion Georgette heartily seconded. 'Yeah, I bet,' Essa said. 'A great white-supremacist tree.'

'Wait,' Paz said to Essa, 'John Wayne's name was *Marion*?' She'd seen a list of the worst movies of the last fifty years, which included *The Conqueror*, a film he'd starred in. Wild horses were chased by helicopters in the Nevada desert a hundred miles from a test site for nuclear bombs. *Live bombs.* During the filming, John Wayne had carried a black box around. It turned out to be a Geiger counter that crackled so loudly everyone thought it was broken.

'There are some cherry tarts from Blum's, if you girls are hungry,' Georgette adds, holding out a plate. 'Not as good as Nana's, but they're not bad.'

'Nana's tarts were gross,' Essa says. 'They were always bitter.'

'Well,' Georgette says, stopping, turning toward Essa, 'that's because I put medicine in them.'

'What kind of medicine?' Essa asks, stretching out each syllable.

'Valium.'

'Jesus H. Now I know why I always felt so weird on the plane. I don't think Valium works the same way on kids.' Essa squints at Georgette. 'Who are you again?'

'Hi, I'm your mother. The person who gave birth to you,' Georgette says, sticking out her hand for Essa to shake, 'without anesthesia.'

Paz takes a tart and they go to Essa's room. After she's unzipped the baby's sleeper and fed Flea her bottle, she follows Essa, who slides open the glass door and lets out the dog. They smoke a joint in the garden. Paz eats almost the whole tart in one bite, the sweet sticky cherries and thick cream filling her throat. Essa has the hiccups as they go back into Essa's room and flop into her bed. A minute goes by. 'Fuck,' Essa says and starts to cry. 'I still can't believe he left me.' She hiccups loudly. She is crying and hiccupping and breathing raggedly. The dog gets up, comes over, and licks her face.

'I should have known it was doomed,' she says, sitting up a little. Paz wonders if Essa is referring to her first night with Old Sumbitch. She'd said it was passionate and violent and not without a certain horror. He'd ripped her favorite skirt.

'Maybe I should call him,' Essa says and hiccups.

'Not on my watch,' Paz says. 'You call him, and I will be forced to kill you.'

After a long silence Essa says, 'I made out with Maarten.'

'What?' Paz suddenly sits up, alert. 'When?'

'Exhibit A,' Essa says, ignoring Paz, 'why you can't take me to a party. I mean' — she pauses — 'he was friends with Ed.' Essa lets out a huge yawn and then says, 'Fuck. I just really need to get out of Oz,' which sends them into a silent fit of laughter, trying not to wake Flea who has passed out in her diaper like she's been anesthetized.

After they lie there in silence for a while, Paz says quietly, 'Ess, I have to tell you something.'

Essa had been the only person growing up who made Paz feel less alone in her ambitions. They could talk about almost everything, except the dark little corners Paz kept to herself. They only had one rough patch, that first year Essa was with Old Sumbitch. Paz was incapable of pretending the situation wasn't awful. She and Essa had been conspirators. They'd gone on fed-up marches. They'd signed a petition to get Susan B. Anthony's face on a coin. They'd smoked cigarettes and talked about going to art school and getting an apartment in New York together, and then suddenly Essa was a wife. Was she fucking kidding her — a *wife*? Paz still feels a twist of guilt around it, all the months she could barely talk to her, but then Essa started calling her again after Ed left. She was really down and Paz was trying to cheer her up. 'Come on, it doesn't sound like you. You are the one person I count on to always like life.' She heard Teddy and the TV in the background. 'Okay, name me something you like,' Paz said. 'It can be anything.' There was a long pause. Paz could faintly hear what she thought was Bugs Bunny's Brooklyn accent. 'Trees,' Essa finally said after a long time. 'I like trees no matter what. See? You can't say I don't like life.'

Paz is drunk and the room is spinning unless she lies on her left side. 'Ess, promise me you won't —' She breathes out. 'I think there might be a chance that Romy is alive.' As she says it, she feels the air go clean out of her. She clears her throat and whispers a little louder, 'I know I sound crazy, but a postcard came with her handwriting and it was postmarked from last week.' She stops. 'I wanted to tell you. Then Fina cornered me at Maarten's and showed me a second postcard. It scared me because I suddenly realize how little I know about what happened that night. I can't stop thinking what if it's some sort of performance, and Romy is with Billy in Rome right now and that's why I haven't heard from him. And I'm trying to —'

When Essa doesn't say anything, she rolls over toward her. She is completely passed out. The baby flings out an arm and hits Paz hard in the face and doesn't wake up. Her brain is churning. She can't bear the thought of losing what she doesn't in fact have. She starts to sweat, her whole body flaming up in Essa's airless room. She coughs through the rattle of the fan. She feels like she is losing control of everything, and having Essa sleeping beside her while she lies there wide awake is only slightly reassuring.

Wednesday

THE ACRYLIC SHEET IS HOT when she gets it out of the truck. She lays it flat on Romy's studio table. She will work this afternoon when the baby has her nap. Suddenly the thought comes into her head that if Romy is alive somewhere, it means she will come back for Flea. For a moment, her body feels loose with relief. She would be able to get her life back in order. She's sunk into glumness, worn herself out. But then she looks down at Flea, her small hand clasping Paz's shoulder, and hates herself with a sharpness reserved for the kind of person who could have such a thought. Her notions of freedom are no better than all the shitty men. Flea has taken her away from making art, but she has also lifted her out of the stream of regular life. Her heart has grown.

She tires Flea out by running around the house, going for a walk in the paralyzing sun. They come inside where the dog is lapping water from his dented metal dish, nosing it to the corner. They play peek-a-boo for a long time. Paz laughs at Flea's logic: anything she can't see, can't see her. She reads all her favorite books, ending with *Goodnight Moon* with the line about saying goodnight to nobody that always kills her. It seems way too dark and existential for a baby. Flea stares up at her with a serious expression as Paz changes her diaper and then gives her some formula. She sits on the couch. Flea's eyes close as she's drinking, and soon her small body twitches and then she finally falls asleep in Paz's arms. Paz puts her heavy sleeping body in the playpen and turns on the fan. She might have as many as three hours to work.

MARCH 1970. *It happened when we were sitting on his couch. Billy told me he'd received the Prix de Rome. A paid apartment and studio for a year in Italy. A year, I repeated. You'll be going soon? It came out in a cold tone I hadn't intended. I felt stung. He looked surprised and said nothing, and somehow it was too late for me to say what I wanted to say. That I wanted him to ask me to come with him. And, if I were to admit it, that I wanted to be the one getting the Prix de Rome. Everything after that felt like it was moving too quickly, impossible to stop. There was a long pause and then he said, looking away from me, I guess you'll want to see other people, then. I felt something snap sharply inside me. And I don't know why, but I said, yes. And somehow with one word everything was undone.*

APRIL 1970. *Red picked me up in her truck and we moved the couple of boxes of art supplies I had. I'm staying with her until I can find my own place. I don't really want to live with anyone, but she doesn't either. She said, I've got no air conditioning, a broken pull-out, and one condition — you have to make art. I've never met a woman who can keep up with the men and still be prolific. She stores sheets of acid in her freezer and pops pills like candy. Sam drops by sometimes. Yesterday I heard him become one of her conversation pieces.*

Sam: You gotta be careful about that space between art and life.
Red: Yeah? What about it?
Sam: You gotta keep it a space.

Red has a big black tomcat, Anarchy, whose name she regrets since he began pissing on everything in the apartment, including most of my books and some of my clothes. He hunts the lizards that shelter in Red's pot plants on the balcony. I've started going out on night walks by myself and have

been taking photos of the ocean. When I get home, I make pencil drawings
of clouds, star fields, the surface of the moon. I make a lot of mistakes, but
they're not mistakes when I can see what's good about them. I've been going
to the library and looking up books on constellations. On a few occasions, I'm
ashamed to admit that I've sliced a photograph out of a book with a razor,
even though planets and stars look like shit in photographs.

Well, well, Red said, looking through the drawings. We've got a woman
among us who isn't afraid of her own talent.

I was talking to Sam about how I wanted to do big light-works in the
desert. I thought about flying. He said, if you get a pilot's license, you'll get
that Duchampian aerial view. I thought of something I read when I was a
kid. The best thing for being sad is to learn something.

SEPTEMBER 1970. Red tore up the cat-piss-gold carpet in the apartment
with an X-Acto knife and was stuffing it into garbage bags when I got home.
The floor looked terrible covered in glue and dirt. It still smells like cat piss in
here, I told her.

Jesus, fuck, she said and flopped down on the couch. She'd already taken
a hit of LSD and needed to do something while she waited to score some hash
from her dealer, and she hated her painting. Amateur hour, she said. I don't
know why I'm making it. The last painting I sold got returned to me when
the man who bought it found out it was painted by a woman. Fucker said it
wouldn't appreciate.

People with money always live in the past. You gotta keep at it.

She poured some cheap red wine into two mugs and passed me one. I'ma try.

I'm surprised you're back to painting, I said to her.

Me? I've always liked painting. It's so direct. You can make it in your
fucking underwear in your own living room. You can talk to it, you know?

We sat there angrily plotting. She sometimes does very cartoonish lewd
drawings that skin magazines occasionally buy, but she limits them because

she hates the idea of anything she makes becoming decorative. It was a good distraction talking to Red. I'd been out with Fina and Cotton and some of the others and overheard people talking about Billy. About how much he likes the co. of women. A poet. An actress who was in an Antonioni film. The wife of a gallerist. A contessa, etc. etc. etc. Yeah, Red shook her head and said, see, now that's a horse you can't put back in the barn.

Paz puts the journal down, looking at it. She's wasting valuable time, she knows. She needs to start working. It's just an object, she thinks. It doesn't mean anything. But the leather is skin in her hands, it feels bodily.

OCTOBER 1970. *Spending so much time with Red has made me want to do performances again. I've been working on one where I get buried with actual dirt. It smells sharp and alive though it's terrifying barely being able to breathe. Cotton and Sam were at the gallery talking to Ora. I saw Sam as I was leaving. I've ruined my jacket, I said. You're a complete mess, he said, stabbing out his cigarette. We went back to the apartment he was staying at. He removed my pants and my jacket, and put them in the bathtub. He ran the water hot and cleaned the dirt off them and then hung them on the door to dry. It made me think of my mother, who believed large appliances were capitalist, bent over the river doing our laundry. Scrubbing our underpants with a wire brush. All the crotches had little holes in them. I sat naked smoking on Sam's couch, the blue upholstery rough against my skin, unsure of what I was doing there.*

NOVEMBER 1970. *Red came in and saw me eating soft-boiled eggs with a spoon. Do you want one? We sat eating our eggs in silence. She was in a bad mood, I could tell.*

The yolk tastes like human being, she finally said.
You've eaten human beings before? I said.
Cock, she said. It tastes like cock.
Hold on, I said, are you recording this?

As Paz walks to the studio, something falls off the shelf — a book — and makes a loud thud. She jumps, sweaty, her heart racing. Flea starts crying and then screaming. She raises her arms to be picked up, and Paz lifts her, walking around the living room, angrily jiggling her, calming her down. Flea cries louder, kicking her legs and pounding her fists on Paz's shoulder. A putrid tang fills the air. The baby appears to have shat herself. She changes her, and then begins walking around with her again. After what seems like an eternity, Flea's body slackens, and Paz calms the jiggling down as her anger subsides. It's as if the universe is conspiring against her making art. Another ten minutes of steady jiggling and the baby is limp and damp. Paz's arms are tired, and sweat is beading across her forehead and dripping down her stomach. She gently shuts the door and walks to the studio.

APRIL 1971. The letters and calls have started from Rome. He said he misses my face. He misses my drawings, which he took seriously, and also my badly rendered projects on little bits of paper. He mentioned the day in the desert when the sun bleached out our pasts. He remembers me saying I wanted to make things that couldn't be drawn. He said important moments in life are the ones your body knows before your mind does. He told me he likes how I look at things, my eyes going over everything, like fingers. In the desert, we had driven out near Death Valley and had been mesmerized by the light burning over everything. We didn't say anything but we both felt it in the same way. He wrote about desert dogs howling and the silent desert creatures

and all that glittering sand. He said the sky had never been as vast or as blue.
I remember that sky. All that blue that I wanted to swallow us up. A telegram,
even. I'm beginning to think I dreamed you STOP standing in the garden
gazing out on the deserted street STOP

Paz reads as the sun drills through the south window. She touches the back of her hand to her forehead but can't feel anything. She feels inanimate. Her eyes go to the shelf with a notebook of Romy's with ROME 1971 on the spine. It's impossible to think that what she has started could ever be stopped.

I know he is working all the time since he left for Rome. But I also know
that at night, there are constant parties and openings. Whole days and
nights disappear. When we were at an opening at Milt's last year, a well-
known actress commented on his 'beautiful Roman profile' with high,
horse cheekbones. 'Roman'? I thought. 'Horse'? I know that women offer
themselves to him, and he takes them.

Paz switches on the saw, wincing at the loud zing. She doesn't even feel like making this piece, but now that she is at the point of avoiding Ora's calls, she needs to produce something. The heat is unbearable. Why hasn't it rained? She is longing for the heavy earth scent, for thick green grass and tiny colorful flowers to sweep across the lawn. She lines up the small pencil mark with the blade, her hands a bit shaky. She feels an ache radiating deep in her skull. Her thoughts had been remote and planetary, but now she's filled with sharp emotion. Her sweat smells like alcohol. In the studio she's already burned her body weight in sage, but nothing can clear the feeling that she doesn't belong in here. Her stomach lurches from hunger, but the idea of food makes her almost retch. She sees Fina hissing in silver, her bare feet, her long fingers holding a cigarette, talking about the postcards. It's just not possible. It's the one thing we know about life. When you die, you disappear and you don't come back. Her face flushes with heat and she wipes her forehead with the back of her hand.

None of it adds up. Romy could be alive. She could be in Rome with Billy at this very moment. Does she have someone dispatching postcards from the desert for her? To do — what? Stage some sort of performance? Paz shakes her head thinking how far-fetched it is, and starts to feel a little sick again. Billy's silence is humiliating. She doesn't love it when he treats her badly, but because of how exquisite it feels when he doesn't. How can she possibly love a man like that? But then the feeling of missing him invades her conviction. Her palms are so damp she wipes them on her shirt and then runs them down her pants before she slowly feeds the panel into the saw. It is satisfying to see the blade go through cleanly. She is working with a combination of terror and seriousness, now barely feeling the vicious heat or the weight of the materials. The work is one of the only things that is her own right now, even if it insists on similarities to Romy's. She might be in some sort of conversation with Romy, and so what? She is interested in making big works, like the ones that had first attracted her at Ora's group show. The kind Romy never got to finish making. To her it seems perfectly natural that she would use Romy's materials that are still right there. She breathes out slowly. There is a humming in her ears. The whole room is humming and her heart catches immediately at the loud erupting thunder of the dog barking wildly, a harsh growl ripping out of his throat, quickly joined by the baby crying, and then there is a loud bump and a flash of black in her eyes. Pain shoots up her entire body and stops her from breathing. She grabs some rags and wraps them around her hand, and they turn completely red.

HER MIND IS SINKING, SINKING, dropping like a stone. She struggles to hang on, thrashes out. She feels the sensation of slowly rolling off a cliff with nothing to hold on to. Her body jerks. 'All falls are about failure,' Billy had told her in New York. 'It's just the moment of gravity taking over the body.'

DECEMBER 1972. *We fall from the moment we are born. Our whole life is one big fall. Falling asleep. Falling ill. Falling pregnant. Falling in love. We fall in love so that we might keep the other from falling.*

Okay, two more steps back, he called down. When you fall, it ends, I said. Sweat dripping down the back of my neck. His arms were hugging the tree, toes bent so that he could grip the bark and hoist his body up to the enormous branch over his head. He said he could see the thin line of the mountains in the distance. He'd only ever lived one meter below sea level in a rainy Dutch town. California was so vast. Fires! Landslides! Earthquakes! Even the disasters here were oversized. When he came here, he felt as though he'd switched off a little black-and-white television and traded it for a huge one of color.

Paz's life before LA comes in flashes. She remembers how in Montreal people could barely recognize each other for half the year, under big puffy jackets, hats, and scarves across their faces. It got so cold that the windows frosted over. Sometimes she slept in a sweater, two pairs of pants, and her snowsuit, next to Ma in a used fur coat. The pillows were cold as ice. She had felt almost comforted in the cold because cold is hard. It's a mobilizing activity. People prepared for it there like animals. She remembers going with her first-grade class to a pioneer house where there were ladies in bonnets making butter and soup beside a fire. She'd sat on a couch that pricked her back and legs. It was some old Victorian horsehair sofa. And she'd thought, those poor pioneers, working all day like dogs, and then when they finally got to sit down, all they had was this piece-of-shit couch that pricked them.

Paz had seen only one photo of her relatives. Their life had been ass-breaking poor. They were supposedly dressed up for a funeral or a wedding, but they all looked like tornado victims to her. Even the sky looked streaked with dirt. They had this tough-as-nails sense of survival. They had lived in places with no heat or indoor toilets, which they thought was squalid and shameful, but Paz found secretly fascinating. They lived in places where people would still ride up on a horse.

NOVEMBER 1972. *Billy said it was hard to believe Ingrid was the one responsible for my feral upbringing, she seemed so refined. He's only met her once, in Rome. She was there for a conference, and we met at a trattoria near the university. She'd barely had any contact with me. She hadn't sent a dime after my grandparents had decided to move back to England and I was struggling to pay for art school. She'd said it would form character. Growing up I wasn't allowed meat, though I once took a watermelon to a remote corner of the property and hollowed out the bright-red insides with my hands like it was a carcass, while a Highland cow watched me through a fence. Sometimes Ingrid baked dense seedy bread and would barely let it cool before tearing into it in a very alarming way. Her lunch often consisted of ten bitter little almonds counted out on the tiled counter that would burn in her till dinner. For years, I kept food diaries detailing what I consumed in a day. Billy's the only one I've ever shown them to. He thought I should use them in my work. Counting it out gave me a vitality the way things that aren't good for you can.*

There is not a single picture of Ingrid and me together, not one. She hates photographs of herself — I think it's because despite her beauty, she never really appears in them, though something comes out around her eyes, all the heaviness she feels about life. My memories are all from a certain lower angle, the bottom portions of Renaissance paintings, Caravaggios, and Raphaels, because I was maybe only six or seven when I left and that was as far up as I could see. At six, I had already seen a Bergman film, but had never watched television. When I was sent to live with my grandparents in America, at first I found the sunshine invasive. I felt it was almost mythical, this land of forbidden pleasures — chewing gum, magazines, Sno-Cones, Dr Pepper. Everything painted in the pastel colors of feminine hygiene. My grandparents had retired to Santa Monica, slept in single beds, and lived together like roommates, as far as I could tell. Everyone laughed when I showed up to school in wooden shoes. I still thought of how my mother would have seen everyone. They seemed all to be working very hard at acquiring two of everything — kids, cars, houses. Ingrid would have sized up the neighbors as consumers. She would have said they all had the same inadequate education, the kind that makes them spend their lives in front of the idiot box, too dumb even to go insane from such a pathetic existence. My grandparents had modern things like whipped cream from a can and salami sandwiches. I tried to eat one and then vomited in the sink.

Ma had been smart. She had been a doctor in Ukraine, and then she was nothing. That was the beginning of the drinking. Paz's dad had been dead since she was born. At least that was the story she'd been told until Aunt May once let slip with a vacant expression, 'He just vanished.' Paz asked if he had named her, but Aunt May said no, it was a border guard who butchered her family's names when they immigrated from Ukraine. They all got stuck with what he wrote down.

Aunt May had told her it was so cold in the old country that every part of your body dried out. Even their asses were like sandpaper. She had moved to California years before Paz and Ma arrived, with her doctor husband from the Midwest who turned out to be crazy. At one point he'd threatened to drive up to Canada and shoot Ma and her. But he'd had an embolism before he could get to it. The doctor was a lot older than Aunt May. He'd bought the bungalow in the forties when it was still squalid in Ocean Park. Things changed when the space-age theme park moved in, until it was eaten by salt air, fires, and neglect, and became a charred hulking ghost that sagged ominously into the pier. Just a few blocks from the bungalow was a gold-bathed universe of large moneyed houses with sparkling pools.

When they moved to LA, it was Aunt May who took care of them on her measly nursing salary. In Canada there had been some sort of clerical error, a mistake that Ma was too proud or didn't have enough English to go in and contest. She ended up working at the hospital, not as a doctor, but as a cleaner. Paz had thought Ma might be different, living with her only sister, but she carried on pretty much the same as before. Paz couldn't believe that people who were related could have so little to say to one another. She occasionally heard Ma and Aunt May speaking in Ukrainian, which they tried not to do. They felt that when a new country accepts you, you have to shed everything. They spoke jerky English together like a badly dubbed karate film. She learned not to correct Ma after the time she'd said that Paz's body was not 'off the racks'. When Paz said, 'It's rack,' Ma had said, 'Fuck rack! When I first came to this country all I could say was "This is a pencil."'

Ma bitterly dismissed everything invented this century. It left Paz with a kajillion cultural blind-spots. 'What is this trash?' Ma had said, lying on the couch furiously smoking, when Paz put on *Abbey Road*. 'Rock and roll, Ma,' Paz told her. She shook her head. 'This is a tragic era.' Ma had never paid attention to her and this was still the only freedom that Paz understood. There was no talking in their house, at least not the kind that gave space, shaped you into being.

There was a little more life in the house when Aunt May got off her shift. The first thing she did was turn on the TV and mix a rum and Coke. She was always on the couch in her robe and ancient pantyhose that bagged around her ankles, watching her shows through all the static. The TV was like another person in the house lighting things up and talking back, filling all the quiet, almost like a sacred object, except that it was a piece of junk. Before the drinking got heavy, she gave the impression that she wanted everything to be over. She cleaned up dinner before they had even sat down to eat. She wanted the mess gone, to get through it. But what is *it*? *It* is life, Paz realized, and possibly Aunt May didn't. But then she let go of the battle with the mess. She just didn't care. Sometimes, they played cards together and ate TV dinners off their own individual fold-up tables. Paz liked lifting off the steaming lid and inspecting the tinfoil compartments to the snap of Aunt May shuffling and dealing out the cards after she'd dropped a spoonful of frozen lemonade into her full glass of vodka. A couple of times she took Paz for a long drive on the weekend. 'Old California,' she said in a tone Paz could only interpret as pride. She would drive to the places still rural, and Paz would roll down the window and smell the lemon groves, and see the hills acid yellow from wild mustard, ocean air breezing through all the clifftop farms along the coastline.

When she graduated early, at sixteen, Essa and her mom came to the ceremony and gave Paz a gold charm bracelet. It was too extravagant a gift, she knew, and Aunt May, standing there in her old shoes and dull hair, her accent thick, said, 'You can't accept it.' Paz's heart sank. 'It's too late,' Georgette said, with able diplomacy, turning Paz's wrist to show the tiny inscription. Paz felt embarrassed at Aunt May's dour appearance next to Georgette, beautiful in a silk dress and pink lipstick. Aunt May seemed to feel the weight of the humiliation too, and quickly mumbled an excuse to leave. She needed to get back to Ma, who was in terrible shape at that point.

When Paz got home, she still had traces of the blue eyeshadow and red lipstick that Essa had put on her before the ceremony. 'You look cheap,' Ma hissed. She looked at Paz with a tight expression and then pulled her to the bathroom where Paz caught a glimpse of herself. She didn't look sexy like Essa did, but more like a tired old hooker at the end of a shift. Ma violently scrubbed off the remaining makeup with Aunt May's nail polish remover. Paz was crying by then, her bare lips appeared raw and wounded. Ma shook her head and sort of crumpled, sitting down on the closed lid of the toilet seat. Paz thought Ma might've been regretting her behavior, that she might start crying too, so she gently touched her arm. 'Get your whore hands off of me,' Ma yelled, batting her away. What had Paz been thinking? Ma was about as fragile as stainless steel. Nothing between them ever took the right course. It was like living with an atom bomb. Paz had been worried about going away to school and leaving Ma and Aunt May, but in the end, it was Aunt May who encouraged her. They had both lived with Ma, a person who had never become what she wanted to be, and for Paz this understanding was in her like a warning.

THE NURSE CRACKS THE BLINDS — 'So you don't have to lie in the dark' — light slicing into the room. Paz winces, and she quickly drops them down again. Her mind feels thick with drugs. She hears a woman's voice low, cutting through the darkness. Romy?

She goes to say something, but her mouth isn't working. It's like it's been stuffed with wool. Her ears feel like she's been out in the cold. The hospital smell had triggered the fire dream, sending a sheet of flame up her body, but now every part of her is freezing, the hairs on her neck standing up, alert. Flickers of light and little clicks as she moves in and out of consciousness.

✻ ✻ ✻

APRIL 1973. *His body is not quite centered in the photo, dwarfed by the enormous trees, the stream black in the lens. I never once thought about harm. The agreement we made in Rome didn't apply to Billy, only to me. I wondered, if it had been me up there, if he would have been able to keep it.*

I was trying to frame it properly. I watched him, arms and legs spidering up the trunk. He was oddly adept at it. He positioned himself and dropped his body down, all six foot five of him, his hands still gripping the branch. Hanging there, he looked long, despite the monumental tree. I took a breath in, held still. Those initial moments felt like an eternity. We had talked about it. The branch would snap eventually — his weight, its thinness. It was

99

a matter of staring down time. He held on for what felt like forever, though it ended up being only twenty-two seconds. He told me that blood pounded into his ears. The muscles in his shoulders felt like they were actually ripping. He could almost hear them, snapping like rubber bands. His legs felt unbearably heavy and began to swing wildly at one point. It looks hilarious when I play it back. And then I see his left hand loosen and drop. In an instant his body hurtles down and thuds into the river below. After he fell, I paused to record the tree, the scene without the body, before dropping the camera to run and help him.

Are you hurt? I hear myself saying on film when I play it back.

He looked at me, wiped his hand on his soaked pants, blood coming through his shin, his arm. No one would ever know that he'd really hurt himself, dislocated his shoulder. The cracking sounds were the bones in his foot.

I told him I had to film it, take photos.

A photo reduces things to a rectangle, he said, reluctant at first.

Well, these rectangles are all we've got.

I took seven contact sheets of images, which became nineteen black-and-white photographs hung in a gallery. Critics would later talk about his isolation. They would say, 'tall, lone figure'. And I thought, just who the hell do they think took the photos?

Paz had seen the falling photos in a catalogue at Billy's New York show. He had walked into the gallery tall, shaky, holding a new baby. Outside it was February, blizzarding. There was snow on his shoulders. Everyone was looking at the baby at first, but Paz saw him. His beauty seemed both masculine and feminine. But he looked hollow. It had only been two months since Romy had died. He'd made this work a year ago, when he was a different person. Paz had the strongest urge to reach her hand out and touch his hair. It was sticking up, covered in snow. All the people coming to him in waves, not knowing what to say. She couldn't stand the things people said about the dead. Rest in peace. In a better place. Fucking hell.

He looked for somewhere he could put the baby down, but there's nowhere you can put down a baby. Paz was right near him and so she offered to take the baby from him, and he was instantly led away. His hands touched her arms when he passed the baby to her, sparking her sweater. The baby's tiny body began to squirm, and she tightened her arm around her. The baby's large outer-space eyes opened, two bright sapphires flashed for an instant. They were Romy's eyes. Paz immediately felt overwhelmed with emotion. The baby's eyes flickered and then closed, revealing eyelids so delicate, with tiny purple and blue veins. It seemed impossible that something so extraordinary could just be passed around the gallery like a coat. She'd never even liked babies, but she liked this one. She felt nervous she would drop her, and then her whole body shifted to a low rhythm, a hypnotic slowness. A warm feeling settled over her. She could hear muffled laughter and high-heels staccato on the gallery's wood floors. A woman in a silk blouse and tight leather skirt eventually took the baby from Paz and grabbed Billy's arm, and she was left standing there, mouth open, not knowing what to do with her hands.

His show consisted of two short films, an installation of photographs, and his writing scrawled on a large white wall. Paz found the work surprisingly moving. She'd been seeing so much machined metal, all the men with their stuff-on-the-floor minimalism. He seemed like a tragic priestess. Dressed head-to-toe in dark blue. Shirt, pants, even his cigarettes. She immediately thought of Romy in dark blue and felt the pain of the entire world playing a trick on her, with the only solution being that she should sleep with him, which she took as a sign of mania.

She had talked to Essa on the phone before coming to the show. She'd told her she was trying to remember when she had last been happy.

She liked the body works she was making, but she missed the Vicks VapoRub smell of eucalyptus, and the smoggy light. It was freezing in New York. 'There are too many rats here,' she'd told her. Essa had said, 'How many would be the right amount?' Paz had said she hadn't seen her legs in weeks. She missed windows open all year round, letting the life in. These closed-up apartments had no air in them. The city was dirt and plastic. Prostitutes scraping along in their high heels when she walked home from the late shift at work. 'Yeah, well, it's beautiful here,' Essa had said exaggeratedly. 'Like heart-stopping fairy-tale beautiful.' When Paz's face stung with cold, walking on certain windy streets in the Lower East Side, she tried to think of night palms. The smell of orange blossoms and sounds of outside. But LA was so far away, it was a parallel universe. She thought of Nabokov writing about how there were no nymphets in polar regions in a library book she'd read in high school. Someone had written in the margin, NABOKOV IS A PERV.

She tried to focus on her work, but she lived in a shitbox that required three jobs to pay for, plus she had to maintain the conditions of her scholarship. For the past year, she'd been sleeping with her Critical Theories professor. He had a big Karl Marx beard and his name was actually Carl. He was quiet and could be a bit unreadable, like he might have a wife and kids at home. Mostly, she was loaded with guilt at having escaped her tragic house. At one point she'd called Aunt May, worried about her caring alone for Ma, saying she was thinking of coming home. 'Don't be a fool. Stay there as long as you can,' Aunt May had said. 'You may never get back.'

❊ ❊ ❊

'Thank you for holding her,' Billy said, readjusting his gaze because he was almost a foot and a half taller than her. She'd forgotten his voice — low, hoarse, deadly.

She nodded.

'Can I get you a drink?'

'I'm trying to stop drinking,' she told him. 'And smoking.' He looked at her. 'Because women artists don't make it until they are old.' She didn't know what to do next, so she dug her hands into her pockets. 'Here,' she said, handing him a small rock.

'What is it?' He turned over the light-veined piece of granite.

'I collect rocks and feathers. They're like charges. They contain the frequency of a place,' she said, adding, 'There's no frequency for me in New York. At least not in the earth way.'

'You're not from here.'

Did he really not recognize her? They'd spoken a few times when she'd been in the group show with Romy. Once she'd even followed him drunk out of the gallery and they'd shared a cigarette. He seemed to think they were just meeting for the first time. She had no choice but to continue awkwardly. She waited for some flicker of recognition from him, but when there was nothing, she said, 'I think you've listened to my tapes.' She hesitated. 'Jolene Arkell.'

'Right,' he said in a tone that didn't tell her anything.

'I still can't get used to it here. Air that smells like bus exhaust, eating takeout from cardboard boxes on the thirty-fourth floor.'

'There's no sky. It's all up close, too tight. The sun goes down, but it never gets dark. It feels like the light is coming from nowhere. You can't even walk out your door and take a piss.'

The baby wriggled. 'I like how babies are good at communicating everything without words,' she said. 'Is there a word for wordless?'

'Silent,' he said, looking at her. Later he would say something about how her unexpected short stature endeared her to him.

'Not the same,' they both said at the same time. This was a revelation, and she needed to say something in the next moment, but he was swiftly pulled away by collectors with oil money guilty enough to spend their cash on art, and she felt a bit ridiculous having given an art star a rock.

When she finally saw him again, he was holding the baby, who was red and wriggling and starting to cry. The gallery assistant came, bringing his coat.

'My apartment is a few blocks from here,' she said. 'You'll never get a taxi in this.' She motioned out the window that framed white on white. She had taken pleasure in just being near him and thought of something she'd heard Romy say to Ora. If you want something from a man, all you have to do is look at him exactly the way you want to go to bed with him. She followed Billy out into the snowstorm. She knew then that she would follow him anywhere.

PAZ'S EYES FLICKER OPEN. SHE can hear a kind of shuffling noise and then the squeak of shoes on the floor growing closer. A hand touches her arm. Air conditioning blows strongly on her face. She wants to tell someone to turn it off, but no words come out. She begins to shiver. There is a prick on her skin and then a slow seep of warmth spreading through her limbs, and she sinks into it.

* * *

Snow was falling when Paz walked with him the four blocks to her apartment on Bond Street. He had the baby strapped to him, his coat was open, and he grabbed each side and wrapped it around so it covered her. They were both slumped forward, snowblind in the headwind, clutching their chests, staggering like they'd been stabbed. It would have been an awkward moment, except that with all the snow and wind, they each needed their own focus to get through.

Inside Paz's small apartment she felt embarrassed by its shabbiness. A stained nylon carpet and almost no heat despite the loud rattling radiators. Piles of ratty books on the floor, and used paint tins and brushes in the sink. Billy fed the baby a bottle and then laid her sleeping on the grotty couch, making a nest for her from his coat, while Paz came out of the kitchen with a quarter of Jim Beam and two glasses. It was all she had. There was virtually no food in the apartment except a couple of moldy bagels and some stale cardboard cereal. Her roommate was at her boyfriend's place, so they were alone. Billy was sitting on the living-room floor. 'So, you aren't on the slow track,' he said as she placed the bottle on the floor and sat beside him.

She didn't know what he meant at first, but then realized he was referring to her drinking. 'Look at it out there,' she said, 'can you blame me?'

'Show me something,' he said. She got up and returned with photos from a piece she was working on, where she glued Carl's beard hair to her own face. She looked like an ugly man, which was what she wanted. Beauty made her nervous. *When you drop beauty, you get something more interesting,* she'd written in a paper for Carl. Something closer to the truth.

'It's good. It's reminding me of the surrealists,' he said, striking a match and lighting his cigarette. 'Except that Duchamp had a total aversion to female body hair.'

Paz, who had a lot of body hair, considered this a blow and remained silent. She hazily recollected Ora saying that when Duchamp was in LA, he mostly just spoke French with the Pasadena Gallery's alcoholic gardener. She contemplated saying this, but there seemed no space for such a useless remark. She drank her bourbon in big nervous gulps. This was not how she'd imagined things would go in the scenario where she had him alone in a room.

'I like your hair,' he said. 'Long and medieval.'

She had thought of this moment, and now here he was, and she felt a strange dislocated energy. It was as if, without Romy, they couldn't even pretend to have a conversation. At first, they had some terse exchanges. If there had been a Valium in this apartment, she would have taken it. He said he had never felt so alone, even though he never was. He told her he'd been up late watching some Western with the baby asleep on his chest, listening to Marilyn Monroe talk about loneliness.

They drank the Jim Beam in more silence. He said it was good he had her — the baby made him focus on something other than the immense pain he felt. Grief made him wander. He'd put the baby in the car and would drive all night. She never woke up if she was in the car and he would just keep driving. 'I would have turned completely to drinking if it weren't for her.' He told Paz about how he'd discovered alcohol in the small Dutch town he was from when he was young, already too tall, and how he'd noticed it was different for him than for his friend Lucas, who remembered everything. He said as he got drunk, bits and pieces of the world came crashing down with him, until he was in a place where every detail became disembodied from its meaning. He said it was like being in a horror dream, where you can't move or speak. He had no control. He called this place Zeroland. As he was speaking he looked up at Paz as though he'd forgotten that he was even talking to someone. He said he'd thought about moving far away, about living a different life. 'I've always wanted to live on a boat.'

'Me too,' she lied. She felt a bit drunk, her hand grazed his belt. 'Shouldn't you still be at your opening?'

'Well, I saw a young artist and I wanted to talk to her.'

'Was she attractive?'

'Ravishingly.'

'We can sleep together if you want,' she said, 'but you should know I'm only doing it theoretically. So you know you're not in Zeroland.'

'Very generous of you.'

She poured them two more gold inches of bourbon. She suddenly wondered if he was sitting here because he just genuinely needed a place close by, out of the storm. As she was thinking this, he reached over and touched her hair, wet from the snow. His fingers brushed her face, touching her so lightly it was surprising, like a leaf or a wing. 'There is snow falling and there's nothing you can do,' he said, looking straight into her eyes. She had never wanted someone so much. It was an intimate moment, and she wanted him to say he wanted her. But his eyes contained a vague awareness that anything he undertook would have consequences. Something shifted in her body that she could do nothing to stop. He kissed her deeply, and his mouth undid her. All the intensity, the thought of Romy between them. She felt his hands move up her ribs and her nipples tighten under his fingers. She slid her hands down his pants and bit his neck as he unbuttoned her pants and pulled them down her hips.

The next morning, he was remote. She thinks that with Romy it would have been like trying to pin down light. But with her, she was salty, land-heavy, of the body. Despite so much desire, the sex was, in the first moments, awkward. All that longing didn't prepare her for the basic facts of it. How their body sizes were at such odds. His feet tangled in his pants, and her elbow hit him in the eye at one point. But then she used her hand to slip him inside her, and she moved her hips slowly until it felt so good that she couldn't see anything clearly anymore, she couldn't think or speak. And then, to her complete surprise, it became something else. A dissolving sensation that took her out of the system of veins and arteries, out of the content of her body, out of normal, ordinary life and into existence in some other place, somewhere on the border of human experience. It was practice for leaving the body. She'd sunk into herself, into her own desire. It felt as though she suddenly could see her way out, a way forward.

* * *

There is a droning sound of a pump, and little clicks and slow beeps which Paz realizes are attached to her. She thinks she can smell Siberian forest scent, live green needles and camphor. Her mind keeps gliding off, into a large, absent space. She blinks but her eyes are blurry when she tries to open them, and she makes out a liquid shape of a woman, tall, gold, light pulsating around her.

Saturday

PAZ OCCUPIES THE HOUSE LIKE a ghost — awake in blue light, while nothing stirs — and then blacks out. Later she wakes up, sitting in a bathtub she doesn't remember filling, gone frigid, her arm bent at an odd angle, water creeping cold into her vagina.

When she opens her eyes again, it's morning. She hears voices outside. One eye is shut tight, the other sees bottles of pills and a cocktail glass of orange juice on the table beside the bed. She's overslept, her head thick with Seconal. The pills are working — the room is vibrating with light and the pain is there, but more like a distant echo. There is the muffled sound of a car engine and then the shower running. She shakily pulls herself out of bed and slowly walks downstairs, gripping the banister, light sparking behind her eyes. Birds are chatty outside. There is the metallic buzz of insects. She has to concentrate on putting one foot in front of the other, as though she's forgotten how to walk. She can't yet look at her hand, wound in white gauze like a mitten. It's her right hand and she is left-handed, which should be better, she knows, but she's already seeing how much she uses her right hand for everything. She can't even do up a button. In school they had tried to switch her to her right hand because they had only right-handed scissors that opened the wrong way and left big red dents across her fingers.

When she makes it downstairs, he is like an illusion, appearing to her taller, more disheveled, more handsome, holding the baby in one arm, making eggs with the other with practiced ease. It's jarring to see him after all these weeks. He's in dark pants, no shirt, bare feet. His hair is still wet. Their eyes meet — her entire body registers this moment. She wonders if he knows his effect on her. She feels stupidly grateful at the sight of him, not somewhere with Romy, but here, in their kitchen. It makes everything seem suddenly manageable. 'You shouldn't be up.' As soon as Flea sees her, she squawks and reaches for her. He rearranges Flea on his chest and puts his arms around Paz. Their bodies stay close. His gestures are like fireworks — sparkling, extravagant. Paz watches him. Everything is reanimated.

'The opening —' she says, swallowing. Her voice is quiet, her mouth is so dry. She's finding it hard to see out of her eyes.

'It was last night. When I was somewhere over the Atlantic,' he says, in a tone she can't interpret. She has completely lost track of what day it is. This is not how she'd wanted things to be when he was finally home — her drugged and him missing the whole point of his time away. 'You scared me,' he says. The phone rings. She turns in slow motion. It's the only way she can move without feeling dizzy. 'How do you feel?' he asks, not answering the phone, saying it can wait, that he wants to talk to her. The phone continues to ring loudly. He puts the baby down on the carpet, walks over, and rips the cord from the jack.

She winces at the sound. 'I'm okay,' she says, even though the pain is present, and the chemicals are coming up through her throat. 'I think the drugs must be working because I can't feel anything.' Her mouth is slow and unreliable. 'I can't believe you're a real person, right here. I was having a lot of fantasies about you while you were gone.' She must be high. That wasn't the first thing she was going to say. He leans down and kisses her. She's too thrown, too shaky to properly take him in, to assess if she'd been out of her mind to think that he was in Rome with Romy.

'Flea has grown,' he says, bringing Paz eggs and coffee, but she feels queasy. How can she explain to him that the six weeks he's been gone were frozen time, hours grown long and full of waiting. The smell coming from the eggs is off-putting, and she has to concentrate on not throwing up. Now that she is aware, the whole house has a rotten-meat smell, like there might be an animal that's gone off and died somewhere in one of the walls. She hears his low voice. 'Tell me what happened.'

'I can't remember a thing. I remember beforehand. Running around like crazy so that I could have a couple of hours to work while the baby slept. And I don't know, then there was a noise, or the dog barking, I'm not sure of the order. And then — I really don't remember.'

'That's probably better,' he says. 'Essa said the doctors were impressed that you'd made it to the hospital on your own, driving with a baby on your lap.'

'Essa?'

'She went to the hospital and brought you here and stayed with you until I got back this morning.'

'How many days has it been?'

'Three.'

Her mind is slurry, unable to hold on to any thoughts. Blood drains from her head, and everything goes dark for a moment. 'Well,' she says, slowly turning to rest her head in his lap. The room moves. 'How was Italy?'

'It was incredible,' he says. Incredible? Is his heart made of stone? For the first time it occurs to her — why didn't she and Flea go with him? He tells her about the Roman streets made with ancient salt, of the priests in long black robes and lace collars walking to cafes, the violets growing from cobblestones. She wants to hear that everything she's been imagining has been wrong. Just thinking about it makes her face get hot, and though she wants to tell him about Fina and the postcards, she decides to say nothing yet. He puts his hand on the side of her face and brushes her hair out of her eyes and starts to say something, but she's already closing her eyes, her mind searching for something after all the nights trying to translate his remoteness, his silence, his indifference to her. As she falls asleep, she sees Rome.

SEPTEMBER 1971. *I'd been nervous leaving for Rome and how everything*
would be with him there. I barely noticed the city streets deserted at
lunchtime, the high old walls, palm trees and pines, the smell of cornetti
and faint lemon. The roofs of the great cathedrals shone in the warm air. My
heart went crazy the second I saw him. He inhaled sharply as if he wanted to
say something, and then just looked at me and pulled me into him. Seeing
him again, I knew I would always be taken by his long body and the electric
thing he gave off. In his apartment, I could hear voices dragging tables back
into the street below, the clatter of silverware. I want to understand what
happened, I said to him. He put his hands on my hips and kissed my open
mouth, and the sensation was so extreme I felt like I was choking. Afterward,
we lay in bed, the big window open to the cobbled street.

When you left, it was hard for me, I said to him honestly.

He told me he'd spent a lot of time alone, drinking, full of self-loathing.
He wanted to make a decision and stick to it for the rest of his life. He wanted
to be a better person. We had sex again, not speaking much. He looked at
me and said, it's not like this with anyone else. I sensed him holding back but
couldn't tell if it was because he was protecting me from hurtful things, or
because he didn't want to make himself so vulnerable again.

I asked if he would do something for me.

Anything.

But when I told him what I needed, the agreement I wanted us to make,
he looked uncomfortable. He didn't want to do it, but I got him to promise
me, though his eyes said something different.

There is a change of air here that is good for us. When he goes to his
studio, I draw, take photos, and walk around in the city's great beauty. I
found a white Saint Laurent dress entirely made of lace and bought it, even
though we haven't yet talked of marriage. He'd wanted to know about who
I had been seeing. I asked him about other women he'd been with. Had he
loved any of them? He looked at me. Only you. He asked me to stay with him
in Rome and I said yes. But already our past felt too heavy for both of us.

✻ ✻ ✻

She must have drifted asleep on the couch. The moon falls into the room and wakes her. She notices a thin line of dark-gray dust on the edge of the fan blade that she'd meant to clean before Billy came back. He came back for her. She half thought she'd never see him again. He came back early and missed his show. The gesture is not lost on her. It means that wherever Romy is, it isn't Rome. Fina's voice and the words from the postcards are smoke in her head. Maybe Romy isn't out there alive and well like some people think. Maybe she really fell off Milt's building and is truly dead. She feels a sharp pain in her skull at the thought of now having to guess at what might be the truth. She had tried not to know.

Slowly, she gets up. The dog trails her, knocking into her heels. She walks upstairs, the blood draining from her head. Near the top of the stairs, she pauses for a moment and then tries to put her foot on the next step, but something stops her. Looking back, there is nothing there. She shakes her head. Maybe the problem isn't in the house. Maybe it's with her.

Since this morning, they haven't really spoken. She slept most of the day, while Billy took Flea out in the car. She remembers trying to talk about how she felt when he was in Rome, but the words were hard in her mouth, they came out broken. He ended up saying he could arrange for more help. 'No, it's just that' — she could barely get it out — 'I missed you.' He looked at her, but the conversation stopped there. It seemed clear that no matter how she tried to angle for his reassurance, he wasn't going to give it.

She continues up the stairs. Her body is still in shock, and she has a bit of fever, but when she slips into bed, it is his skin that feels hot on hers when she touches it, waking him. 'Lie on your back,' he says. Her whole life she had tried to be like a man about sex, and all it did was make her feel so unlovable, like there was something wrong with her.

His skin stops her from shivering. She does everything he wants. She is devotional. She forgets about her hand.

After, she looks over at Billy sleeping. How can he always sleep? She's always flopping around like a fish that's been caught. She sits on the bed holding her knees to her chest, wishing she still smoked. Her eyelids flicker. She's taken a sleeping pill and is fighting it. The curtains move in the breeze and she gets up, hearing a little clicking noise that she follows downstairs, walking slowly. She sits on the couch, the sound of crickets loudly coming through the windows. After a few minutes she walks out onto the porch. In her half-sleep state, she thinks of him sleeping above. He gets to come and go, sleep with her, not give anything away. She lets it happen, but still she can't help thinking how much power he has. He told her he was glad to be back, and she believed him. But what gets said in the middle of the night doesn't matter. Daylight cancels everything, and you always have to start again.

Tuesday

AT BREAKFAST BILLY POURS COFFEE. 'I'm going to take Flea to Romy's mother, Ingrid,' he says, placing a mug in front of her. 'To stay with her for a few days.'

'Romy's mother?' She swallows. 'Does she live here now?' She's trying to make her voice sound normal.

'She's staying in Santa Barbara for a couple of weeks before she flies back to London.'

After a pause she says, 'Do you really think it's okay to just leave the baby with her? She doesn't —'

'Paz,' he says, 'I don't know if you are in any shape to look after the baby right now. She asked for this. I'm doing what is required of me.'

Paz puts a bowl down in front of Flea, who senses something is up. Mechanically, she spoons cereal into the baby's mouth, but Flea clamps it shut with a suspicious glare which conveys that she thinks Paz has somehow been seized by madness, and that she's suddenly aware that having a spoon poked into her mouth isn't a dignified way to eat. She spits. Paz cleans her shirt and Flea's face with a damp cloth, feeling a bit dazed by the thought of sudden freedom from the slow tick of all the days with Flea that take little bites out of her. But then she feels a growing sense of dread. A rigidity settles over her body. Her jaw is stiff. A pain hollows her stomach. At first she can't understand what it is. It feels like nausea, a strange sensation like she is going to be sick. It isn't until she thinks about Billy mentioning Romy's mother that she knows what it is. She is jealous. Her anguish seems completely unrelated to reality. She is nervous at the thought of leaving Flea with a total stranger, even if the stranger is her grandmother. But if she's truthful, that isn't it. It's Billy. Talking to Romy's mother behind her back. Making arrangements without her. Her continuing to have sex with him, out of some desperate, naive hope that it will change something.

She hears Billy's sleeping-pill voice saying her name and then he hands her the phone. She hadn't even heard it ring.

'You sound a bit stoned,' Essa says. 'Don't take too many of those horse pills. They'll put you out of touch with what's really happening.'

'That's fine with me, Ess,' Paz says. 'That's how I like to be when I've chopped off a body part. The farther the better.' Though she wishes there was a pill that could erase every annihilating detail she has ever felt. Essa is getting Keith to make a kind of metal cover for her once the bandages come off. 'You are going to look so punk,' she says, which makes Paz feel better for a moment. But every time she feels okay, a horrific thought enters her brain, and then she remembers the finger. It makes her feel her own mortality. She'd started this world with ten fingers, and then she lost one. *Lost one!* Only a complete moron loses a part of their body.

Yesterday, when she and Billy were pulling out of the hospital parking lot after having her bandages changed, there had been a funeral procession. A long stream of black shiny cars with mirrored windows reflecting the sun, the drivers wearing mirrored sunglasses, sweat rolling down their faces, while she and Billy waited forever to cross the intersection. Losing her finger made her feel like she herself had touched a hearse. And then she looked down at the white mitt. There was the simple fact that it made you grotesque as a woman to have a deformity. A man could be missing a finger and it would give him character. A woman would just be considered not, quote unquote, all woman.

* * *

Billy is getting ready to leave for Ingrid's when Maarten pulls up. Paz is upstairs folding Flea's clothes. Through the open windows she can hear him say, 'Maarten.' He's outside in his bare feet greeting him. She sees them hug one another. The first time she'd seen Billy, at Maarten's opening, he'd walked up to Maarten and hugged him, so moved by the work there were tears in his eyes. She'd said to Essa, 'God's honest truth, I want a man who can hug another man with tears in his eyes.'

Out there standing in the sun, Billy looks like something is melting down. She hasn't considered how he feels until seeing him out there now.

'You okay?' Maarten says.

'Did you sell some work?' Billy says, referring to Maarten's 1968 Mustang GT.

'I bought it the American way.'

'What way is that?'

'The installment plan,' Maarten says, lighting a cigarette. They both stand there silently in the sun. 'You okay?' Maarten asks again.

'I don't know. I have no mood,' Billy says. He leans against the car. 'This morning the baby put something in her mouth and I pulled it out. I felt teeth. I don't remember teeth. She used to like to clamp down on my finger when she was small. It felt so strange — those sharp gums, like something primal, something animal.' He tells Maarten that he hasn't seen his daughter in weeks, and it makes him uneasy. Paz has taken care of all Flea's routines — the laundry and feeding and cooking and playing, he's missed it all. It's not just that he's missed the practical things, but what comes with them, that closeness. 'There's no room in my life to express anything. She's in my head,' he says. The words are so jarring they shock Paz as she understands he means Romy. She stops folding Flea's sleeper. She holds it up, looking at it as though trying to understand what sort of object it is. She puts it carefully down, Maarten's and Billy's voices a kind of buzzing noise outside. She sits down on the bed and breathes out slowly. She can't tell what's worse. Feeling like nothing, or feeling grateful, because now she knows for certain that if Romy is alive, there is no way she was with him in Rome.

'I see her in the baby's eyes and it makes me shaky. Her art is still hanging everywhere, her clothes are still in our room,' he continues. 'She was always interested in places where things had been left and the meaning was not clear, like Stonehenge or Chichén Itzá.' He pauses.

'But they are still ruins,' Maarten says.

'And yet we find ruins beautiful.'

Billy is looking out at the light, made sharp in all the dryness. He tells Maarten he was just in Rome, damp and gray. 'It's funny,' he says after a long time.

'What's funny?'

'Death is maybe the only way you can understand someone's full resonance.'

Maarten waits a moment and then says carefully, 'How does Paz feel about all this?'

'I'm not sure. I can't talk about it with her. I'm fucked up, Maarten,' he says. 'I wonder if Romy's the only one who could make me feel like I properly exist. If that's even something I could have with someone else. And I know what you're going to say — you're going to say, why did I marry Paz.'

'Actually, I wasn't,' Maarten says. 'But a lot of people —'

'A lot of people,' Billy repeats, cutting him off.

'You know, if you ever want to talk about what happened —'

Paz had heard it was Maarten who Billy called that night, yelling into the phone. Billy had called 911 from Milt's apartment where only Milt remained, completely passed out. It was so late it was morning. Maarten had been stunned awake by the loud ringing of the phone.

'Billy,' Maarten says, looking at his friend. He says he never suspected him capable of any violence, though who the hell knows what goes on between two people. 'I understand it's unbearable — this— state.'

Billy stands looking out and then after a while clears his throat. 'It's like with art, how hard it is for the viewer to locate what is fiction and what is fact.'

'Reminds me of that joke,' Maarten says.

'What joke?'

'The one where the guy says to the abstract painting, "What do you represent?" and the painting says, "What the fuck do *you* represent?!"'

✽ ✽ ✽

NOVEMBER 1972. *I think the performances, the body work, are stopping me because the body is what I've tried to get away from my whole life. I don't want it to be as Red says, defined by the hole between my legs. Men get to make art as though they don't have a body. But performance is a new form, which means not male-dominated. Billy is probably relieved I'm moving away from it. We haven't talked about the agreement since Rome, but I know it makes him uncomfortable, and it makes me worry that he won't be able to keep it. The light stuff is confounding. I'm using flammable gases and having trouble controlling them. Red helped me today. I could do them outside with wind, but in the gallery, things caught fire. I had to grab an extinguisher. Fuck's sake, Red said, don't wreck it. She was in a bad mood. Pissed at some trashy-ass deodorant billboard that had gone up across from her studio. Now she had to stare at* MAKE YOURSELF HAPPY WITH A LITTLE TICKLE! *from her window. Yeah, people, she said, anything is a dildo if you are brave enough! Standing in the gallery, a red stain spread across the seat of her white work pants, and instead of shrinking with embarrassment, she turned to the gallerist and the assistants. You should see your faces! You should be happy I'm menstruating in front of you! It's probably the first*

*real thing that's happened in this gallery in years, she said and stormed off.
I tried to give her a pad in the washroom and she said, great, so now the
whole precinct has hit the same cycle. She lit a cigarette and took the pad
and looked up at me. Jesus. You use these two-by-fours? I showed her some
Francis Bacon sketches, knowing it only took a good drawing to make her
happy. When I drove back home alone, I held on to the rushing-hot thrill I
was getting with the fire experiments. That strange border between wonder
and annihilation. Driving to the house Billy and I now have, lush with giant
birds-of-paradise and towering palms, and a porch with hours of sun. We
haven't told anyone yet, but we got married in Rome. We want to keep it
between us for as long as we can. When we saw Maarten he said, what are
you on? You're both lit up like stars.*

'What are you doing?'

Paz looks up at Billy with alarm. She doesn't know how long she's
been sitting there. She didn't hear Maarten leave.

'I was talking to you but you weren't responding,' he says.

Her heart is beating very hard as she looks into his dark eyes, his
gaze steady. A panic floods her. *Is this when it happens?* She blinks several
times and looks down, but she's put the journal away. For a moment she
thought it might blurt into view. She's trying to think of what to say, but
her brain feels muffled and strange, like it's full of dead birds.

'LISTEN, PAZ,' COTTON SAYS OVER the phone. 'It's critical that you follow my pre-performance instructions.'

'Which are?'

'Don't eat, don't drink, don't fuck.'

'Jesus, Cotton.' She hates the idea of being the subject and not the maker, but Cotton had called her right after Billy left with Flea for Ingrid's and begged. His model had backed out. He promised he would help her with her work. Drive her out to Plan-it Plastics where she gets materials. He offered up his car, a white Mercedes-Benz W113 coupe, while Billy had the truck. 'Okay, okay,' she said, backing down, though she wondered how many people he'd called before her. She decides not to mention the pills.

NOVEMBER 1970. *I've been working all the time and am going to graduate a semester early. I bought a black suit from the thrift shop on S. Broadway, and Sondra lent me a short dark wig. Red helped glue on sideburns. When we were done, she looked at me approvingly and said, I always knew you were a big lez. Then she got serious. You're gonna pass. Can't help your brains, though. That's the most important part. But all I could hear was the sound of my own blood in my ears. I wanted to walk out and pass as a man. People have always thought because I want to be around men that I want their attention. I don't want their attention. I want to be them. I've consciously used what people would call sex appeal for power. It turns out it's cheap, all women have it. But it's not really power. Not really. This, on the other hand, felt like the blazing endpoint of power.*

JANUARY 13, 1971. *I asked Red if feeling a bit insane preparing for a performance piece is normal, this obsessive tunnel vision I'm getting. She looked at me. Turner strapped himself to the goddamn mast of a ship in the middle of a storm to see and feel the real storm, so he could paint it later, she said. What a fucking nutjob. But that's the kind of driven that turns me on.*

JANUARY 16, 1971. *I ended up performing the burial piece at Ora's gallery. Not being able to breathe, my lungs straining for air, I felt pain in my spine. My legs started trembling out of control, and after that passed, I had an intense feeling of harmony with everything around me. A powerful sense of myself. I could feel it in my whole nervous system, my intestines, everything. I was attuned to sound waves and light and colors, and especially smell. I could smell every object in the room like a dog. Sam's scent, the smell of his skin, I can't explain it. He came up to me behind the building after the performance. Somewhere in Rome at his gallery there, Billy was probably performing too. We didn't say anything. He pulled me toward him. We stood still for a moment. I could feel his breath on my neck. His mouth was open and warm, we kissed slowly, and I ran my tongue up his tongue. I want to stop. I don't want to stop. He turned me around against the wall, lifted up my dress, pulled down my underwear, and came. It was just in that one moment, an intense energy, and then it was gone. I think I confuse the powerful feeling after a performance with sex. It's the only other thing of intensity I know. It is a total narcotic to me.*

❊ ❊ ❊

Large rolls of paper have been taped to the floor. Everything is white. Paz can hear people filling the gallery. She unzips her dress in the bathroom with difficulty and takes it off. Unhooks her bra, steps out of her underwear, removes her sandals, leaving everything in a pile on the concrete floor where little bits of hair and dust have gathered in the corners. There is no mirror in here, which is better. It's hot and windowless and smells of urine cut with Lysol. She lets out a breath, waits a few beats, and then turns the door handle. She walks out in measured steps, naked, glazing her gaze so as not to make eye contact with anyone in the audience. She lies down in the center of the floor on cool white paper under the bright synthetic light, pressing her body against the ground as forcefully as possible. There is a smell of cigarette smoke, and cheap pink champagne. The thin buzz of overstrained electricity from the fluorescent lights stops when Cotton flips off the switch. Paz waits, keeping her body still, even though she feels jangly with anticipation.

Cotton is sitting with his knees up, a stony expression, in his white T-shirt and jeans. All the titterings and shufflings and coughings and laughings have dulled to a very complete soundlessness, the whole audience seated, perfectly still. The first sound of the match striking rips the silence. All Paz can register is the intoxicating smell of the match, which jerks her alive. Her head is full of blood. Cotton throws it at her body. Misses. Extinguished in the air. Out of the corner of her eye she sees an arc of white smoke. While she waits for the next one, she becomes attuned to the sounds and smells in the room, separating them in her mind — the deodorant forming white little balls in the creases of some woman's underarms, the butcher smell of some guy in the front, the rubber soles that have stepped in dogshit mostly rubbed off, menthol cigarettes, the wilted gardenia behind a woman's ear, also a strong smell of Irish Spring and sex. She feels warmth coming off the bodies. Billy is there, standing at the back with Juke, but she can't think about him. She stops the flow of her thoughts, right down to the bad things. Pushing out the postcards. Pushing out Billy's voice, *she's in my head*. Lying there on the white paper she feels something sharp and rare. She feels no fear. Cotton does it two more times until a lit match lands on her shoulder. It feels like being skinned alive, and she wants to scream, but the deal is she can't move until the performance is over. There is a disturbing smell, which she realizes is the smell of her own flesh burning. She lies like that, time dragging, willing her body not to move, for her hand not to touch the red welt, until eventually Cotton gets up slowly and walks out of the room. This is her signal. Paz gets up, pivots, and walks back to the bathroom, aware that everyone's eyes have nothing to do but to follow her crotch and, when she turns, her ass. Normally, feeling burning-hard stares would have made her self-conscious, but she isn't going to be embarrassed. She feels an intense, exquisite stinging on her arm, her thigh, the top of her foot, where the matches grazed, but the pain on her shoulder is unbearably strong, almost religious. She runs the water in the sink until it is very cold, and then awkwardly leans her shoulder under the stream for as long as she can take it. It was the only match that landed square on her skin and stayed there. She folds toilet paper and dabs the burn. In the cramped bathroom she zips up her dress and walks out. She's sweating, and her hair is damp at her temples. The lights are on again, so bright she squints. Her body, which she normally hates for its curves and its smallness, feels right to her in this moment. Not like when men say they like your ass, but when some woman you admire gives you a compliment and you are lit up, right up from inside.

PAZ WALKS OVER TO THE table and picks up a glass of champagne in a clear plastic cup. Its bubbles pricking cool on her fingers. Cotton is being interviewed by an *L. A. Times* writer and she hears him saying, 'It's a double bind for the viewer between the moral compulsion to intervene in crisis and the institutional taboo against touching artworks.' It makes her drink down the whole glass of champagne. She eats a couple of salty green olives and sweaty cubes of cheese. Her eyes move around the gallery until she sees Billy leaning on the wall, talking to Juke, and she watches as a woman in a shimmering gold top and extremely long white jeans that drag on the floor walks over to him and kisses him on the mouth. Jealousy spreads through her body. The woman laughs a little too loudly, trying to get his attention.

'Paz!' Sondra says, pulling her into a circle of people she doesn't know. She's wearing patrol-officer sunglasses, has a mustache, and is leering at a woman whose breasts appear on display through her keyhole dress. 'Hello, Fantastic Being,' Paz says to Sondra. It's part of the performance she's been doing for a while, where she shows up playing her male opposite extreme, complete with filthy masculine habits like ogling women and adjusting invisible balls.

'In seven billion years our sun will die and become a big piece of glitter in the center of our galaxy. And no one will be able to see its shimmering light,' Maarten says.

'Uh, yeah,' Red says, throwing back a glass of champagne. 'Because we'll all be dead.' She shakes her head at him. 'Man, you live in a floaty state.' The Fantastic Being has put his arm around Red, who looks him up and down and says, 'I mean, I love your aviators, obviously.'

Paz walks right up to Billy and kisses him. His hand brushes her hip, which feels illicit in a way that she likes. This is what the performance has done, because all she wants is to feel his weight pressing on her.

'Paz, you were fan-fucking-tastic,' Juke says and clinks his glass with hers. 'How's the hand?' he asks, nodding to the white bandage which she has hacked into, to make less of a mitt and so she could undress herself.

'I'll live,' she says, and then immediately realizes the wrong choice of words and feels her face get hot.

'You should have filmed it,' he says, motioning to her hand. 'It would've been heavy.'

She looks at him and mouths, *Sicko*, and then asks Billy, smiling, 'What's up with him?'

Billy looks at Juke and then back at her and says, 'Substances.'

'Cotton was lucky to have you. You were fearless,' Billy says. She is happy he's said that. She tells him she is easily seduced by people who compliment her, and he says he is easily seduced by people who are braver than him. She takes his hand and leads him through the gallery to the cramped bathroom. It's hot and so small they press up against each other. He puts his hands on her breasts and she bites his lip. She undoes his belt and kneels in front of him, and he puts his hand on the ceiling to steady himself. Right as she finishes, the door opens. No one is there, which is odd. Paz sees the Fantastic Being talking up Tammy the art student. Neither of them sees Billy doing up his belt and walking with Paz back to the main gallery space, where some of the glasses have spilled from the table and there is an inch of cheap champagne on the floor. Paz sees Essa who is talking to Fina, easily and cleverly working her way in. It bothers her, though she doesn't let it show. She is always hiding her jealousy when it takes over her.

Milt takes Billy to meet with a critic from some magazine in New York and leaves Paz standing there, so she walks over to the bar and picks up another glass of champagne and swallows the entire glass, then another one. Everyone has already been drinking heavily, and it will be too dull unless she catches up.

'It's about the inverse of the American dream,' Essa says, sounding a little drunk when Paz walks up. 'Hey, you did great,' she says, taking Paz's good hand. 'God, is it ever good to see you out. How are you feeling?' One of the women walks away as soon as Paz approaches, but Fina and a few others are now looking at her.

'Better,' she says. 'The painkillers are spectacular.'

'How did it feel out there?' Essa asks.

'I like how every time you think you have found a truth, it changes,' Paz says, suddenly aware that Romy might have said this, feeling heat on her face. 'You feel real, which is really the only thing that keeps you from dying.'

'Making art doesn't keep you from dying unless you get paid,' Essa says, lighting a cigarette.

'Did you see that Margaret Miller is here?' a woman wearing see-through pants says.

'I'm not in any hurry to talk to her,' Fina says, holding herself perfectly rigid. 'You know how much she's eviscerated me in the past. Remember when she wrote that my vagina was "as familiar as an old shoe?" Would anyone ever say that of, for instance, Doug Cotton's dick?'

The Fantastic Being comes over and says, 'Excuse me, ladies, did someone say "dick"?'

Fina walks away, and a few moments later, on the other side of the gallery, Paz sees her talking to Billy and her whole body stiffens. Is she telling him about the postcards? She sees Fina's head tilted up at him, and then she moves closer and at one point touches Billy's arm, but he jerks it away like she's slapped him.

Essa leans in. 'There's some tension because Milt's ex-wife, Makiko, is here with her new husband.' Paz looks over her shoulder to see that Billy is now talking to Maarten and feels relieved. 'Apparently he's also a gallerist, a very calculating one. The men can't stand him for some reason, maybe out of loyalty to Milt. Or maybe because he looks like Cary Grant. But really, who could blame her? I mean, remember when Milt went missing for five days and everyone was looking for him all over the city?' Paz had been in New York then, but has heard how Makiko lost her mind, going crazy trying to find Milt. Police were involved. Eventually they found him. He had been in their attic the whole time. No one could understand how she could put up with him, his addiction, his philandering. 'The last straw might have been when their daughter found his stash in her Barbie camper,' Essa says. 'When I talked to her, Makiko seemed very mature about it. She said there was no way she could ever live with him, but she still respected his vision.' Paz knew what it was that inspired him to find new, groundbreaking work in the gallery. He'd told her too. It was the simplest thing. It was that art offered the possibility of love with strangers.

Paz goes to get more champagne. When she turns around, Fina asks if they can talk. She doesn't want to talk about anything because she wants it all to go away. She hesitates and then reluctantly says, 'Okay.' Her delusions about Romy and Billy together in Rome had been wrong, but the thought of hearing Fina say Romy's name is enough to make the weight drop down on her. They walk outside. On the steps, the warm night air hits them. There are people drinking, and her husband, who doesn't see her, smoking Colts with two different women. They go around the corner, and Fina takes her bag off her shoulder, pulls out a postcard, and hands it to Paz.

'Another one?' Paz asks.

Fina nods. It's the same A6 cream paper and has the tiniest of pinprick pencil marks. She wants to wrench it out of her hands, tear it up, and destroy — what? Some part of her own future, the version where Romy comes back and claims, without a hint of cruelty, the place Paz occupies. *Listen, I'm really sorry. It was a performance. You didn't know?*

Fina passes it to her, and she stares at it for a moment and flips it over. DARK MATTER. This one has a clear postmark — it's from the desert, Shoshone. She wants to sit down.

'Fina?' Paz asks. 'Did you tell Billy just now?'

'Tell Billy what,' Fina says, looking annoyed.

'About the postcards.' Fina exhales a thin stream of smoke and shakes her head.

'I saw you talking to him,' Paz says, searching Fina's face for some sort of acknowledgment of what she'd seen across the gallery, but there is none. 'Why are you showing this to me — not him?'

'Because I think it's you this most affects.'

This strikes Paz as surprisingly humane. Too humane. 'You don't want to take this to the police?'

'The police?' she laughs sarcastically. 'Never tell the police anything.' Fina's hair blows across her face, though a sweep of it is pinned back with a silver clip. 'Besides,' she says, 'I'm not sure I trust Billy anymore.'

'Fina,' Paz says, ignoring her comment about Billy. 'I admired Romy more than you think.'

'I know,' she says, stubbing out her cigarette. 'I know. You admired her enough to want her husband, her baby, her work. I guess you could call that admiration.'

'You have to stop this,' Paz says, starting to feel the pain in her shoulder and her hand. 'If you two were so close, why do you never come to see the baby? A good friend might want some involvement in her life. But you seem so focused on Billy, which makes me think he's the only one you are interested in.'

Fina laughs. 'Good.'

'Good?'

'There's a bit of fight in you. You're not the pushover everyone says you are.'

Paz's throat hurts like she's going to cry, though she's too angry for that.

'You had to know that people would be upset,' Fina says.

'I was never trying to steal Romy's life,' Paz says. 'Though I don't know what exactly entitles you to an explanation of my actions.' The pain is now intense. She feels around in her bag for her painkillers and breathes all the air from her lungs. 'I would never — I just — really liked her,' Paz says, unsure why she is defending herself to Fina. Surprised to find she's full of emotion, her eyes shining with wet.

'You married her husband because you liked her so much. Is that it?'

Paz goes quiet. She feels the terror of Fina. Or maybe it is the terror of Romy. It could be the terror behind all women artists. Is Fina helping her, or hurting her? Paz can't tell, though it almost doesn't matter because she knows she has to put her body through the work if she's going to get out of this. The heat suddenly feels murderous, and Paz is finding it hard to move. She knows now that she needs to find Romy, and that she needs to do it alone.

THEY'VE DRUNK SO MUCH CHAMPAGNE, and now that they're home, she feels drunker than she was at the gallery. Paz walks up the steps past the dried-out roses, and Billy says something about how before Dylan Thomas drank himself into a coma, he fell into a rosebush and scratched his eyeball. 'Even his slapstick was poetic,' Paz says. Billy takes out the dog, drunk in his suit, and then he comes back and opens the fridge door, standing in the glow of it, clinking some jars. Something about making pasta and then deciding it is too much work. Her guard is down and so is his. She thinks about telling him about the postcards. Every time she thinks of them, a slow spool of images flashes through her brain, ending with him and Romy and the baby. She is full with all the questions she wants to ask him. About Romy, about the calls from Milt. But instead she finds herself asking, 'Who was the woman in the gold top?'

'Who?'

'Who was she?'

'I don't really know.'

'She seemed like a big fan of yours.'

'People act that way when they want something from you,' he says in a way that ends the conversation. Billy stands there at the window, smoking and looking out. He doesn't say anything for a long time, and neither does Paz.

'I meant to ask you what Milt wanted,' she finally asks. 'You saw him today, didn't you?'

'Why?'

'He called a lot while you were in Rome. It seemed urgent.' Paz looks at him.

'He wanted to talk about the show. It's all — happening a bit sooner,' Billy says.

She feels certain that she is being lied to. The conversation lapses into silence, and they both sit on the couch while he smokes, his other hand on the bare legs she's resting in his lap. She's feeling light-headed and leans her head on his shoulder, the one covered by a scar. Not covered, that was lazy, but it took up most of his left shoulder. He had once been struck by lightning. *Tall, thunderstorm, dreamer,* Romy had written. The closeness of his body has always had a sedative effect. The feeling that comes over her when he is beside her is so total, it makes it impossible to see him clearly. 'What are you thinking?' Paz asks him, her face burning a little. She feels like she is staring at two separate people. Not even two — many. He is in so many fragments, but she only ever gets one. She thinks how little she actually knows him. If she were to admit it, she knows more about him from Romy's journals, and is not unembarrassed by the voyeurism.

After a long silence he says, 'I have some things' — he coughs — 'I need to sort out,' and he moves his hand over her hair. She knows he isn't talking about work. She finds it unbearable. It almost doesn't matter what it is that has made him remote, it just makes her feel like she has always felt — that there is something wrong about her that no one could love.

'Billy?'

'Yes.'

'What did you talk about with Fina? At the gallery.' He looks at her and she feels a bit stupid, but she doesn't stop herself. 'It seemed — intense.'

Billy closes his eyes. 'It was nothing.'

'It honestly didn't look like nothing.'

'It was just — nothing you need to worry about.'

'Worry about?' She swallows hard. 'Why can't you just tell me what she said?'

There is a violence in his expression. 'What do you want me to tell you?' His voice turns hard. 'Do you want me to tell you that Fina asked me to fuck? Is that what you want me to tell you, because that's what happened. I didn't want to tell you because I knew it would upset you. It's nothing she hasn't said before.'

'Why did you think it would upset me?' she says, something switching inside her. 'How well do you think you know me?'

There is a long silence and then he says, 'Paz, don't.' She can't tell if he is holding back out of a desire to protect her, or if he is just incapable of closeness with her. Maybe because of the pills, or the performance, or because she is also very drunk, she does something she never does. She presses him on it. She gets up off the couch. He stands up and levels his gaze at her. 'Drop it,' he says severely. Like she is a dog. He must have realized his tone is too harsh, because he softens his voice and says again, 'Paz, I don't want to do this.' His harshness has frightened her, she doesn't know how to act, and suddenly Romy seems to be speaking through her.

'Fina did this when you were with Romy?' she says, anger breaking through.

'Fina knows where I stand on the issue.'

'I don't know how to believe you when you tell me nothing,' Paz says, shoving him a little. He grabs her jaw. A look crosses his face that she can't name. He stares directly into her eyes, puts his hands on her shoulders, and she winces. Then he leans toward her and kisses her, hard on the mouth. This is what he does to her — he drowns her in him. And always, she lets him. He grabs her hair roughly and pushes her up against the cool wall and runs his hands up her ribs. She feels a beat of pleasure. His mouth on her neck. Then he picks her up and pulls down her underwear and fucks her against the wall, and she lets herself believe this is the truth and not a way around it. It feels so good to her that she doesn't know what she is saying. He pushes harder against her, her hair all over, their bodies moving, slick with sweat, her thinking, What if this is the only real thing? And then she thinks of nothing at all. After they move slowly down, limbs threaded, her head on the hard floor, she hears a distant sound of sirens, or maybe it's coyotes, the ones she sometimes hears coming from the mountains. By then it seems normal not to say any of the things that need saying.

Wednesday

SWEAT TRICKLES DOWN HER BACK. She hadn't woken Billy when she'd left early this morning. The food on the passenger seat is already scorching in the sun, but it means she won't have to stop. She wishes she was one of those women who got too distraught to eat, but the truth is she is always hungry no matter what. A sharp frightened feeling runs through her body at the sight of white lace poking out of the bag she packed as a half-formed thought. The bottles of pills roll off and rattle around on the car floor, like hail on a rooftop, as she takes a huge bite out of an apple, already warmed by the sun. She's got Cotton's car, only for a day. The freeway was almost empty when the sun rose from the mountains and got the sea glittering and shining. At night the Pacific just lies there like a big black terrifying void of dark.

Paz exits onto the CA-127 as a plane flies above through big gulps of blue. The air is shimmering. Even the planes seem beautiful to her right now. It is easy to see why light is a historic occupation here. The movie business is here because of the light. The highway temperature clock is already reading 104 degrees as she drives past a whole section in the road where palm trees are bending over, as though they can no longer carry the weight of their own heads. She turns on the radio. It buzzes with fire reports. And then shootings. Men shooting each other. All they ever report are shootings. A woman is raped every two minutes. Why don't they report rapes? How many rapes happened in this city last night? She tries to roll down the window farther. Damn it. The crank has fallen off and now she has to fit it back on, turning slowly while using her other hand to carefully push down the glass. It's so hot she gives up and keeps it where it is. There are planes throwing chemicals on the fires to no effect. At least three more towns are burning. People are evacuating. Paz switches the radio off.

* * *

The fires had started when she'd first moved back in April, when all the star-shaped blossoms were emerging from the mock orange tree on Aunt May's lawn. Before she moved in with Billy, she talked to Essa a lot on the phone. She was packing up Aunt May's house and Essa was reading *Woman Hating*. Essa read something aloud about power imbalances with female virginity and how 'the man' brings 'the woman' to life through sex, which made her laugh like crazy.

Paz thought of her own first time, the lead up to which involved French-kissing a skater named Pete on Essa's couch in the basement, his jeans pressing into her, moving up and down for such a long time she almost wondered if they'd done it, though at the end of it, they both still had their pants on. 'You definitely know when you've done it,' Essa said with the sweeping authority of someone who has had sex once. The following weekend, Essa had a party, and after a lot of straight vodka drunk through a straw, Pete, who worked on the zipper of her pants but could not get them over her ankles, pulled them down to her knees and fucked her like it was a job someone had given him, and then passed out on the bathroom floor while Paz stared up at the ceiling, noticing a line of tiny black ants. She found Essa outside smoking a joint. She pressed it to her lips and took a big haul, watching the red ember shoot up and burn the paper. And then Paz leaned into the planter of azaleas and threw up.

'You okay?'

Paz wiped her mouth with a sharp leaf. 'Yeah.'

She thought she might feel better about it if she could turn it into something, so she gave Pete her number and attempted to look like she was not waiting near the phone. At some point, Aunt May, who seemed totally unaware by then, surprised her by saying, 'He's not gonna call, honey.'

'Who?'

'Whoever you are waiting for.'

How was that six years ago? When she'd returned from grad school, she was shocked at how much Aunt May had nosedived. She looked a hundred and seven. Her hands shook visibly. It seemed like she had been drunk since Paz had left and everything had passed her by. Her brain wasn't working right. And when the LAPD returned her in the middle of the night, barefoot in her nightgown, Paz had no choice but to sell her house and get her into assisted living. Aunt May didn't want to go to the home, the kind where everyone already looks dead, with pamphlets everywhere about accepting Christ as your savior.

Essa, who was getting over her own misery with Old Sumbitch having left a few months before, helped talk Paz through it. Paz remembers packing up Aunt May's house while on the phone with her. 'What are you doing?' Essa had asked her after hearing a long pause.

'Just feeling sort of empty,' Paz said. She felt a flatness, seeing where she'd spent her childhood, its own unspecified value spent. She'd seen everything moving at such a clip, except Aunt May and Ma, their lives trailing off like cigarette smoke.

The phone cord stretched to the living room, where Paz lay on her back with her legs propped up on the wall. 'I don't know how to explain it. It's just, I've been painting for years, and then I woke up and realized —' She stopped. 'That I hate being a painter.'

Georgette got on the phone for a moment. 'You're such a good painter, honey, why don't you just paint?' Essa managed to wrest the receiver from her. 'God, Mom,' she said. 'Sorry. Well, what are you going to do now?'

'Focus on ideas.' She didn't have the heart to tell Essa that she'd destroyed all her paintings from her entire MFA. She'd spent almost all her money shipping them back to LA. They had been so important to her. But then that desire just left her body. After leaving Aunt May at assisted living, Paz had cried all the way home, the way you do when you have left someone in such an unbearable way. Then she'd called Jay about borrowing his van. He'd been her only friend other than Essa in high school, one of the surfers who'd had a crush on Essa. He was one of those guys you call who would do anything for you. It just took a while because he was usually stoned.

The beach near Dogtown could get seedy. At night it rippled with meanness. The crash of waves drowned out the ugly sound of people fighting and fucking and punching each other after dark. She thought she and Jay were going to get murdered. She gathered all the canvases and boards and arranged them into a pyramid. shape. She glugged an entire jerry can of gasoline over the canvases and lit them all on fire. She instructed Jay how to shoot a grainy video with her Super 8 camera. She watched the flames and felt a little chill, a flicker of what it is to be human. It was when she knew she'd done the right thing. She burned almost one hundred paintings. One of the skaters came up to her eventually and said, 'What's that?' pointing to the fire.

'Art,' she said.

'Cool,' he said and high-fived her.

❊ ❊ ❊

Paz squints at something up ahead in the road. After all that time hypnotized by the desert landscape, driving through sky, two tumbleweeds the size of giant beach balls roll across the highway and she swerves. She's embarrassed she could have caused an accident over some twigs and air, but it wakes her up.

SHE REMEMBERS HEARING ROMY'S NAME on the radio the day after the accident. That's how they referred to it. They said 'accident' and 'no foul play suspected'. 'Foul play' always struck Paz as an odd term. It sounded like baseball, not murder. They quoted *New York* and *L.A. Times* critics, longtime enthusiasts of Billy's work, saying he was a gifted, internationally recognized artist. They didn't mention that Romy had also won a Prix de Rome and a Guggenheim fellowship. A shock went through the art world for a day, literally one day, and then it was quiet.

The wind rips through the window and she tries to block out an image that comes to her like a knife. The image of Romy on the edge of Milt's roof, glinting and lunar under the neon, the feeling of cells dividing, that Romy herself is splintering out there on the roof. People say she had to fake her death to start again. They say the disappearance itself was a performance — a narrative too tempting for any of them to resist. For the first time, Paz realizes she doesn't know what she'll do if she actually finds Romy.

Paz's face is already damp with perspiration. She dangles her arm out the window, swallows another Percodan and washes it down with Coke, but it sticks uncomfortably in her throat. The present has begun to fall forward and backward in a way that is making her feel a bit off. Suddenly the thought comes over her in an icy panic. In her sedated fog of narcotics, she hadn't thought to ask. Where is her finger? The thought horrifies her. Is it still lying on the studio floor? She can feel the sting on her shoulder in all the wind. Everyone had had too much to drink at the opening. No one had thought to treat her burn.

What if Romy has been just a hundred miles inland all this time? But even if she had planned to disappear, Paz knows Romy would want her life back. The desert blurs by in flashes of blue radiance. There's nobody on the highway in either direction. When a car does finally appear on the other side, she thinks of how crazy this pact we make to not kill is, hurtling toward each other at death speed, narrowly missing each time. She's written out rough directions, but there must be a map in the glove box. She reaches around and pulls out a piece of paper that turns out to be the car registration with something stuck to it. She shakes it, and out drops a condom. Fucking Cotton. The original pussy-hounder, Red calls him. He'd sleep with anything. He'd French his own dog. 'No I wouldn't,' he'd said to Red, grinning. 'Too much fur.'

The landscape pares itself down. The treed hills and glinting ocean give way to towns, clusters of low buildings framed by light, slowly thinning out. Past the odd homestead, the abandoned freight cars. The soft rolling earth is cut with bright-blue sky. It makes her want to strip her life clean. Down to what is most essential. The sand glitters a blinding white on either side of the road, and she thinks of it as time. What she is looking at is ground-out time, and she realizes that she has always been pulled by this feeling, a feeling between wanting to be somewhere and wanting to be nowhere.

The sand billows past the car. The glare of midday sun, its luminous, beautiful force. She hasn't seen anything in miles and then drives past a hand-scrawled sign, SHADY LADY, announcing out of nowhere, in front of a desert mountain range, a low building with a tin roof that could contain supplies, but instead contains women you pay for sex. Who is even around here to service? It's just like America to be lipsticked in the unassuming moment, revealing itself to already be corrupt. Insects tick the windscreen, their bodies candescent droplets of bright yellow, pale gray, and green, like a palette.

She feels a low-level emptiness and then realizes she misses the baby. Really misses her. A few miles ago she started to hear her crying, in the back seat. Aunt May had once told her that they had a streak of insanity in their family and it had always terrified her. But this is different. It makes her feel like an actual mother, which she's always felt awkward about since becoming a mother when she was twenty-two, to a long-legged baby that isn't hers. When it first happened, she had called Essa, who said, 'Oh yeah, the phantom crying thing.' It made her feel better to know it was a thing. Essa also said that a therapist had told her that if the baby — the actual baby — has been crying for an alarmingly long time and you feel unable to go on, and you are about to lose control, you've got to get out of there.

'Where would I go?' said Paz.

'Well, if you're alone and no one can take the baby, go somewhere else.'

Paz thought about this. 'Where?' she said.

'You have to leave the baby in a safe place and go to another room, or even take a few steps back.' There was a pause, and then Paz started laughing. 'What?' Essa said, in dead seriousness.

'I don't know, it just sounds like you are talking about a bomb.'

She cracks the can of salted almonds, tipping her head back and pouring some down her throat, washing them down with Coca-Cola, while steering with one wrist. She's reminded of being with Billy and Juke going a hundred and twenty on the highway when Juke eighty-sixed a clock out of the car window and that was it — that was the piece. He just turned to them and said, grinning, 'Done, man, *hecho*.' It bothered her to admit that in the end it was a kind of show business, in a way.

Paz spins the radio dial through a wilderness of static until she hears 'Love Is the Drug' fading into 'Crazy on You'. She turns it up very loud and drives with her arm resting on the car door. Something about the music and the hot wind and the speed of the car feels like freedom to her. At the next payphone she decides to pull over at the side of the road. She drops a dime into the slot.

'Cotton?'

'You know it,' he says, sounding tranquilized.

'Listen, can I return your car tomorrow?' Paz hears music, and then the phone sounds like it has been dropped under water and then passed to someone else. 'Who is this?' she says, impatiently, the phone scorching against her ear.

'Who's this?' a woman's voice says, part laughing. The woman is sucking on some sort of candy.

'Can you put Cotton back on the phone?'

There are some muffled sounds and then Cotton talks into the phone. He also seems to be sucking something. 'I can't hear what you're saying,' Paz says.

'Keith brought over a bag of blackballs.'

'Okay.'

'Where've you been?'

'Nowhere.'

Cotton suddenly lowers his voice to a whisper. 'There's a mouse in the john,' he says. 'And the mouse is' — he pauses — 'eating a blackball.' He laughs. 'Some blackballs must have rolled into the bathroom when the bag opened. They rolled out everywhere.' He continues, whispering, 'Every time I go to take a piss, I see this mouse, crazy fucking thing — it's holding the blackball in its paw like a bowling ball. And each time I go in there, it's a different color, it's chewed off another layer. First it was blue. Then it was purple. Now it's sort of a pink color. It's really fucking trippy.'

'Cotton.'

'Yeah.'

'What are you on?'

'White lightning.'

'*White lightning?* That is, like, cop-level bad.' She pauses. 'Okay,' she says, exaggeratedly slow. 'I'm letting you know I'm going to need your car for another day. I think that by the sound of it, you won't need to be driving for a while,' she says. There's a long silence. She feels like she could almost faint in the heat. She's worried the phone has gone dead and yells, 'Hey! Pal! I have at least one sacrificial burn in the name of your art.' The air is searing so clear she can see every spike on the cactus yards away, and the sharp desert grasses poking through sand. She can feel the minerals under her feet. Nothing moves, not even the highest palms. She overwhelmingly feels the desert's pull, but to do what? Swallow it? Get lost in it? And even then it wouldn't be enough to get what she wants from it.

'Pazzy. Keep the car, man,' Cotton finally says. 'It's cool. I don't need it for a while. Lucky for you.' There is more laughter and then just dial tone as she hangs up the receiver, still hot in her hand.

A desert thistle brushes her leg as she gets back into the car. It makes her think of John Wayne and his Geiger counter. The desert is full of radioactive tumbleweeds. It turns out that half the people on that movie set got cancer, and a quarter of them died, including John Wayne. What did survive was the Russian thistle.

Talking to Cotton reminds her of the party at Essa's house in high school when they took LSD. She remembers being in Essa's bedroom with Essa's boyfriend at the time, a guy named Brad. Brad handed them a tiny square with a badly rendered Mickey Mouse that seemed a bit perverse to her, and said, 'After you, my dear,' and she died a little. He was the lead singer in a band. His singing was clichéd and his guitar playing was crap, but she liked watching him onstage. He had a big nose, big in the right way, and worked at giving off a look of despair that gave him more dimension than he probably had. She looked down at the tab. It was smaller than her baby fingernail. They waited and waited until suddenly everything seemed off, like the world had been shaken and sprayed with a hose. Everything was shimmering, and it looked like there was a puddle on the floor where really it was just wall-to-wall carpeting. Paz's mouth tasted like blood. She tried to draw in her sketchbook but felt woozy, putting it back into her backpack. There were rainbows forming around the curtain rods. Things looked glittery, and she could feel dampness in the crotch of her underwear. She felt moisture everywhere — her eyes, her throat, under her arms. *Oh my god,* she thought, *I'm a plant.* Essa had long wandered out by that point, and when she looked down, Brad's head was in her lap. He was staring up at her. It might have been a minute, but it might have been a lot longer than that, because later, when she went to the bathroom, she saw a dint on her thigh from a button on his shirt. 'You're not beautiful,' he said. 'You've got a chipped tooth.' He rubbed his finger under her front tooth, which felt kind of erotic. 'You've got black hair all over your sweater.' He took a sip of rum. 'But what an ass.'

'Thanks.' Her voice sounded high and strange. She actually thanked him. This is where her mind gets shaky. She remembers him brushing her hair off her face, his mouth on hers, his hand up her skirt. She sipped from his sticky glass and felt it burn her throat. She felt a flash of shame bloom hot across her face. What had she done? He popped an ice cube into his mouth and started chewing it. She put her ear on the top of his head. It was the most amazing sound she'd ever heard. She was bursting with love at this incredible sound. She told him she wanted to chew ice for him so he could hear it too, but then Essa came back looking stunned. She took Essa's hand. It felt fresh and rough in hers. 'You okay?' Essa looked at Paz's hand, and then followed it up Paz's arm and looked into her face blankly. After a while Essa slow-blinked and mouthed, *Who are you?*

＊ ＊ ＊

Paz is suddenly ravenous. She fishes around but she's already finished most of what's on the passenger seat. She kicks off her sandals and drives in her bare feet. She looks at herself in the rear-view mirror and sees that her shirt is inside out. The heat makes the scenery look almost two-dimensional. It gives it a radical geometry. She's driving a speed addict's car in an inside-out shirt, on painkillers, with a hand wrapped in gauze, on her way to find her husband's dead ex-wife. If she concentrates hard enough, these things will snap into a logical pattern.

A SIGN PIERCES THE BLUE and she pulls off the highway into the parking lot of The Desert Inn. She slams the car door shut, grabs her bag, and walks across the asphalt, her sandals slapping against her heels. It feels even hotter here. Sweat trickles. She licks it off her upper lip, which is already cracked, and smooths down her hair, feeling the prick of salt around her hairline. The motel diner is lined with huge flowering rosemary bushes that send their sharp dusky scent into the air. The small tiled lobby inside is air-conditioned, thank god. There are eggs popping on the grill, and slabs of bacon frying, and the smell of old, slightly burnt coffee. A waitress sits her down at the counter, giving Paz a view of the grill and the orders written on paper, clipped onto a metal circle that the cook turns as he reads them. She can see the bubbling deep fryer. It reminds her too much of the late-night donut shift she worked in New York at art school, and how her clothes and even her hair would smell like old grease from the fryer for days after. And it strikes her that no matter where you go, everything resembles something else, and that everyone is also made up of the same things, electrons and forces that stop us from flying off in all directions.

Paz asks for a booth. 'Will someone be joining you?' the waitress, whose nametag reads Linda, asks, a bit sarcastically. She shakes her head. The place is virtually empty except for a teenager in a wheelchair eating alone, and an old man smoking and eating eggs, yelling to the cook, 'Lord knows, we need rain.'

Linda hands her a menu and says, 'Suit yourself.'

Paz orders a coffee, a hamburger, and a side of toast. Linda doesn't exactly bust her ass to get it. And when she does, the coffee is black and sour and Paz sips it so quickly it burns.

❈ ❈ ❈

One of the only times she was alone with Romy, they had gone for a diner breakfast during the group show at Ora's. At some point, Romy had said something about how she didn't really have a mother, and Paz had told her she didn't either. 'But honestly, for me,' Romy said, 'I think it's just made everything clear. It helped me in the sense that I've always understood I can't really count on anyone. No one can. You have to figure it out alone or you will always be stuck.' Paz nodded in agreement, though she wondered where Romy's husband fit in to this worldview. She noticed that Romy didn't touch her food. Romy stretched her long legs out under the banquette and leaned back. 'I wish I could cut myself off from social contact sometimes. There's already not enough time to do all the things I'm thinking about.' She blew on the murderously hot coffee and took a sip. 'I hate wasting art-time on people I can't stand. I keep thinking about disappearing, checking out. Still working, but cutting myself off from all the distractions. I guess I can't shake how I grew up. My mother was a classicist, so all my thinking has been about things that last,' she said. 'When I was little, I was surrounded by images of saints and martyrs. My mother liked everything that was dead. She was convinced even birds communicated in Latin.' She laughed. 'I never asked her what they were saying because that was where she was most at home. Explaining arcane things to people.'

They had certain things in common, but for some reason, Paz was unable to figure out how to engage with her. Everything Romy said assumed importance. She lived her life so strongly. It made Paz want to approach her with the purest sincerity, but this only made her feel empty and young, like an acolyte. She ended up nodding a lot, slightly shredding her napkin. In Romy's company, she was tense with constraint. She felt she had no personality and ate her entire breakfast far too quickly. 'What made you start to work with light?' she asked, hating herself for this inane question.

'I think it really was when I went to Crystal Cove near Laguna Beach one summer, and I watched tide pools fill with abalone and other colorful sea creatures. I was hypnotized by them. After, my grandparents took me to see a traveling circus near by. I remember being crushed by synthetic smells — cotton candy, hotdogs, and a sickening sunscreen smell, the kind with chemicals. The carnies were all stoned and focused on their tasks. Everything felt unrecognizable to me — food, even people were roasted hotdog red. My grandmother bought me my first ice-cream cone. It was almost frightening, that secret sting of sweet. Inside the tent, I took my seat and wiped my sugary hands on my shorts. I was overwhelmed by the spectacle. Even then I was always making calculations. I could never just relax and enjoy everything at face value. When we were leaving the tent, a thick swarm of bodies pushed through. A tanned boy with a ripped T-shirt, and hair sticking up, walked by me. He might have been smoking, even though he was barely twelve. I felt sex come off him like heat. I was probably only about nine, maybe ten. It hit me somewhere in my stomach, at least that's the only way I could understand it. I remember my grandmother's hand reaching in, pulling me away, as though she somehow knew, and needed to stop it. Even though it was just a frequency. A feeling of a frequency. As I was leaving, I saw the boy standing beside his friend, a thin boy selling photographs of sharks by the parking lot. My grandmother wouldn't let me buy one. "They're all dead," she said, pulling me away.'

Romy sat back in her chair. 'I thought about the boy for a long time after. It's funny, but telling you now I realize that the revelation of light came with this visceral experience of desire. I always wanted art to feel that way.' She took a long sip of coffee. 'At first I couldn't shake the notion that I'd failed as a painter somehow.'

'Me too,' Paz said. 'I have that same feeling of failure.' God, she sounded like an idiot, though she really had been contemplating giving up painting to focus on her performance pieces. Still, she wasn't able to translate herself properly to Romy.

'Well, I think failure that comes from trying new things is okay. It's not the same as those mistakes that take you away from yourself. But sometimes you don't want to overthink a feeling. When I first talked about it with my husband, he said to me, "If performance isn't what you want to do, then fuck it, quit. Do what gives you pleasure."'

What she hadn't expected was how she felt in Romy's presence. She couldn't stop staring at her, realizing how a beautiful face can't really be explained. It overwhelmed her, made her feel a kind of full-body flood-of-warmth excitement. She asked Romy if she was going to the upcoming women's meeting Essa had told her about.

'I don't like the whole "you are either with us or against us" mentality. Also, I don't like being called a woman artist. I mean, can't we just be artists?' she said. 'No adjective? Everyone's always going around using so many adjectives, I just lose it.' She had a point. There were a lot of groups starting and it was confusing about which one to align yourself with. Women were divided. Even Sondra, who headed up so many of the meetings, was torn as a Black woman leading groups of mostly middle-class white women. And then there were the lesbian separatists who were anti-art because they considered art bourgeois.

They were interrupted by a boy in the booth next to them who kept asking his mother, 'Why is the sky blue?' The mother's hair was full of curlers wrapped in a chiffon headscarf. Paz always wondered what occasion these women were all waiting for to reveal the curled hair. Leaving the house clearly wasn't one. He repeated his question until

Romy shifted her gaze to him. There was total silence from the mother, who was blowing smoke with a stunned look on her face. The boy poked his head around the booth and looked at them searchingly. Even the woman's own kid could tell his mother was an asshole.

Romy said to him, 'The short answer?'

'Hit me.' The kid was sharp, she'd give him that.

'Nitrogen,' Romy said.

The kid stared at Romy like she was television. She turned back to Paz with a slight, drifting smile. They fell into silence for a moment, backgrounded by low-level voices. Paz placed her mug down and leaned back. 'Do you think you will ever have a baby?'

'I have other plans,' Romy said and went on talking about her work. She said that light was a subject that, thank god, had no gender. 'Anyway,' she said. 'Man, woman, I'm never really sure which one I am.'

Paz found that hard to believe because Romy's feminine beauty seemed so undeniable. 'Really?' she asked.

'Yep,' she said in a voice that made it clear it was the last thing she wanted to discuss. Romy told her that she had gone to one of those women's meetings early on and heard a woman say in a loud voice, 'Tomboys always turn out to be the biggest sluts.' And then a woman she didn't know, who had been studying her for a while, had walked up to her and said, 'You don't like yourself, I can tell.' And Romy had said, 'I like myself,' and then she walked the hell out.

The feminism Paz had witnessed was all about rewriting the rules of society. But she could see that Romy was outside of that. She'd been blowing up objects, flying through deserts. Not for their shock value, but to defy the kind of inner constraint that makes the agreed-upon forms of living unbearable. She wasn't interested in rewriting anything. She didn't seem to understand the limits of who she was and where she was. Or maybe she did.

When Paz talked about the work she was making, she somehow wound up telling Romy about caring for Ma when she was going downhill. Being back in LA made it all come back to her in sharp relief. She'd always worried she was never going to escape her miserable past. The only place that was hers had always come through art, but she also saw that the jewel-like joy of making something, getting to be outside of herself, required withdrawal from all other realms of life.

And then Romy said something that surprised her. 'I can see why you were selected for the group show.' Words that sounded like fireworks to her, said in a consoling tone that brought to Paz's attention that she was in need of consoling.

SHE FINISHES HER HAMBURGER AND drains her coffee. The bun was toasted hard and has ground up her palate. She asks Linda, who finally passes by, for more coffee and then for the menu back. Linda, who eyes Paz buttering both sides of her toast, says, 'You got a bun in the oven or something?' It makes her think of how almost immediately after she'd first moved back to LA, she'd thought she was pregnant. They agreed she wouldn't keep it. Though, in her darker moments, she wondered if it was more how Billy thought it would look to everyone than anything else. Paz secretly swore that she would never complain about another thing again as long as a baby didn't come. It had been eight weeks. She'd known she wanted her art to hang in a museum since she was fourteen. She had worked incessantly, lived cheaply, was careful about contraception, and now she couldn't believe this was where years of bleeding and cramps had led her. It was just like her body to get up to this kind of dirty work. She tried to imagine their child. She had no doubt a boy would be beautiful. Things might not work out so well for a girl. She remembers the doctor's office where she took a blood test. A woman next to her in the waiting room, who had plucked her eyebrows into such terrifying arches she looked insane, leaned over and said, 'How far along are you?' Paz said nothing, mortified at the lack of anonymity. After an excruciatingly long time sitting in the fluorescent-lit waiting room with radically outdated magazines, she was called in. The nurse said, 'You're not pregnant, dearie,' in a voice rinsed entirely of human sympathy.

Paz looked her in the eye and said, 'Good.'

'Well, aren't you a cool customer.'

* * *

She finishes her coffee and gets up to pay the check. Beside the counter is a moon-faced teenager with a side ponytail, wearing a pink velour tracksuit, in a wheelchair. She says she was born in the desert and that her name is Veronica. 'After Veronica Lake,' she says, which strikes Paz as cruel somehow, given that she couldn't look less like Veronica Lake.

Desert Veronica Lake appears to want Paz to comment, so she says, 'So. Your parents were into femmes fatales?'

'I guess.'

'Well, she was quite beautiful,' Paz says, trying to get Linda's attention so she can pay.

'Yeah. But she sort of had a sad life. In the end.'

'Sad how?'

'Well, you know her signature —' She motions hair over one eye.

Paz nods.

'Yeah, well, during the war, apparently government officials made her change it.'

'I didn't know top brass weighed in about women's *hair*.'

'A lot of women had her hairstyle. I guess they thought women who were working on assembly lines during the war with hair over one eye were going to get it all caught up in machines or something.'

'Actually, now that you mention it,' Paz says, 'I don't remember seeing her with another hairstyle.'

'That's because she only got a few crappy bit-parts after she changed it. Anyway, she became an alcoholic and died as a cocktail waitress married to her fourth husband, a commercial fisherman known as Captain Bob.'

'Bummer,' Paz replies, not sure what to say, thinking no one should ever be named after anyone else.

'Are you here to see the eclipse?' Desert Veronica Lake asks. Paz shakes her head, distractedly. 'It's a total lunar eclipse. Which means Earth is going to block most of the sun from reaching the moon, so it will look red. A blood moon.'

Paz nods. She's suddenly feeling very hungover and shaky, and steps awkwardly into the stand of sunglasses, knocking them over. There are cassette tapes. Nothing she recognizes except Johnny Cash.

'Excuse me.' Paz pulls out the postcard, holding it toward Linda as she walks by. 'Do you know where this postmark comes from? It says Shoshone.' Linda snatches it from her. Her hands are surprisingly strong. 'No,' she says, quickly handing it back.

'Do you think you could take a look —'

'I have a table,' Linda says, pushing past Paz, tripping a little over one of Desert Veronica Lake's wheels. Desert Veronica Lake examines the postcard. 'It looks like the old post office?'

'Where is that?' Paz says, wondering why she said it like a question.

'Well, up the Fifteen, past Barstow, just north of Tecopa,' Desert Veronica Lake says, trailing off.

'What is it?' Paz asks.

'Well.' She hesitates. 'Is this an old postcard?'

Paz shakes her head. 'Why?'

Desert Veronica Lake looks at it again and says, 'It's just. That post office was part of an old hotel.' She looks confused. 'The post office has been closed for years. And no one's been in the hotel since the artist who was working there, well, died.'

JANUARY 1977. *I've found an abandoned hotel in the middle of the desert and am leasing it from some Texans out of Nevada. I'm saving to buy it. I'm not interested in selling any work, so I've been flying to make money, doing aerial burials, scattering people's ashes on mountain tops or into the sea for the Neptune Society, which is run by a guy who plays the Mother Earth's Plantasia album to his houseplants every morning and likes that I don't mind flying his old Cessna that pulls to the left a little. I've always kept my money separate from Billy's, even when he started getting big commissions. I knew I had to do something for myself before he came back from working in Germany. The question is, what do I want at my center? I felt like I was growing dimmer every day, so I drove out here to clear everything from my life and live in a way I believe in. I've charted out a new regimen. I've set aside two rooms at the front of the hotel. To block out the light, I've sealed them off, and painted the walls and ceiling with thick matte white ceiling paint. I make coffee but it burns in the gut. There is an old fridge, but it doesn't keep cold and most food spoils in the heat, so I buy bags of sunflower seeds and very slowly crack my way through them. I often forget to eat. The project is emerging. In the day, shafts of sunlight move slowly across a section of wall or floor. Twice a day the light levels exactly mirror each other.*

These skies have a glittering, healing light that gets in your clothes, and head, and hair. I can't stop dreaming of light. I walk out, absorb the light, and then come back in to work. Sometimes, when I go too long without eating, I start to see something that isn't there. Often it is just an object, a glass of water or a shirt draped over the bed. And then I look up and discover that it is already night. I've been reading about dark matter. I can't believe nobody talks about the giant black hole at the center of the universe. Circling oblivion, it seems, isn't good for conversation. After a few weeks of observations, I made some carefully calibrated openings that allowed light to enter rooms under controlled conditions. I had to redo the first one because I'd fucked up the cut — it was too large and too square. But when I saw it the next day, I thought, this is such a beautiful, divine thing. If you spend enough time, something else comes into play. That's what I wait for.

SEPTEMBER 1977. *When Billy got back from Germany, he drove straight out here. He couldn't find it at first. Blew out two tires. I can only work on the building in the daylight, so I've been doing night work, hundreds of studies, sketches in pencil and eraser of the surface of the moon, hunched under a goosenecked desk lamp.*

Billy looked at the moon sketches. This is what you've been doing when night falls?

Night doesn't fall, I said. It rises.

These are remarkable. His voice was filled with admiration. If you keep this up, they're going to name a crater of the moon after you.

They don't name craters of the moon after women.

Well, it's the kind of work people get remembered for.

You can say that because you immediately get recognition for your work, because you and everything you make are recognizable to the outside world. For me, the more I work, the more isolated I become. I can already picture what the critics will say. They'll say, 'This isn't art. It's carpentry.'

I knew he was moved by what I was making because he could also be brutal with me, with my work. In a fight before he left the last time, he said, can't we just go back to before? When you were still painting instead of trying to sell a piece of the blue sky? I'm just trying to be honest, he said.

Honest? I thought. We'd let things go too far and we both knew it.

He focused his attention on the rectangles, looking up at the night sky.

I'm going to gather starlight that's over two billion years old. Older than the solar system.

It reminds me of a line of Simone Weil's.

What line? I said. The fact that he was equating me with a fasting mystic was not lost on me.

Love is not consolation. It is light.

I handed him a typewritten piece of paper without looking up. He sat up and read it. Oh no. No. I'm so sorry. The hotel had been bought by developers. I had to be out by the end of the month. He came over and put his arms around me and held me for a long time. I'm going to fly over the desert until I find a new site, I said. And though we didn't say it, we both doubted this was possible. He could hear it in my voice, as I could. Something had crashed in me.

STANDING BACK FROM A DUSTY untrafficked road, the hotel is bleached as a seashell, surrounded by tufts of sharp weeds. The sun has washed out the foliage. Paz takes the key out of the ignition but keeps her hands on the steering wheel. She's had so much caffeine she feels almost holy, her body sped up, the scenery looking like it is designed for her alone. The engine and the tape deck have cut out and there is no sound at all, no birds singing, nothing. Her heart begins thudding in her ears. The sun is high above. It must be at least 110 degrees. *110 DEGREES*. A little shiver goes through her despite the gushes of coppery heat that hit as she slams the car door. Her bladder feels heavy as a sandbag. Beside the building, she pulls down her underwear and tries to direct the stream between her feet, but some gets on her ankles. Son of a bitch. There are little thistles sticking out of the sand. She sees what looks like quartz glinting in the sun but decides not to pick it up. At the front door, a faded paper is nailed to the wood saying the building is set for demolition, dated over a year ago.

A dead cottonwood stands in front of the post office boxes. The building's windows have been boarded up. A door, almost off its hinges, flaps in the slight breeze. She swats at the flies that circle and land on her, as though checking to see if she's become food yet. The air shimmers. She swallows another Percodan and a Librium and washes them down with Coke that foams warm in her mouth. She closes her eyes to the sun. She's taken so many pills she buzzes all over. She hasn't really played out what she will do if she finds her. Paz's life has become so frozen with questions it is impossible not to want to put her foot through all of it. She's left herself undefended, which makes her feel a soft shock of alertness. Every possible outcome scares her, but she finds herself moving forward, her legs carrying her toward the dirty white building lit by the sun.

FEBRUARY 1977. *Space has three dimensions and time has only one dimension, which we call the fourth dimension. The event horizon is a boundary in a space-time continuum. If a person is outside this boundary, the events taking place will not affect the person.*

The rooms have been sealed off, and smoothed with plaster, all painted what must have once been white. Light throws beams across the floor, illuminating swirling dust. A rectangle of light shines on her face. She follows it up to a square cut out of the ceiling. To see what's happening, she lies down on her back, though the floor is filthy. The Coke sloshes in her stomach.

* * *

The nearest she has been to here was in May, after she'd moved back from New York. She'd gone way out to the shaggy wilds of the desert with one of Sondra's classes, collaborating on a twenty-four-hour performance along the highway, before everyone had started to turn on her. It was in the early days with Billy and she wanted to get back to him right after, so she borrowed Essa's car instead of piling in the van with the other women. She drove six hours straight. By the time she was on the 138, she really had to piss. She wanted to make it to Billy's class for seven. She was trying to decide what to do. If she pulled off the highway, she wouldn't make it. And then she just slid down her pants and pissed into a Styrofoam cup she'd found on the floor of the car so she wouldn't have to stop. She didn't know what to do with it when it filled up, so she threw it out the window and then felt bad about littering, and also about being someone so crazy they'd piss in a cup instead of stopping at a gas station like a normal person. She could see herself in the rear-view mirror, dirty, with tangled hair, looking like a genuine lunatic. Billy's class had already started when she came in and sat at the back as the slide projector clicked through images. Her scholarship in New York had been given up so she could come to LA to be with him, though she wouldn't have put it that way to anyone, especially him. She had never done this before — submit completely to someone's control. But there was a disquiet around him that she picked up on in his class. Earlier, during their critiques, he had severely admonished a student for a performance that seemed to borrow heavily from his falling works. Paz wondered if what was troubling him was that if someone could make work like his, it made what he did of no significance at all.

After the class, while he spoke to some students, she went to the washroom and sat in the stall for a moment. She was exhausted. There was sand stuck to her skin and in her hair. Even her eyes were gritty. Through the crack in the stall she saw that two of Billy's students had walked in, and didn't feel like facing them so she sat and waited it out. 'I don't know if I'll ever learn anything from that man when all I want to do is sleep with him.' There was a short pause. 'I think he's taken,' the other one said. The first one said, 'They always are.' The second one said, 'That's why you'll have to steal him.' They both laughed. 'Who do you think that was in the back of class today?' the first one said. There was silence for a moment. 'You mean the one who looked like she'd been through a nuclear war? Rapunzel with the fucked-up hair?' There was another pause, and then Paz heard one of them say, 'No one.'

And then the door slammed, and she could hear their laughter echoing down the hall.

When she drove back to Billy's house, she tried to put it out of her mind. The car filled with their silent respective uneasiness. They got out, and the air around his house smelled like flowers. The babysitter left, and then he turned to her and said he felt so unburdened with her. It was better. She made everything better. This surprised her. She hadn't known what he was thinking. At the end of the night when she was getting ready to leave, he said, 'You really have been supportive of me, with the baby. With what I've been going through.'

'You don't owe me anything.'

'I didn't mean that.'

She got up to go and he touched her arm. 'I thought it was obvious I want you to stay.' She didn't find it at all obvious what he wanted, and she felt the pleasure of him telling her this. He said this relationship was something he'd never imagined for himself so soon. She had a sharp curious brain that drew him in. But he said she was hard to get to know. Her small body turned him on, cracked open his need in a way he'd forgotten existed.

Are you sure this is what you want? she wanted to ask him. But she knew that would make the conversation serious and she didn't want to corner him into anything. She silenced all her questions so as not to risk this fragile thing that was happening. 'I am going to see Aunt May tomorrow,' she began, a bit taken aback by this unexpected declaration, 'but after, I can —'

He pulled her closer. 'Or just come back and never leave.'

SHE HAS NO IDEA HOW long she's been lying there, but the heat is making her feel heavy, full of pressure. She keeps coughing in all the dust. There is a sink on one wall, and she sits up and brushes herself off. She feels blood rush to her head. She turns the faucet, and nothing comes out. Her mouth feels like sand. She's suddenly aware that she has brought no water. She is so parched she walks outside, into sun like the staggered flash of a thousand photographers. There is nothing to drink except a can of Coca-Cola that has been rolling around on the back seat. She cracks it and it froths down her fingers, and she drinks it in long gulps. It's mouth-warm and so sweet she almost spits it out. She wipes her mouth with the back of her hand, dirtying the white gauze, which is now sticky and rusted with blood. She feels pressure in her hand like a heartbeat. When she looks up, she sees something move through the door. A quick flash. Her stomach drops. Very slowly, still looking ahead, she reaches for her bag and feels for her camera and pulls it out. Breathing fast, she turns the key enough to keep the car radio on. She doesn't want to drain the battery, but she wants the feeling that she is not alone out here. It's just her and the tape deck for company.

Her sandals click on the cement, her breath catching at every sound. Inside, she aims her camera at the square on the floor, at the walls. She drops her bag to the floor and takes out the white dress. This morning she'd opened the closet knowing she wasn't going to find what she wanted. She'd long lapsed into wearing mostly jeans and T-shirts, and felt a sudden unraveling staring at the sad collection of her worn, stained clothes, wondering if Billy had noticed how little attention she paid to beauty. And because it was hanging right there, instead of her own, she grabbed Romy's wedding dress. It was beautiful white lace, high-necked, long. Something she'd never dared to touch.

She sheds her clothes on the dusty floor and carefully steps into the dress. She zips up the back as far as she can get it with one hand. They had completely different bodies, and though the sleeves are too long and it drags on the ground, it fits tightly on Paz. She holds the camera out as far as she can and takes a photo of herself. It will only catch her wild hair and part of the lace. She's not sure what she plans to do with it exactly. A performance? *Second Wife. Light Death.* It seems ridiculous now — nothing she could conceive of could ever touch what she's done in this serious space. She's entered the intensity of it with Romy. It feels ritualistic. Sweat erupts from every pore in her body, her slow-moving flesh submerged between states. She walks around taking several photos and sees pencil drawings of the moon, and a list on a piece of paper. Flowers? No, it's baby names — she sees the baby's name on the list and it makes tears well. There is a series of photos taped to the wall of Romy falling. A lot of them. She is wearing her dark-blue pants, her long thin arms sticking out of her rolled-up shirtsleeves. Her body is tilting dramatically to the left. In others she is lying on the ground, just fallen, like a saint warmed by the sun. She sees something Romy has written on the back of a pencil drawing. *So much light running through my body. I don't know what to do with all this light.* Paz steps back, tripping over the uneven floor, grabbing the cupboard door that is slightly ajar. The cupboard is empty and full of thick colorless dust. In the back corner she sees a small box with papers and some books — *NASA Book of Clouds*, a book on galaxies, and Susan Sontag's *Against Interpretation*, pages curled with sun — and, in a bin, wedged at the bottom, she recognizes the blue edge of a notebook. She can feel her heart beat in her ears, the amphetamines surge through her body. Nothing will bring her down. Billy had said he had all Romy's sketchbooks. It's stuffed with loose papers, drawings, and Polaroids of light studies.

She flips the page.

APRIL 11, 1976. *He was coming around the corner with an intense look, eyes fixed on a short woman with very long dark hair. I couldn't see her face or the color of her eyes, but he could. I could tell by the way he moved that he had been drinking. The girl was rapt, gazing up at him. I felt my face fill with blood, my eyes stinging, a high-pitched sound in my ears. Everything about him seemed repulsive to me in that moment. Slovenly, with his stubble and wild hair, his wrinkled jacket. I'd come to the gallery, where he'd said he was going, after it had been hours. I'd come to find him. There was a dinner for Juke at Martoni's. I knew what he wanted. He wanted a woman who wanted only his body. I'd become a woman who needed more than that — a difficult woman. I was so disgusted by his ugly, predictable male vanity. Stupid self-centered ego, after everything between us. And him feeling no need to explain. He, of course, denied it was anything. We went to the dinner and fought, and then drank martinis like they were water. When we got home, I felt his presence in a way the dark-haired girl brought sharply into being. I am certain I'd never noticed him so fully. It was an oddly erotic moment. A momentous fucking. Maybe the best yet. He fell into a deep contented sleep. I couldn't sleep at all. What kept me awake was thinking what a fatal mistake it was to put everything I had into one person.*

The last line jumps out, an unsettling feeling moves through her. Paz puts the sketchbook back carefully and sits down on the floor, and then lies down again. She should be feeling pain in her shoulder, her hand, her excruciatingly dry throat, but she can't feel anything. She is wild with vulnerability. All she can think is that, like so many women before her, Romy's genius was ground into dust, by a man. A man. By some fuckings done in a blackout that didn't even mean anything to him except a possible glimmer of shame the next day. Romy, like so many artists she knew, so often seemed to wind up with men who had something to teach — usually older, established — maybe because their hunger to know was so great these women just couldn't help themselves. And then a terrible thought crosses her mind. She is one of these women. Now, looking at Romy's notebook, Paz feels sick. Not because she is the dark-haired girl, but because she isn't. She would have been in New York studying for her finals. He wasn't any different than anybody else. He loved and betrayed like everybody else. On one of the only nights she'd had enough wine to question him, he'd looked at her and said, 'I'm sorry, but this is all I'm capable of right now.' He asked her to accept him for who he was. Fucker, she thought, wanting to slap him. Instead she got up and cried over the bathroom sink, running the faucet so he wouldn't hear her. Everyone thinks that no one has ever loved or suffered as much, yet they all suffer and love in the exact same ways.

She puts the notebook back carefully, breathing out very slowly, so slowly she is barely breathing at all. Blood pounds in her ears as she shuts her eyes and opens them, only now really seeing the gold light radiating through the room, overcome by what is happening in this place, this divine work. Every color blazes through, the sky hovering like a floating infinite portal through which Paz feels she has lost all sense of dimension and is staring at her own mortality. She can only take in shallow breaths. She feels her lungs struggling. Why is she breathing like this, or is it really her? Maybe it's the organs inside her body pumping and circulating, not her at all. So, who is it, then? Who is it that's breathing?

There is a miracle in it, even half-done. She feels like she has stared into the sun until it has come into her body. She luminesces. Every single cell in her is lit up. It is not a human feeling. Her body feels ridiculously light and brittle, like it's made of Styrofoam. Energy drains from her as she slowly draws her body into the fetal position, feeling a deep nausea. She wants to throw up, something vital, something incandescent. She feels all her life she's been an empty object, the long disintegration of her whole self to be a receptacle for images and words and sounds and wrecked people. Heat and light flicker over her. Her eyes are blinking stars. She's seeing images in reverse, like negatives. She clings to this thin thread of light. To the chilling, freezing, broiling sense of herself. To the idea that every single thing in life is a part of it. She can smell desert flowers baking in the sun, and she hears voices from the radio blooming in her head, and this rectangle of light and *love and hope and sex and dreams* and *look at me! I'm in tatters.*

The light crosses the walls and all this time it's felt wrong because *I know there's nothing to say, someone has taken my place.* She's in trouble, she's sunk, and she *went down down down and the flames went higher.*

THEY'D HAD ONLY ONE DAY together, in a dusty vacant lot, but for Paz, it felt like something had flown open and anything could rush in. 'I was lucky to discover art,' Romy had told her. Paz had got in the truck around the time the sun burned off the last of the morning's haze. 'Because on some level I could have ended up doing something a lot worse,' she said. 'I've always liked blowing things up.'

Romy was going to do some colored-smoke tests on a piece of vacant land out of town, and Paz had asked if she could come. She had only one day before she had to fly back to New York.

They stopped at Ka-Boom first. Paz wanted to go in with her, but Romy put out her cigarette and said, 'I'd rather you didn't. They're both creeps.'

In the truck, Paz was nervous. She felt she had to start from ground zero after talking too much to Romy after the opening, when they'd all gathered at a cramped apartment on Hollywood and Vine. Paz wasn't sure what to say now that she was in the truck alone with her, so she ended up talking about the review of the group show that had only mentioned Romy, saying she made work like Georgia O'Keeffe and looked like Monica Vitti. Romy shook her head. 'It always gets you, even if it doesn't get you.' Paz wasn't sure if that was all she was going to say on the subject. There was a long uncomfortable silence. 'I know I'm supposed to be grateful that I got an inch of type when no one else did,' Romy told her irritably, 'but that work was nothing like Georgia

O'Keeffe's.' Which was true — it was light panels made from projectors. Paz remembered a photographer stopping to take Romy's photo. She hadn't smiled. 'Besides,' she said, 'they would never say that Billy made work like Duchamp and looked like Paul Newman.'

'It was an impossible feat you pulled off,' Paz said. 'Being a woman *and* an artist.' Romy laughed. Paz felt better having found camaraderie at a wry distance. They drove out of town, past dirty mattresses, dented old Buicks with leaky oil pans parked on front lawns, men sitting out in plastic chairs shirtless and smoking. It was so hot in the truck that Paz felt sweat pooling in her bra. By the time they reached the plot of vacant land, she was so starving her stomach made loud noises as Romy parked the truck. Romy got the boxes out of the back and saw the Ka-Boom guys had forgotten some of the tubes. She threw her hands up. 'Why is everything so inhospitable to women artists!' Paz wasn't sure what was going on when Romy began lining up cans of spray paint that had been rolling around the pickup bed on the dirt. She came back from the truck carrying a rifle. It made Paz's stomach flip. There was a danger in Romy. It was the same danger that came out in her work because she was willing to go anywhere. 'What are you doing?'

Romy stiffened her legs, hoisted the gun, closed her left eye, aimed, and shot. She hit two of the cans and they exploded, bright pink and purple. The echo ricocheted richly through the vacant land. 'Here,' she said, handing Paz the gun. 'Try it.' Paz took it, almost dropping it. It was unbelievably heavy.

'Does anyone know you can shoot like that?'

'As the French say, no.'

The gun felt frightening in Paz's hands. She'd never held one. Her heart raced wildly as she leveled it and aimed. 'Just relax your shoulders.' It was hard to steady. 'And summon your rage,' Romy said, 'it'll focus your attention.' Paz immediately thought of how Ma saw the ugliness in everything, never the good, and pulled the trigger. The rifle jumped in her damp hands. She missed. She thought of how when Ma got violent, she had sometimes hit her with the prickly side of her brush. She missed. She thought of her high-school art teacher saying that she could draw, but to forget about being an artist because she was a girl. She missed again. She tried until she was self-conscious that she would never hit anything with Romy's eyes fixed so intensely on her, as though she'd dropped from the sky. Sweat trickled down her forehead. She took aim, and to her relief, a can exploded, spurting pale blue on the ground, gray and dusty like elephant skin. She laughed. It felt surprisingly satisfying.

'It's good, isn't it,' Romy said.

Paz smiled. 'Is it for something?'

Romy met her eyes. 'I'm not sure I want to get into the system,' she said. 'As it is.'

'Hmm,' Paz said, realizing she'd never thought of not trying to get into the system. As it was. 'Do you think art matters beyond the commercial and institutional bubbles of the art world?' Paz asked. 'Places I probably have no hope of entering into anyway.'

'Don't do that to yourself. You're a grad student and you already have a show at Ora's gallery,' Romy said. 'Despite being set in its ways, it's still possible to throw a bomb.' She turned to face Paz. 'You have to find the value in how making it changes you. You can't let it bother you — what anyone else says.'

'It doesn't bother you — what critics say?'

'Of course it bothers me.'

Romy cleared the remaining spray-paint cans and threw the gun in the back of the truck. It made a heart-stoppingly loud clunk. The leather seat was so hot under Paz's legs when she got back in, she couldn't believe it didn't ignite.

Romy turned to her when she started the engine. 'Do you know what you want to do with your work?'

There were a few moments of silence and then Paz said, 'I want to bridge the material and the immaterial.' She wasn't sure why she said that. It just came out. They drove for a while through all that sky. They didn't talk much. They didn't need to. It felt like something had just happened.

Thursday

EVERY OBJECT THROWS OFF THE strong scent of cigarette smoke. Whoever lives here has a habit. Paz feels a shrill pain in her head as she blinks. Hardened grease is splattered on the wall above a stove. Silver spots sail through her vision as she sits up. It's dark and cool, the blinds shutting out the light's sharp points. All the heaviness she felt before is not in her body. For some reason, wherever she is, she's not scared. Maybe it's because of all the books. Solzhenitsyn's *The Gulag Archipelago* is face down on the kitchen table. Anyone who reads can't be a complete psychopath. There is writing everywhere, papers covered in sketches and measurements and notes tacked around the room with a kind of military precision. Military precision with a bit of a drinking problem. Her eyes must be playing tricks because the writing looks familiar. She blinks. The sheets feel sandy and smell like something gone off, and she is reminded how even bad smells can sometimes be good. Something pulls at her skin. She touches her shoulder and feels tape and gauze through the wedding dress. Oh god, the wedding dress. Everything comes pinwheeling into her brain like a firework.

The door swings open. 'Aloe. There's a plant out back. It'll help the burn,' he says as he walks into the trailer, his heavy work boots thudding across the floor. Sam is wearing a CAT trucker hat, pants covered with diesel and plaster dust. He puts down the mug he's holding and grabs a glass. He wipes it with his shirt, fills it with water, and hands it to her.

'Thank you,' she says and drinks down the entire glass. He refills it.

'It's not really a thank-you situation. You either drink it or you die,' he says. 'You should bring some of this along the next time you decide to come out here. There's not a lot around. From here to Nevada all you got is cults.'

She nods, swallowing her last two pills. Sam eyes all the empty bottles in her bag. 'That's a lot of pills.'

'I hurt everywhere,' Paz says.

'That bandage isn't helping you either,' he says, motioning to the gauze on her hand, which is unspeakably dirty. 'I can change it for you.' She cringes at the thought of him seeing her hand. She hasn't even been able to look at it yet.

'How did you find me?'

'I was driving back out here and I heard Johnny Cash, and then I saw Cotton's car parked outside The Cielo, which struck me as odd. And then I went in and found you lying there. Out cold.'

'God, thank you,' she says, taking another sip. 'I owe you.'

'Yeah, I don't believe in debt. I can take you back to the car if you want, but you'll need a boost. I think that battery'll be dead. If you want to go tomorrow morning, it has to be early. I start working by six.'

Paz is amazed at his total indifference to her, whether she stays the night. Where would she sleep in this small trailer? Though as she thinks this, she realizes she must have been here last night. She knows his silences are well documented, but she can't imagine a person could be so uncurious. This neutrality is also what makes him interesting. He's completely undomesticated. She had no idea Sam's site was even remotely near The Cielo. They both existed out here in this existentialist landscape. The faint throb in her hand is making her aware that those were her last two Demerols.

'I —' She clears her throat. She is aware of an odd feeling in her body. 'I came out here because —' She pauses. How can she explain it? 'There were postcards.' She tries again. 'Fina says —'

He cuts her off. 'You might want to rethink that,' he says, leaning against the doorframe. 'A person's things should be left alone.' His eyes meet hers and hesitate. He is holding something back.

MAY 1977. *I know his trailer well. When Sam has women living with him, or when I am deep in my work, I stay away. But there are nights when I sit on the steps with him and crack beers after working, our shoulders touching. It isn't even sexual, but I feel something almost as a courtesy to his reputation. And for a moment, in the scale of this place, we are just two people working. We are equals. I rib him about his girlfriends. How many more women are you going to have toss drinks in your face? He said he didn't believe in love. It's just disappointment. He told me he hated social commitments and all the futile, pointless conversations when you are only going to die abandoned anyway. God, I thought, I really had underestimated how alone he truly was. Yeah, he said to me. Well, according to you, the only way to love someone is to let them treat you like shit. We often smoked cigarettes in silence. Two bodies sitting there under the sky.*

After some tequila one night, I told him about the last trip to Rome back in March where Billy met me after working in Germany. It had been years since Billy and I got married. At first, when we were apart, Billy called me constantly. He said he longed for me. Then he started getting shows and flying to Europe, and a lot was being written about him, and not much was happening to me though I was working like an ox. He was under pressure with all of the shows, and started drinking. We'd begun arguing. You don't have to make excuses for leaving anymore. I can live without you, I told him, the phone going dead. I stood for hours arguing, slamming down the receiver and him calling me back, the phone booth steamed up. By then, when we were together, he said the only time I'd really look into his eyes was to see if he was lit.

When I got to Rome, I could tell Billy was keeping something from me. At first, he said nothing had really happened. He'd woken in the apartment alone and didn't remember anything. He was disturbed by how little he remembered. All he knew was that he'd lost control. Zeroland.

The apartment hadn't changed much in the years since we got married except that it now contained a kind of sadness. A reminder of how things once were, and were no longer. When I walked through the door, he told me I had the radiance of when I was happiest, which filled him with shame. He said a line from Milton — which way I fly is Hell; myself am Hell. He had a lecture that day at the Galleria Gian Enzo Sperone, I roamed the markets with nerves like a wild animal. He saw me come into the lecture as he was delivering the last lines, standing as though he hated the space he occupied. The minute I came in I knew it, and he knew I knew it. He was ashamed of something.

He said he had to tell me something. He hadn't wanted to meet my eyes. We walked up the steps and unlocked the apartment, sat down on the bed, and opened the window. The sounds of Italian church bells and car horns and children laughing came suddenly into the room. Would you like some wine? he asked.

Please, I said.

He'd been so drunk he didn't remember anything, except that he was filled with shame the next morning. He'd done it and now he couldn't undo it. Flashes of it came back to him. A woman he swore he'd never met laughing underneath him, undoing his pants, grabbing his belt, hearing the buckle as it hit the floor, pulling down her underwear.

The sounds from the street below were fading in and out of my ears. The weight went out of my body.

The next morning, I put the coffee on. Scrambled some eggs, made some toast. He ate mechanically and left the plate on the table, unable to get any words out. I didn't eat anything. There was a heavy space between us. For the rest of my time there we argued. We fought late at night on Via Margutta off Piazza del Popolo. I got angry and he grew distant. He was so full of shame. He vowed to become a better person. I was amazed that two people who had *burned for each other could end up so miserable. Over the course of that time, all the talking and honesty and rawness, something else had opened up between us, and that's when I realized I was pregnant.*

WHEN PAZ WAKES UP IN the trailer, it's pitch black outside. There's no sign of Sam. She opens the door and stands on the metal steps for a moment, and then sees the flickering light of a fire in the near distance. When she looks up at the blanket of stars, they are so staggering she almost falls down. There are so many she can't find a single one she could name. There is a low-level buzzing in her body, not uncomfortable, but something she's aware of. She feels light-headed as she walks toward Sam, sitting by the fire smoking a cigarette. He knows how to make a fire. Something about this makes her love him a little.

She sees enormous mounds of stone, dark in the distance. 'God, I had no idea you were working on something so — monumental.'

'Size is deceptive out here. My sculpture is just an ancient way of formatting space,' he says as they both stare, mesmerized by the fire. 'You've got to let things be the size they actually are.' Everything he says hangs in the air like an unintentional piece of wisdom.

'Well, it's clearly set to outlast humanity,' she says, making a joke, one that he takes at face value.

'Look, I'm not like other artists who are running around expressing themselves. I feel I'm performing a function for society. What I'm doing here is important. This work isn't some sort of bullshit generic hotel art. It isn't for galleries,' he says, leaning back into his chair. 'It's going to stick around.'

She's only partly listening. There's something odd going on in her body. Like the prick of champagne running through her insides.

'I'm not saying everything needs to be at this scale. You can make revolutionary art from a number six pencil and a piece of paper. Size and money have nothing to do with it.' He pauses. 'Money just means you can buy better paper.' He looks over at her. 'You okay?'

She nods.

He shoots her a kind of lethal smile and takes a drag on his cigarette, its orange ember glowing luridly. 'You should just go back and make your work and forget mucking around out here,' he says, blowing out smoke. 'Forget about all the other noise.' There is something good about being here, though, because partly she has been longing for some sort of incident of her own.

'How do you do it?' she asks. 'I mean, forget about all the other noise.' The buzzing climbs her spine. It feels like electricity, as though she is the antenna, her body the wire.

'Making work isn't the problem, it's not making it,' he says, exhaling smoke. 'The personal stuff is beside the point.'

She's not sure how to respond, so they just sit there in silence for a while. He throws a large piece of split wood onto the fire. It sparks and cracks.

'I've never even considered people,' he says.

'What about when you're finished here? Aren't people going to have to come to look at it?'

'I have no intention to turn this place into some goddamn circus for the jet set. I've been living out here for the past twelve years and I have an obligation to the people who live here not to bring a bunch of nutcases who are going to pollute their land and kill their livestock, because that's what fucking humans do.' She hadn't thought anyone lived around here but doesn't say anything. He runs his hand through his damp hair. 'You want a drink?'

He is persuasive, the way cult leaders and alcoholics are persuasive, that undeniable charisma and dedication to their own belief that you can't help but want to participate in, warped and doomed as it may be. He's a completely different person than the one who opened the trailer door today, when she was interrupting his work. She scans the black landscape, holes of various depths everywhere. Oh my god, she thinks to herself, looking around, I'm on fucking Mercury. Her hand is beginning to throb.

He comes back and pours tequila into roughed-up metal mugs and tells her about how he's made drawings since he was two, and how he went to Paris when he was twelve just to look at art. 'I saw everything, went to every single museum,' he says. 'You have to see it firsthand. No one can go to school and learn about art by looking at a bunch of slides projected on a wall.'

She wants to say that when she was twelve, she scrubbed the toilet Ma got sick in because by that point she was a raging bed-ridden alcoholic. She had to work two jobs and get a scholarship so that she could look at a bunch of slides projected on a wall. Still, she finds herself telling him she's tired of everything and just wants to drop out for a while. 'But drop out *and* produce work,' she adds.

'You should go away and work. Get to things before your number's up.'

'I'm finding it hard to know where to start.'

'When things are moving too fast, fix your eyes on one thing.' A look crosses Paz's face. 'He'll be fine. He'll find some young girl.'

Of course, this is what he'd reduce her situation to. 'Younger than me?'

'Well, you're getting on, aren't you?' She laughs and he shakes his head and says, 'I don't know why people always forget the basic principle about making art.'

'Which is?'

'If you don't work, there won't be any.'

She brings her legs up, hugging her knees against her chest. It's the first time she's felt cold in a long time. Sam takes off his flannel shirt and passes it to her. She wraps it around herself. It smells like cigarettes and woodsmoke. They sit in silence like that for a while. She finally says, 'Do you know if Romy ever made falling works?' She pauses. 'I saw a lot of work in The Cielo that looked —'

He looks at her for a split-second. 'Do I know?' he says, monotone. 'All I know is that his work got a lot better once he met her.' Sam refills her glass and kicks a piece of wood farther into the fire, making it pop. An ember shoots up. They both follow it, looking up at the night sky. 'That's what I like about it out here. It's the only place that makes the stars feel closer than they are.'

A dazzling pain shoots up her hand and he sees her wince.

'Stay right there.'

He comes back with a metal box that clinks as he walks. 'Give me your hand,' he demands. She doesn't want him to see her hand but she has no energy for resistance. He sits so close to her that she smells soap on his neck. He slowly works off the dirty bandage, very carefully sliding a small blade up the center and cutting through it. It takes an excruciatingly long time, and she bites the inside of her cheek until there is blood in her mouth. She's turned away from him so when the bandage is off, she doesn't have to look. She can only see his face, outlined by the light of the fire. He looks brutally handsome. With the bandage off, it feels like her whole hand is missing after having it wrapped up for so long. It's naked and vulnerable in contact with the cool air and feels lighter than anything she's ever known. More like a cloud than a body part. He washes it with some sort of cold liquid that stings, looking at it intensely. She is so tired that she doesn't care he's seeing it. His finger grazes her palm and it gives her a chill. 'You're a lot tougher than you look,' he says, with what sounds like admiration. And then he lines up the gauze and winds the bandage around and around, and cuts the tape in his teeth before fastening it lightly on the back of her hand. It strikes her that this is the first time in a long time that anyone has truly taken care of her.

The fire flickers in the dark, illuminating their faces, their knees touching. She is so close to him now she can feel his breath on her mouth.

Friday

SAM LEANS OVER THE ENGINE of Cotton's car outside The Cielo. He unclamps the jumper cables and slams down the hood. He says to run it for a while longer and then he'll go. The sun behind him makes him glint. After her time in New York she can see why all those women would fall for him. His quiet, his need for nothing, is a bit of a relief. It could give a person some space. And she is an idiot who couldn't even remember to drink water. Let the sun burn it out.

He goes back to his truck and they both sit, engines running, looking through their windshields at each other like some kind of vehicular showdown. His truck is radiant, hit by the rising sun, and she is struck by the feeling that she wants to stay like this forever, in separate shimmering cars with separate destinies. She had wanted to ask more about Romy, but in the hour or so it took to drive back here, they'd said almost nothing. She had her bare feet on the dashboard and her eyes felt heavy, her head resting on her knees. She had lost her nerve. She was bone tired. A thought had occurred to her on the road — that the postcards are just someone's art. It made her think of what Ma would say. *It's poor people's art. Anyone could do it if they had the time and a couple of stamps.* But they don't, Paz thinks. That's the point. It's the simplest things that are the hardest to do. The postcards were Romy's drawings and her handwriting, but it was clear that no mail had left The Cielo in years. Romy wouldn't have left there either if she hadn't been forced out — Paz can see that now. It was the work of a lifetime. It had brought her to the edge of what she could do. Looking out at the half-formed Cielo, Paz is hit with a grief, the kind that feels like an abyss. *So much light running through my body. I don't know what to do with all this light.* Tears stand in her eyes but don't fall. She feels sadness for all Romy lost. It's the first time, in all this time, that she knows Romy is dead.

She can't shake the pictures of her falling, her body angled and long. In some she is alive but dying actively, choosing darkness. In none of them is she truly dead. In none is she beneath a sheet in an ambulance at the side of the road, lights blazing, the sun not yet risen, the streets quiet around her. Someone would have tucked her under the sheet so no parts of her could be seen the way she wouldn't have wanted to be seen. Where had Billy been?

Sam waits a moment longer, and she makes an okay sign with her fingers. He nods, touching his hand to the brim of his hat, and drives off, his truck sending rocks and dust into the air. The sun is slowly appearing, and the entire landscape is sunrise, flaming pink against violet hills. She sits silent for a while. The whole desert sparkles like the skin of a fish. The bright luminosity of a new day. And that's when it hits her. That's when she knows what she has to do out here. She's chased down the disquiet, put herself in proximity to a larger question. She's made a discovery. The story is not about Romy, as she'd expected. It's about her. She needs to fill in every blank with her own name. She puts the car in reverse, and snakes come out from under it in every direction.

IT'S EVENING BY THE TIME she walks up the porch steps. The dog wags his tail, a low whine in his throat, his nails clacking as he leaps from paw to paw. She unclips the long leash tied to the porch, and he licks her face. 'Did it ever occur to you that I could get another dog?' she says, looking into his eyes. She's made up with him, even if he is partly responsible for her losing a finger. His tail thumps. He tilts his head. The look in his eyes says, Did it ever occur to you that I used to be a wolf? She goes inside. Flea is still with Ingrid and Billy is gone, the house empty. She sees there are messages flashing red but can't check them yet. It's impossible to think it was only just the day before yesterday that she left this house with Cotton's keys in her hand. She is relieved that Billy's not home. She's feeling a kind of strange energy that she isn't ready to disrupt. She opens a bottle of beer and comes back out, sitting on the porch with the dog resting his nose on her feet. The desert is still on her skin. She can't stop thinking about the rectangle of light and how she feels this light inside her. The buzzing has been moving up her body, into her jaw, it even radiates under her fingernails. She wonders how it will come out.

After a while she notices the moon rising, a big ball of burning red, a once-in-a-lifetime moon, Desert Veronica Lake's blood moon. There is no way it's not trying to tell her something.

'I'm coming over,' Essa says on the phone. Paz says it's too late, but Essa has already hung up. She goes outside with her sketchbook and sits with it on her knees and begins drawing. Her hand gets a bit stiff, so she shakes out her wrist and takes a break, lying on her back with a big bag of salty pretzels resting on her stomach. It's so big she can eat it without worrying that the pleasure will end. She's always wanted Billy to love food the way she does, but he's always preferred alcohol to anything. The dog is gazing at her with his head tilted to one side, and she gives him a handful. She eventually feels sleepy, three beers in, and lies there on the porch, slowly drifting in the dark.

Paz wakes up to a car pulling up, throwing off heat, its two bright headlights startling. She must have fallen asleep. The bag of pretzels falls off her.

'So, is this your get-fat-and-lazy piece?' Essa says, slamming the car door and walking up the steps.

'That was fast.'

'Have you checked your messages?'

'What?' Paz says, looking up. 'No.'

'You sound weird.'

'I am weird.'

Essa has brought over a bottle of vodka. Paz feels the buzzing in her body getting louder, or maybe it's just changed pitch. Something is different. She wonders how it would be to get something so intense out of your body. 'What was it like giving birth?' she blurts out before she can stop it. A conversation, she realizes, they've surprisingly never had.

'Why? You're not pregnant, are you?' she asks on her way inside to get glasses.

'Not with a baby,' Paz says.

Essa gives her a puzzled look and sits on the porch. 'It's a bit like being thrown through a window. Actually, no, it's not really like being thrown through a window. But' — she pauses dramatically — 'it wasn't at all like the divine lady power I'd been reading about in *Spiritual Midwifery*. I mean, let's be real, we're talking about a human coming out of your vagina.' There's only a bit of cherry juice that Essa has found to mix with the vodka. 'All that woowoo hippie crap about lighting candles, having rushes while you smooch your old man, and then out comes your lovechild in one big orgasm.' She stops and hands a glass to Paz. 'I couldn't reach Ed, who was out getting bombed at Juke's studio, and I was left with hot nauseating pain in a fluorescent-lit hall in the hospital where I could hear other women groaning. And then, to my horror, out of nowhere a starched nurse in a cap suddenly began shaving my crotch as I yelled at her, "Is that really necessary?" I mean, I'm sort of fascinated by the blood, piss, vomit part of it, but they completely tried to erase all that. The nurse didn't even look up. Later, when I was mid-contraction, another nurse leaned in and said, "Don't push that way, honey. You've got to push from your rear end, like you're taking a you-know-what." *Honey, honey, push.* "Did she really just liken childbirth to taking a shit?" I remember thinking. A doctor came in at the last second from on-call, in what must have been his going-out clothes. I felt crazy. "Is that a *leather* tie?" I asked, and then began laughing hysterically.'

She takes a big sip of vodka. 'Paz.' She winces slightly. A pained expression crosses her face. 'Billy was taken in for questioning today.'

Paz instantly feels a horror so deep. All the troubling stories that have circulated immediately come into her head. A dinner when everyone had drunk far too much and Billy had threatened Romy if she didn't stop arguing with him. She has heard about these wild fights with Romy, but it doesn't add up. Paz has never fought with Billy. Not once. He and Romy had apparently kicked things and thrown things and shouted at parties and in crowded restaurants. There was mention of another woman, an artist in Paris. And possibly another in Berlin. 'Complete horseshit,' Milt had said. Though she had also heard all the things women said. *He's a genius. He is too good-looking. He's an operator.* Operator. She thought about that word. It sounded like he was driving a machine. A woman wouldn't be called that. The woman wouldn't be the one operating anything. Was he an operator? Maybe.

'What?' Paz says, turning to Essa, stunned.

'He called me because he didn't know where you were. He asked me about looking after the dog if I didn't hear from you. He was with Milt and his attorney. They are opening an official inquest, a grand-jury indictment into Romy's death. They brought him down for questioning,' Essa says, speaking rapid-fire. 'No matter what, Milt says he is facing at least five days in custody.'

'Where is he?' Paz asks. Something about Essa's tone makes her reassemble.

'I'm not sure, but Milt said he is being held without bail at his arraignment. The judge refused art as bail, and some sort of bond is being fixed.'

'Held?' she repeats. 'Bail?' Her throat catches. She suddenly feels intensely present.

'I didn't want you to hear over the phone,' Essa says. 'Milt made it all sound very straightforward. "You sit down with the DA, eye to eye, and make a deal,"' she says. 'I'm sure it will be okay.' Though she's not sounding entirely convincing. 'I mean, this is Billy we're talking about. Of all the men brutalizing things, he's the one weeping and arranging flowers.'

'Are you saying that men who subvert illusions of masculinity in their art are not capable of —'

'Maybe?' she says, and they both laugh a little.

'Fuck. This isn't funny,' Paz says and starts to cry. 'It's shit. It's just all going to shit.' It's at the center of everything between them. She has always suspected that one day she would be forced to give up this love with its dark heart.

'Do you think —'

'Do I think what?' Essa says.

'Do you think he could have — harmed her?' Her throat catches.

Essa turns to look at Paz and breathes out. 'No,' she finally says. 'I don't think he did it. I know people have talked. He's quiet and sensitive and a bit alone, but that doesn't make him capable of anything other than making decent art.'

Paz can see that sensitive is something people always think is a good quality, but in the group of artists, it often means being so wrapped up in yourself you think of no one else. He is a person who is capable of anything, she thinks. He has always related to women better. But when he drinks, a shadow passes over him that eclipses every part of his being. She'd seen it in Ma and Aunt May, darkened by something so brutal and fierce it burned holes where life should have been. The thing is, he loves drinking. Loves it.

There is a long silence. 'God, Ess,' Paz says, wiping her face. 'I was such a jerk when you married Old Sumbitch. And then look what I did? Went and got myself married with a baby, all at once. I'm sorry I was mean.'

'You weren't mean.'

'Well, thanks for saying that.'

The cherry juice has run out, so she and Essa have switched to pouring the vodka straight up. They're sitting on the porch in silence, which is unusual for them. Two women undone by men, Paz thinks and then can't unthink. Her whole life has been about things being undone, about empty spaces where the real things should be. Paz looks up, watching the eclipse perform, wishing she knew more science.

'I went to The Cielo,' she finally says, 'the place in the desert where Romy was working right before she died.'

Essa looks at her. 'Oh.'

'Aren't you going to ask me about it?' Paz says.

'Do you want to talk about it?'

'Why are you talking like a therapist?'

'Because lately you haven't really talked about your feelings,' Essa says.

Paz feels something drop inside of her. Essa's right, of course, but she felt this had somehow gone unnoticed.

'God, it was so —' She can't find words to explain what happened at The Cielo. None of them sound right. She decides not to start with the champagne feeling. Instead, she talks about getting there. About Linda and Desert Veronica Lake. About knocking over a bunch of sunglasses and feeling she had to buy a pair. 'And so I wore the dark glasses and followed the road and the movement of the sun, which I know sounds like I was going to have a nervous breakdown any second. And then when I pulled up in front of the hotel, it was like I was walking into a kind of sacred temple, except I hadn't yet passed the tests to enter, even though it drew me in, made me lie down in Romy's wedding dress and —'

'Romy's wedding dress?' Essa says. 'Lie down?'

'I guess I eventually passed out, because I woke up in Sam's trailer with a weird feeling like somehow the light had got into my body —'

'Okay, whoa. Back up,' Essa says. 'Sam's trailer? I'm going to need way more information.'

'I guess I was really dehydrated. It might've partly been the painkillers. I feel like I've been dried out from the inside. I have maybe been taking too many. There is something about veiling the functions of the body — it makes you a ghost. I felt separate from my own body. I also saw that Romy was there, Ess,' she says, taking a deep sip of vodka. She feels something shake loose inside her, the words pouring out. 'She was there, in that work. It's still — I don't know how to describe it. It's still sending particles through my brain. I think the best way to look at something someone has made is with no feedback, in silence.'

They are now drinking straight from the bottle, taking slugs and passing it back and forth. She takes another sip. It burns her stomach but makes her feel sharp. She wipes her mouth with the back of her hand and tells Essa about the postcards from Fina.

After a moment Essa says, 'That's weird.'

'What's weird?'

'Well —' She fishes in her bag and pulls out a postcard. DISAPPEARANCE PIECE.

Paz is confused. 'I got this yesterday,' Essa says. 'We all got them. I just assumed it was some sort of serial mail piece. One in very poor taste, I might add.'

'Ess, it is really disturbing,' Paz says, stopping. 'Romy wrote about how she would disappear, and about how she was having premonitions of her death. I mean, this was someone who was pregnant. You can't get more alive than that. But when Fina gave me a postcard at Sondra's, for a moment I felt she might actually be alive. All those rumors about her death being a performance were no longer unimaginable. It felt like these last few months with Billy have been disorienting. I've been so threatened by Romy's presence, but at the same time, thinking about her, wanting her approval. It occurs to me that I am the ghost of this house, wandering from room to room, never certain of my purpose.' Her voice catches. 'And after going to the desert — I can't explain it, but I understand now that she is dead.' She takes a long sip from the bottle.

'The geometry of it — three can only ever be a triangle or a straight line. But I know now that nothing consists of just two people, or even three. And all along I've felt like when Billy got back from Rome we could start again. I saw a house covered in bougainvillea off Sunset in West Hollywood for rent. I never understood why he still wanted to live here, with all of the memories. But then I realized he *wants* to live with a ghost.' And then she's crying a little.

Essa reaches over and hugs her. 'You know, it's okay, Paz. I honestly don't know who wouldn't have done the same thing if they'd been in your position.'

'Would you have?' Paz asks, sitting up, wiping her face with her hand. 'Well, no,' she says, and they both laugh.

Paz dries her eyes on her shirt, she has so many questions but right now can't think of a single one. After a long silence she asks Essa what she thinks about the postcards. They are, after all, Romy's handwriting. 'What are you, nuts? Everybody's done anonymous serial mail pieces,' Essa says, taking another sip. 'Okay, let's just play this out for a second,' she continues. 'If she were alive, are we supposed to think that she walked out of the morgue, called her dealer to apologize, and then left her baby, her husband, her work, and LA for some two-bit town some place in the middle of desert nowhere, and is renting a room by the week so that she can harass you — by mail?'

'I know. I know that now.'

'Have you ever heard of a ghost who doesn't eventually refuse to play dead?' Essa says. 'I mean, the one true drag about life is that the people who leave don't come back.'

'She was so young, Ess. She was way too young to die, and that is just always tragic.'

'Tragic? I mean, yes, of course that's objectively true. But think about what would have happened if she'd stuck around to care for a baby, walking around in a sad stained sweatshirt and unbrushed hair, a career like a tumbleweed, while her husband shot to fame surrounded by ardent fans. Think of that if you want to talk about what's tragic.'

They are silent for a while, and then a look comes over Paz's face and she becomes rigid. 'Do you think he could actually be responsible?'

Essa breathes in deeply and then says, 'I think you have to think less about him right now and more about yourself, because —'

'Because?'

'Because lately I feel like it's you I'm watching disappear.'

'I didn't think you had been noticing what was going on with me,' Paz says, looking down.

'What?' Essa says, surprised.

'I don't know. You seem to be hanging around with Fina a lot these days.'

'Fina? I've gone out with her a couple of times. I find her compelling, but I've never been sure if she's an ally. She acts like a friend, but it's just competition.' She pauses. 'You know, she asked me if she could "use" lint in something she was doing and without thinking it through, I said yes. Now guess who's making cunts out of washing-machine lint.'

'No!' Paz says. 'I'm so sorry.'

'Yeah, well, it's my own damn fault.'

Essa lights a cigarette, and Paz is suddenly ravenous. She offers some pretzels to Essa and takes her own big handful of them and then licks the salt off her lips. The vibration shifts a bit, moving up her left side.

'I love him,' Paz says after a long silence. She feels so stupid thinking of that little rush when she feels power over him, for a brief moment, with her body. Immediately after, she has to shed parts of herself to be with him, and it is humiliating.

'Do you?' Essa hesitates. 'From what you've said, it sounds like what you love is what he does to you.'

While she is thinking of this, she feels the buzzing again, climbing up her spine, warm and full, and she holds on to the intense sensation.

Saturday

PAZ WAITS AT THE KITSCHY Polynesian restaurant in Beverly Hills, which Ingrid, to her surprise, proposed. The phone call late this morning was terse. 'Fine,' Ingrid said after Paz agreed. 'Meet me in an hour.' The restaurant serves enormous rum drinks with floating gardenias. She orders one and sips it slowly, trying not to think of where Billy is being held, or how long Ingrid is taking, making her wait it out. She watches the large aquarium full of poor fish just swimming around waiting to be killed. Juke was once escorted out of here high on mescaline for eating one live, right out of the tank. She goes to the washroom and catches herself in the mirror as she's washing her hands. The bruisy shadows under her eyes are gone, and her skin is a very deep brown. She looks better than she ever remembers, which surprises her because she's never felt good-looking in her own eyes. When she gets back to her table, Ingrid still hasn't arrived. She sips the rum and feels heat in her stomach. The anticipation she feels waiting for the baby is excruciating, her leg jiggling under the table. She has missed her and hadn't realized how much until this very moment, though she is dreading the encounter with Ingrid. She agonized over what to wear, and in the end just ran a brush through her hair and put on her only clean shirt, along with the large black glasses she got in the desert.

Ingrid finally arrives, holding Flea, who looks like she just woke up and is not too happy about it. She's wearing a pink smocked dress with a Peter Pan collar that Paz has never seen before. She is overcome with the same feeling she had when she first saw her — that she has to protect her. She seems to have grown, is bigger, even in four days. Paz had forgotten her bright eyes and her meaty little forearms, the way she swings her legs when she gets excited. Her heart skips a beat. She's feeling flushed from the rum and her sunburn, and from the excitement of seeing the baby. Every detail of the baby's face is more familiar than her own. Paz kisses the top of her head, which smells like White Shoulders, made somehow perverse coming off a baby. Flea is oddly shy at first, but then she screeches almost angrily, slapping her palms together, and now, in Paz's arms, puts a fistful of Paz's hair in her mouth, and Paz feels the hot place in her heart only the baby can touch.

'Ingrid,' the woman says, extending her hand formally. The air is rigid between them.

'Paz,' she says. This could work, Paz thinks. They could be polite. Ingrid is quite tall, which is unusual for a woman of her generation, and has a stern beauty that makes her somehow seem invincible. The confident lipstick, the ice-blonde hair, and the dress of non-machine-washable fabric that immediately makes Paz question how she is able to look after the baby in it. The dress is very fitted with a zipper up the back, and she's in two-inch heels, which, when caring for a baby, is two inches too many. Her body is very thin, the kind that looks kept that way by hard work and anger. She is beautiful and clearly intends to carry on being beautiful until she dies. In this town, age is treated as a natural disaster for women. They tend to go into hiding with their sparse diets and intense beauty regimes once it hits, forced into the private horror of their wreckage.

At first, they are quiet, but once she is settled in her chair, Ingrid takes in Paz with disturbing intensity. 'You're no bigger than a child,' she remarks. 'And what did you do to your hand — are you all right to care for the baby?'

'It was an accident,' Paz says.

'Well, whatever it was, I would suggest you devote yourself to less dangerous pursuits. It's ridiculous for grown adults to engage in high-risk activities.'

Does she consider making art a high-risk activity?

As though Ingrid has read her thoughts, she says, 'You are a *performance artist* as well, I presume?'

Has Billy really not told Ingrid anything about her? Her cheeks burn. A performance artist seems to be Ingrid's enemy in art form. She might as well have said *war criminal* or *psychopath*.

'I've always thought that performance art rather lacks a future,' Ingrid continues.

Paz veers away from the subject, which she knows will just infuriate her. 'How did it go with the baby?' she asks, genuinely wanting to know.

'I'm her grandmother,' Ingrid says, as though that somehow answers the question. She has a presence that is impossible not to take seriously. She has Romy's eyes, Paz notices, that same startling blue. Ingrid looks at the baby and then back to her and takes a second to manifest her opinion plainly. 'People must mistake you for the nanny.'

Paz is stung. She is trying to hold back the tears she can feel welling from the cruelty of this remark, half said but fully understood. She can't decide if what she's feeling is some sort of racism, given her name and dark looks, or if Ingrid actually feels she is in some way protecting Romy. Either way, the conversation is like chewing on razor blades.

After an awkward silence, Paz says, 'I feel so close with her I don't see the differences between us.' She's trying to think of something to say that will not begin a fight. In the presence of this very proper woman, the only way she can calm her anxiety is to do what she's always done to take her mind off something stressful — think about sex. Her arms, legs, wrapped around, fucking this woman's son-in-law with such intensity that her face gets hot. 'So, you like Polynesian food?'

'Pardon me?'

'Is that why you wanted to meet here? The Polynesian food?'

'That's what you want to ask me?' she says. 'You really are a naïf. I have no interest in what the Polynesians eat. It was Stravinsky's favorite restaurant, and I wanted to see it for myself. The first time I heard *The Firebird* I felt a soaring —' She stops and stares at Paz. 'I suppose you wouldn't be familiar with his compositions.'

She tries to remember back to when Ma still listened to her records. Essa's dad had known Stravinsky. She'd met him at their house once. She pictures a long horsey face that for some reason scared her. 'Atonal?' she says.

Ingrid ignores her. 'Of course, my daughter preferred Bach, especially his *Goldberg Variations* played by the Canadian who used to hammer away on that ridiculous child's chair. She listened to them over and over. We had no television, no car, no telephone —' She stops. 'It's not because I was some sort of hippie. I am a classicist,' she says, straightening her already perfect posture, her body an antenna in her chair. What Paz hears is, *I am a classist.*

'I was very interested in my daughter's education, you know. Before she came to America, I took her to Rome to see all the most important Italian churches and museums.'

Very interested in my daughter's education? This from the mother who'd told Romy she wished she'd been a boy because the world neglects girls. This from the mother who'd sent her daughter away. Paz doesn't tell her that, Stravinsky or not, it's a tacky restaurant that only children like.

'I assume you already know that I have nothing to say to you,' Ingrid says. 'Anyone can marry a man with a baby whose wife has only been dead for a few months.' She shakes her head slowly, affecting a look of sadness. 'But as far as I'm concerned, anyone who actually does is a little monster. I think I would not be alone in this assessment. I am deeply concerned about the current situation with my son-in-law, given that he's set up house with a complete stranger, someone of such extreme youth. Especially as I am to be back to my teaching position at Oxford in two weeks. I hope this indictment — that everything will be cleared by then. I expect we will need to communicate if future custody arrangements are required.'

'Custody?' Paz swallows.

'In the event that the situation with my son-in-law is not resolved, and given that you are, as I can only imagine, temporary.'

The waiter comes over with large laminated menus that Ingrid waves away.

'The baby will stay with us, with me. She will not be sent to England,' Paz says, unable to control the anger rising in her. 'Romy wouldn't have wanted that.' The light that vibrates, radiant in her, is shifting things around. It doesn't matter that Ingrid is awful. It only makes her feel more protective of the baby and aligned with Romy. A mother who is beautiful and accomplished has been Paz's fantasy her entire life, but now that she is in front of such a mother, she is truly horrified. It makes her feel that Romy was remarkable to have survived this cruel woman and done what she had. Romy had never compromised on anything, and it had made everything about her life less safe, but it was hers.

'I don't think you could presume to know what my daughter would have wanted. I am the child's grandmother and you are —'

'Her mother,' Paz says firmly as the baby launches a spoon off the table and then twists wildly trying to retrieve it.

'Stepmother,' she corrects. 'And are you even — legally?' she says, taking a sip of water. Ingrid's skin is pale, and her forehead has no pores whatsoever. She looks like a sculpture. 'No one ever wants the truth,' she says and then takes another sip of her ice water.

Stepmother. It's the first time she's ever thought of herself that way. As though there is an obstacle between her and the baby. She'd taken to the baby from the moment she'd held her at the gallery in New York, but had felt abandoned and out of her depth with Billy gone. There were moments of despair because of her failures, but also a kind of gratification that was new to her. She's the only mother the baby has ever known, and she knows this is the way it has to stay.

'I don't know why you are so hostile with me. I am caring for your granddaughter. I don't want anything from you, if that's what you're thinking.'

Ingrid seems to consider this. Paz can see that she finds her some sort of low-class moneygrubber incapable of basic human emotions.

'Then what are you doing here?'

Paz tightens her arm on the baby, who squirms at the restriction. 'I'm picking up my daughter,' she says, and feels a kind of unexpected happiness in declaring this. She is getting used to the feeling of being happy and unhappy at the same time, as if it were the only possible outcome of doing something as idiotic as following your heart.

Ingrid gets up, collects her handbag, and says, 'You should thank me. I've spared you having to sit through drawn-out false pleasantries.' She says a formal goodbye, literally, to the baby, and leaves Paz sitting there stunned.

The waiter comes and asks her if she'll be ordering any food. She tilts her head back and finishes the rest of the rum. 'No. Just the check, please.'

Flea plunges her fist into the glass and pulls out the gardenia and jams it in her mouth. Paz rests her cheek on her flower-gentle skin. What had she been thinking? As if she could charm someone whose own charismatic daughter was unable to win her over. Paz can be a lot of things, none of which is charming. Despite the horrible encounter, she feels light, being here with the baby. It was Ingrid against them. She had stood up for them. With Flea on her lap, she feels a shift from the belief that freedom and responsibility are opposites. Her desire for freedom, she now sees, has been the desire for a distinctly male kind of power that has always been unavailable to her. But for all their freedom, men don't seem to enjoy it all that much, or do much with it — except limit women's access to it.

Her body is warm with the vibrating inside her, and the unexpected force of her feelings for the baby, and for Romy. She turns to Flea and whispers, 'You're going to have to remember all this, because it's your story.'

The waiter lingers at the table. 'I couldn't help but ask —' He leans in. 'But was that *the* Ingrid, as in Bergman?'

Just as Paz starts to speak, she feels a tap on her shoulder and turns around to see a woman with a mass of hair that makes her think of Lady Lazarus rising out of the ash with her red hair, eating men like air. 'It's you,' Paz says, aware of the unbelievable luck. 'I've been wanting to talk to you.'

'I know,' the tarot card reader says, looking at Paz with a smile that shows her teeth.

Paz feels panic but tries to shake it off. 'I need to ask you about what happened with Romy,' Paz says. 'I know you saw her before she died.'

'Honey, that's not objective fact.' She studies Paz. 'You've got to stop going around with that wounded look on your face. You look like a bird in distress. You were once a hot wire. You've got ideas. Dollar bills under the sink. Don't let the heat burn all your thoughts away.'

Paz is getting impatient with the tarot reader as the baby squirms in her sweating arms. 'But what about Billy?' she begs.

'Who?'

'Billy.'

'What about him?'

'Is he guilty?'

She looks at Paz and then at the baby. 'Very guilty, I suspect.'

JUNE 1977. *Before I went back to The Cielo, I had been sharpening a pencil with a knife, and the shavings fell on a card I'd forgotten about. The tarot card reader had handed it to me at a party. She must have been hard up for business. Maybe because my life was about to radically change, or maybe just out of sheer desperation to understand the weather in my head, I found myself driving, turning up Glendale, and eventually looking for the number that was at the bottom of the card. The tarot card reader's house was up on a short steep hill in Eagle Rock, and she led me into the first room, small and incensey with stoner plants covering the fogged-up windows. I hate snake plants, the only plant that looks fake dead or alive. When the tarot card reader was in the kitchen making her tea, I ran my hand over the leaves. Fuck me, they're plastic. The tarot card reader came back into the room and asked me why I was there, and I said, you know why.*

You are a bully, she said, squinting her eyes a little, as though in concentration. Are you the man in the family? Is it you who pays the bills? she asked.

I see violence. She paused to look at me. You have hit a man in the face?

Aren't I the one who's supposed to be asking the questions here? I said.

Honey, she said, what do you want to know?

I need catharsis, I told her, and then coughed. My worst fear is being held captive.

And yet you are.

The tarot card reader said that I could ask her three questions, but there was only one I wanted the answer to. I didn't trust her, but I could tell she was seriously devoted to her practice. First, I needed to see if she had actual telepathic powers. What am I thinking now? I asked her in my mind. I thought of Fishing for Sea Bass, a short film I'd made when Billy and I had driven to the ocean after a fight. Some girl leaving her number on our answering machine. I sat on the end of the Santa Monica pier while Billy fished. I ended up filming him. I told him that once he caught a fish that would be the end. Eventually he caught a sea bass. I kept the camera going as he pushed the fish's head into the ground, and I heard its neck crack, though its gills kept fanning rapidly. Billy took out a knife, slid it into the white belly, and slit it head to tail. He did it so expertly, so cleanly. Hook, line, and sink-her. He gently pulled with his fingers, and in the bloody gelatinous insides, its heart was still beating right there on the cement. Billy felt around. There was something hard in there. Sticking out of the blood was a blue dice. That's where I cut the film.

Christ, what luck, he'd said.

Why are you thinking of luck? the tarot card reader said, leaning over, her turquoise clacking. I felt less in control if she actually had some psychic power. Though she still hadn't seemed to 'read' the big secret that I was carrying. Is it because you worry yours has run its course?

I'm pregnant, I blurted, hoping to throw her off.

Yeah, this is just your reading, honey. She eyed my necklace and said, more on that later. I can read your cards, she said. I mean, isn't that why you are here?

I don't want my cards read.

Really? she said. Okay. Give me your hand.

I reluctantly offered it up. The tarot card reader turned it palm up and looked at it and then up at me. And then back down at my hand.

What is it?

Look, I'm not sure how to tell you this.

Tell me what?

You're already dead.

THE BABY IS KICKING HER legs against the seat of the broiling hot car as Paz fastens the seatbelt. She can't shake the thought that it should have been Romy having lunch with Ingrid and Flea, not her. She doesn't remember ever having a meal out with her own mother, not once, though she and Aunt May sometimes ordered in Chicken Delight.

* * *

She'd never talked to anyone about Ma's death, not even Essa. But when Paz sat next to Romy when they'd all gone out after their opening at Ora's, Romy lit a Camel — the same brand as Ma's. She didn't know why, but she found herself telling Romy about her. Romy asked what she'd died of. Of nothing, Paz said. Her heart just finally gave out. The thought had come into Paz's head that Ma had been like an old jukebox with only two songs left, and you couldn't dance to either one.

It had got unbearable in the years before she'd left for New York. Ma's entire life was reduced to her bed, lying on her back listening to radio soaps and smoking, even though the doctor said she had to quit. They'd put an asbestos apron on her in the hospital when she insisted on smoking in her room. When she was back at home, Paz had found her smoking in bed again.

'You're not supposed to smoke, Ma.'

'I'm not.'

'You're smoking, Ma.'

She had looked at Paz, irritated. 'I'm on fire.'

Paz had had to buy groceries with food stamps because Aunt May mostly worked the night shift and Ma didn't go out. The fridge had held murky jars of pickles, mustard with a crust grown over it, gummy salami, and bread furred with mold. She'd spent most of her time at Essa's house because it was so unbearable at hers. Ma, toward the end, had started to take on a distinct smell. It wasn't bad, but it was strong, a bit animal. She remembers walking by Ma's bed, and Ma, in one big snip, had cut off most of Paz's hair as she leaned over to empty her ashtray. It's why Paz never cuts it now. Ma had slurred and said, 'It makes you look short when you wear it so long.' Paz, who wondered how Ma had got the scissors, had said, 'I am short, Ma.' She always had to be tough with her. Any sign of breaking and Ma would take it. As she told this to Romy, she ran her fingers down her long braid, as though checking to see if it was still there. Old habit.

On the phone, Aunt May had relayed something that Ma had said right before she died. She'd sat upright and said, 'Paz is a watering can. I have confidence.' Paz wasn't sure if Aunt May had got the translation right — she will never know — but Aunt May seemed to be satisfied that Ma's dying words were that her only child was a watering can. Was she the watering can or the water? And what was a watering can without water, other than an old useless object? Aunt May had stuck to a hopeful interpretation that it was Paz who made things grow. Ma, who had never said anything charitable, had said that she had confidence. The idea, odd and unsubstantiated as it was, worked inside her and in the end helped her. She was determined to prove her right, even if the words seemed counter to the mother she'd known. That's when she'd understood that life, when it goes, can bring a kind of uncertainty, not a clarity.

When Paz had got off the phone with Aunt May, her body was shaking. Being so far away, she had wanted to mark Ma's death with some kind of gesture. What gesture? She couldn't have a drink, or light anything on fire. Should she break a plate? In the end, she had walked toward the Hudson, eyes watering in the cold. Thinking of years so bleak they flashed by as objects — sticky bottles of rye, the old radio crackling like broken glass, a royal-blue velour robe with stained cuffs, a cloudy glass of something by her bed, greasy plates Ma had eaten off with her fingers. All those years Paz had cared for her, though 'cared for' wasn't exactly correct. She'd skulked around dark corners trying not to disturb her. She was terrified of her, always drunk in an ugly mood. Lying sick in bed, beached on her stomach, Ma's nightgown hiked up to her enormous haunches, saying, *If there is a God in this world, why am I not dead yet?* Sometimes Paz would wake in the night to Ma screaming. She'd go into her room and find her sheets pulled up to her chin, mouth open, crying. Or mornings when Ma stumbled around, turning up everything to look for a bottle after Paz had cleared them all away. Most of the time, though, she lay in bed quiet as a stone, staring at nothing, smoking.

This image was in Paz's head as she stopped walking. She'd looked out onto the Hudson, feeling a hollow emptiness. But then what raced through her was rage. It was Ma's rage and it raged in her. She leaned her whole body into it and spat in the river. Somehow, that seemed like the appropriate gesture.

❖ ❖ ❖

NOVEMBER 1977. *Inside the event horizon, the events that take place will simply kill a person. In fact, the boundary is actually a point of no return. Anything that steps inside the boundary will never return and will be destroyed. The gravitational pull inside the boundary is so strong that escaping it is impossible.*

Paz pulls into Ka-Boom. She has to be quick because Flea is squirmy and hot and starting to fuss. The teenager is filing her nails into red points in the office trailer. Paz asks about the Kevins. 'Out back,' she says, not looking up. Kevin Two is doing pushups, clapping in the middle of each one like a marine, while Kevin One is doing some sort of cleanup work wearing puffy oven mitts that look like boxing gloves.

'Did you lose a bet or something?' she asks Kevin Two.

'Don't ask,' he says, veins popping on his neck, his face in a red grimace. He doesn't seem to register the baby.

'Well, if it isn't our favorite nine-fingered lady student,' Kevin One says, taking off an oven mitt. Paz shoots him a shut-up look, and oddly, he does. 'Hey, no offense, *hombre*,' he says, and then brass-knuckles her head in some sort of intended affectionate gesture that mats her hair and irritates her.

'I know it's last minute, but I'm going to need to get a bunch of wire and igniter clips — also, I have a couple of questions and a diagram I was hoping to get your consultation on.'

Kevin Two hops up and wipes his sweaty hands on his shorts. 'Ten four,' he says, suddenly getting a rush at the thought of blowing something up. 'I've got all the inventory categorized,' he says, bossy in his excitement. 'Let's get inside. I'm sweating like a whore in church out here.'

Monday

THE NEXT MORNING IS THE hottest yet. It is shimmering and windless as Paz spray-paints marks on the sand. She'd gone out for fish tacos last night with Essa and left Flea with her so she could drive back to the house to collect a few things. Milt had called when she was there and said that they expected a verdict soon. She should have been thinking of Billy, the balance of her life hanging on the decision, but she was far too distracted. She hadn't been able to think of anything to say to Milt. Still, it was there under everything, like an animal-frequency hum before a natural disaster. She was conscious of a throbbing sensation in her hand but felt a kind of odd clarity, and wondered if it was because it's the longest she has gone without pills. Driving back out to the desert, the road was lit by stars, the sky wild. An intensity she could relate to. She slept on the old mattress in The Cielo and woke up to squares of light, the way Romy must have done.

Paz walks back to the car to get some water and sees Sam's truck pull up. The sun is reflecting off his sunglasses as he walks toward her, and she suddenly feels nervous, the heat pressing in on them.

'I know this isn't the time,' he says, slamming the truck door, his white T-shirt radiant against his deeply brown skin. She sees her own face doubled in his mirrored lenses, glowing with a sheen of sweat. 'But I wanted to apologize.'

'For what?'

'I wasn't straight with you.' He looks at her without taking off his glasses, which makes it awkward. She feels he should remove them for this kind of conversation.

He stops for a moment. 'Romy told me about wanting to drop out of the art world and focus on the light work. And then when The Cielo sold, she got really low. But later, when I saw her, she said something had shifted. There was a performance that she didn't want to talk about yet.'

Paz can see beads of her own sweat mirrored in Sam's glasses. 'You asked me about those falling studies in The Cielo,' he says, looking at her. 'That's what she was working on. When I last saw her.' There is a tense silence. 'Billy's' — he pauses — 'extra-curricular activities were also wearing on her. I don't know if she planned on leaving him, but it seemed she had something going on.' Paz looks at herself looking at him in his lenses. She sees how similar Romy was to Sam. All their stakes were in their work. They both had projects so big they would have died for them.

'I told her to forget all the bullshit and just confront him. She said she was planning to, but she needed to get things into place first.' Sam stops and pulls off his sunglasses. 'Next I heard, she was dead.'

She can feel the sharpness of his emotion, though his face says nothing.

'Billy's in custody.'

He stops and takes this in. 'Right after she died, a lot of people thought that justice would be served.' They keep their eyes on each other, a kind of awareness between them. 'I thought that there should be a trial. But in the end, I spoke with police, and not a single other person stepped forward to say anything against Billy —' He stops. 'Because all of them want a shot at a fucking show in Milt's gallery.'

PROJECT RULES (DECEMBER 1977)

No fixed living place	*Energy from within*
No contact	*No rehearsal*
Risks as opportunities	*Follow instincts*
Open to chance	*No predicted end*

'What do you think happened?' she finally asks.

'It doesn't matter what I think,' he says, looking over at the open trunk of Cotton's car.

'You're not going to ask what I'm doing with a car full of explosives and a hundred yards of connecting wire?'

'That's your business.'

'Sam?'

'Yeah.'

She isn't sure what she wants to ask him. Seeing him in the bright sun confuses her. She wants him to be a joke, one that she and Essa could laugh at, with his silences and thousand-yard stare, but it doesn't feel that way standing next to him at all. There is a gold stripe of sun on his neck distracting her. What he said struck her, but she is unable to make sense of it. The falling studies were that last thing Romy was working on, but it is unclear what she was planning to do with them. Sam said confronting Billy meant the end of Romy. Confronting what? Romy had obviously known of his transgressions. She thinks of the agreement with Billy that Romy wrote about in her notebooks. But she doesn't know what was meant by it. She still doesn't understand what any of this means except that there is no way Billy is not implicated. He has never acknowledged any guilt. Even though it radiates off him, he seems incapable of bearing any. Though guilt isn't worth anything, she knew. The little Paz had tried to press him, the colder and harder he became. There are so many questions she needs to ask Sam, but the one that comes out, idiotically, is, 'Did you love her?' The sun is beating down on both of them. As soon as she says it, she regrets it.

'We got along.'

Paz shuts her eyes. Sunlight leaves sparks behind them. She sees what Romy had found in Sam. Something she found in no one else. It wasn't love, exactly, but something that possibly held up better than love. He saw her for what she was — an artist, no adjective.

Sam is quiet for a few seconds. 'She always wanted the truth told square,' he says. He looks at Paz. They've found common ground, but she still couldn't speak. 'She wouldn't have wanted people judging anything half-done. That would have been the worst thing,' he says, gesturing to The Cielo.

Paz looks at him and feels certain he is aware that this is something she deeply knows. She wants to say that he can trust her, but why should he? He looks at the trunk and back at Paz. 'You know where I am,' he says, 'if you need anything.'

She could have been undone by what he's just said about Billy — that he thinks he's responsible, that Romy confronting him led to her death. But she feels completely possessed by what she has now set in motion. He can feel it too, she knows. He of all people understands what it means to be fixated on seeing something through.

PAZ'S KNEES TOUCH THE BURNING sand as she places the chain fuse and begins cutting and measuring the tape. Essa has arrived with Flea. Sondra, Ora, Red, Luanne, and at least a dozen other women have all shown up and are moving on the sand to the spots where they will place fuses, white spray-painted Xs. She sees Fina in the distance. 'Fina?'

Essa shrugs. 'I put out the call to all the women artists in all the groups.'

Paz is overcome with gratitude. She honestly didn't know if anyone would show. Fina approaches and asks what she needs to do, Paz instructs her and hands her fuses and a lighting torch. Perspiration drips down her forehead. The options between them have dissolved. They look at each other and something shifts. Their bodies have made a decision — they will work together.

THE PROSECUTOR PUNCHES A CASSETTE INTO THE CHEAP
PORTABLE, CRANKS THE VOLUME, THE DEFENDANT'S VOICE
PITCHES LOW. THE POLICE REPORT CONFIRMS THEY RECEIVED
A CALL ABOUT A JUMPER ON WILSHIRE AT 4.53 AM.

Her brief conversation with Billy plays and replays. It will be a few more days. He'd said on the phone, 'I will tell you everything.' She could hear him breathe in and out into the receiver. 'I'm sorry,' he'd said. 'I'm so sorry to put you through this.' A mistake, not for him but for her. She knew it all at once, but it was too late.

IN THE INDICTMENT OF THE PEOPLE V. XANDER RIJKER,
WILL THE DEFENDANT PLEASE RECOUNT THE EVENTS ON THE
EARLY MORNING OF DECEMBER 22, 1977.

Paz is attaching the shooting wire, making knots so that it won't get yanked apart in case someone trips. She twists the yellow and blue wires in opposite directions like the Kevins have shown her. Going through everything with ritual attention. Resistance equals voltage divided by current.

I DON'T REMEMBER.

She is calculating the maximum lengths of wire she can use for this configuration.

WILL THE DEFENDANT PLEASE STATE WHAT IS KNOWN ABOUT
THE NIGHT IN QUESTION.

Ora's photographer has the cameras set up. Paz will count down and then time for the first lighting.

ON THE EVENING OF DECEMBER 21, 1977, THERE WAS A
PARTY THROWN BY MY GALLERIST, MILTON BERLIN, AT HIS
RESIDENCE IN 3355 WILSHIRE BOULEVARD TO CELEBRATE
A WORK ACQUIRED BY THE MUSEUM OF MODERN ART IN NEW
YORK.

Essa is holding Flea now so Paz can check the wiring, careful not to damage the cut wires, stripping the insulation with her fingernails. Essa is eating a rapidly melting ice-cream sandwich and letting Flea lick it. She is keeping the baby a safe distance away because Paz wants her to be part of what's happening. Sondra and Red are deep in conversation. They've been together since Cotton's opening. When Cotton had ribbed her about it, Red said, 'A relationship without any of the accompanying male bullshit? It's about as close to a pretty decent definition of utopia I've ever known.'

Paz shows them the diagram she's made to outline where they need to position themselves. She shades her eyes with her hand. 'Thank you,' she says to Red, knowing how close she was with Romy. Red salutes and then says, 'I'm sick and tired of the shitty treatment of artists by each other.'

```
LET THE RECORD SHOW THAT THE PROSECUTION PRESENTS
STATEMENTS FROM SEVERAL WITNESSES AT THE PARTY
CONFIRMING THE COUPLE HAD BEEN SEEN ARGUING.
THE DECEASED WAS LAST SEEN LEAVING THE PARTY IN
POSSESSION OF A BOTTLE OF ALCOHOL AT APPROXIMATELY
1.30 AM.
```

Paz's body feels light and strange and full of purpose.

```
NO WITNESSES CAN CONFIRM THE TIME THE DEFENDANT
FOLLOWED THE DECEASED UP TO THE ROOF OF THE BUILDING.
THE DEFENDANT'S ORIGINAL STATEMENT INDICATES THE TIME
WOULD HAVE BEEN APPROXIMATELY 2.40 AM. THE DEFENDANT
ALSO STATED THAT THEY HAD BOTH DRUNK, QUOTE UNQUOTE,
A TREMENDOUS AMOUNT, AND THAT NO ONE KNEW THEY WERE
UP ON THE ROOF.
```

There is no room for error.

```
THE DEFENDANT IS RECORDED AS SAYING DURING THE 911
CALL, QUOTE UNQUOTE, SHE WAS SO ALIVE AND THEN SHE
```

```
WASN'T ALIVE AT ALL. SHE FELL.
```

Sondra signals to her that the fuses are in place.

```
THE DEFENDANT ALSO SAID IN HIS STATEMENT THAT HE,
QUOTE UNQUOTE, FELT SUCH A DEEP PAIN, IT WAS AS
THOUGH A SHARP KNIFE HAD ENTERED MY CHEST, SLOWLY
PIERCING ALL THE SOFT TISSUE AND ORGANS, AND IT
STAYED THERE [PAUSE] IS THERE STILL.
```

The photographer checks her light meter and gives a thumbs-up.

```
ACCORDING TO THE PROSECUTION, THE BODY OF THE
DECEASED WAS EXAMINED BY A JUNIOR CORONER WHO WASN'T
THOROUGH ENOUGH. (HEARSAY.) THERE WAS ALSO A FRESH
CUT ON THE DEFENDANT'S FACE THAT WAS NOTED BUT NEVER
DOCUMENTED BY THE POLICE. (INADMISSIBLE.)
```

Paz carefully rips open the tape on the last box of copper wire with the tip of the wire cutters.

```
ON THE NIGHT IN QUESTION, THE DOORMAN OF THE GAYLORD
AT 3355 WILSHIRE BOULEVARD HEARD A COUPLE ARGUING
AND A WOMAN SCREAMING, 'NO, NO, NO.' THE DOORMAN, A
VIETNAM VETERAN, WAS TAKING HALDOL AT THE TIME, AN
ANTI-PSYCHOTIC PHARMACEUTICAL. (INADMISSIBLE.)
```

Paz wipes away the sweat that has dripped down her forehead. She is trying not to think of Billy's voice, hoarse and low on the telephone. She looks over and squints. Fina is carefully positioning the fuse on the mark.

THE DECEASED'S FUTURE PLANS FOR EXHIBITIONS, HER
GUGGENHEIM GRANT, AND THE CREATION OF A LONG-TERM
PROJECT HAVE BEEN OFFERED UP BY THE PROSECUTORS TO
RULE OUT ANY NOTION OF SUICIDE. (OF NO CONSEQUENCE.)

Paz signals to the women and the igniters are lit. A thin, high hissing
sound echoes across the sand. The lit fuses glow with an almost celestial
intensity.

EVIDENCE SHOWS THAT THE DECEASED WAS GIVEN TO
IRRATIONAL OUTBURSTS OVER MINOR OCCURRENCES AND WAS
PRONE TO HYSTERIA, PARTICULARLY AS A POST-PARTUM
FEMALE. (ADMISSIBLE.)

The baby, who she sees is streaked with dirt and tears and ice cream,
blinks slowly and stares ahead with large eyes.

WITNESSES SAY SHE LIVED FOR HER WORK. (HEARSAY.)

Paz feels the old glint of pleasure at inhabiting herself inside her body,
even to know this is still right there, possible for her.

ACCORDING TO SEVERAL REPUTABLE SOURCES, THE
DECEASED'S WORK HAD, QUOTE UNQUOTE, DEATH VIBES TO
IT.

Everyone is in position, a slight bending of vision already happening in
the desert heat. The hills bleached out in their faded moth colors edging
to pink, cut gem-like against the infinite blue. Paz sees the sky all around
her, not just above her. The desert surroundings have become a stage.

CONFLICTING STATEMENTS THE DEFENDANT MADE TO THE
POLICE IMMEDIATELY FOLLOWING THE INCIDENT REPRESENT
A CONFUSED ATTEMPT AT BOTH RECONSTRUCTION AND
SUBCONSCIOUSLY BLOCKING OUT THE MEMORY OF THE
TRAUMATIC EXPERIENCE. (INADMISSIBLE.)

There is a moment of synchronizing, where all lightings must happen together. In the deepest moments of it, she doesn't separate herself from Romy, so evidently a part of everything Paz is doing that she cannot shake the vertigo.

VERTIGO HAS BEEN DESCRIBED AS THE LONGING TO FALL.

The match is lit, the jittery flame rolling into a bright line of fire. Lines of color shoot upward into the sky and flay into points. The sky flashes with pink and blue and green and white light, hypnotically, while the women stand on the sand looking up. There is a whistling sound, and then the colors silently explode and arc, the noise of their explosions off-time, coming once they are already on the descent. Glittering shapes of colored light continue to crack and bang with startling intensity and fill the entire sky. Paz motions to the women, who bend to light their marks, and then there is the brightest purple-and-pink smoke filling the whole area around The Cielo, moving in wide waves that expand with the wind. It's igniting and softening all the land around her. All the bodies and landscape barely visible.

Essa hands the baby to Paz. She feels light. Essa has taken off her diaper, which was bloated beyond all recognition and sticky with ice cream. For the first time all day, she's completely still in Paz's arms, transfixed by what is happening in the sky.

She thinks of Billy and wonders where he is right now. It is hard to know how he really feels. He deflects. His images and films that embrace despair so resonantly, they all seem to say, all you need to know is to know enough not to ask. He never notices that she is withering without making any work. She doesn't know how he feels about her as a mother to his daughter. Or even how he feels about her as his wife. She's been so fixated on his past with Romy that she failed to see his utter lack of curiosity about hers. All her love, its excess, hanging out of her — it was embarrassing. When he'd first told her he had feelings for her, she'd felt so different, not like how it had ever been with any other person. But then she'd heard him telling Maarten how much he missed Romy. All she remembers was how insignificant she felt. She would never occupy as much space as Romy. She would never be an equal collaborator, or his first love. It was like he was simply enduring her. She knows this feeling well. It's how she grew up. She'd worked so hard to remake herself, but now here she is, having outrun nothing. She'd hidden everything so completely that she can barely recognize who she's become. She pretended she was okay with the little Billy offered her, when she wasn't. Pretended she wasn't jealous of Romy, when she was. Standing there in the bright sun she is scared at how damaged she's let her life become. She is so upset by this thought, it feels almost physical. Something is leaking over her body. She feels a warm liquid spread down her legs. She looks down. The baby, bare under her dress, is peeing on her.

The women are scattered across the open landscape cracked by drought, showered in light. She passes Flea to Essa, and the women stand there watching as she ignites the final fuse and billows of purple smoke begin pouring out, filling up the space, tumbling across the sand, and eventually diffuse into the desert air. It's the most beautiful thing she's ever done. Every part of her has been activated. Hope takes a wild leap inside her. She thinks of something Romy had said about a work that was good. It should be like falling in love, all the senses waking up.

After the last of the colored smoke drifts off, a regular black cloud rises, and soon the air smells like burning. The women walk as if in formation, an army moving over sand dunes, taking their positions and forming a wall around The Cielo, now engulfed in fire. Her skin feels hot, and that's when it hits her. It's the dream. It's the recurring dream, the one she's been dreaming all this time. Only it's not frightening, as she's always interpreted it. It's powerful, something total in its transformation. She stands there vibrating with consciousness as she watches the flames, ghostly in the sun.

Thursday

THE RINGING STARTLES THE AFTERNOON silence. Paz has been waiting for this call for days and goes to the phone on the wall with its long curling cord, picks up the heavy receiver that slips in her damp hand. She's too distracted by what she's just read to receive it properly.

DECEMBER 1977. *The days feel swallowed since the baby was born. My body is shaky, provisional. I feel the flap, flap, flap of my own mind. After giving birth, the edges have melted. The world seems too bright, too harsh for a baby. As soon as I had her, I wanted to fold her right back into my body.*

Ora asked how the baby was when I went by the gallery today, and I looked at her. I didn't know how to sum up my condition in an answer. I could tell her that Billy had come inside me when I hadn't wanted him to, and this is what happened. If that hadn't happened, I wouldn't have had to wear white underwear for weeks to call on bleeding. And when that didn't happen, I wouldn't have had to carry her around, wrapped in my insides, foot stuck in my rib for three months, rearranging my internal organs, softening my bones, making me sick. I wouldn't have had to undergo this unfair deformation of a woman's body. I know that's not what someone is supposed to think when they think of their baby, but it's like how transparency contains all the colors, life can hold every thought, one beside the other. But once I'd had the baby, and Billy and I were both holding her in our arms, I was shocked, completely shocked, to find that what we held was love.

When I was leaving the gallery, I saw Paz. She said she was home for the holidays. I hadn't seen her since the group show. I admired her skill, I knew she was going to be good, and her performance was the last thing I expected to come from her — the husky voice, the small body, soot-wet mascara, the cowgirl get-up. An unsafe strangeness that seemed uncomfortable for her to do. She had sent tapes from New York that Billy and I had listened to. Her music infected us for a while. We hadn't found her. She'd found us. But I couldn't shake the feeling that she was going to take something from me.

After I got my check from Ora, Paz walked with me back to my car. I was unsteady in the hallucinogenic heat. The sun was making everything inert. I walked slowly, carefully. I hadn't been outside the house since the baby was born.

You really should be resting, she said, concerned. Where is your husband? He should be here with you.

She seemed more adult, more grown-up, even though I was the one who'd just had the baby, and she was just a kid. Now, looking at her, what I felt was affection for her. It seemed remarkable to me that after everything she'd been through, she had managed not to be destroyed by life. She'd outstripped the brutality of it, made it into something else. She understood that art can do the impossible. It can outdo nature.

Paz has read and re-read the entry several times. She is struck by Romy's generosity toward her. She notices something she's never noticed before. All this time, and there it was. Small, angular, beside her name — a heart.

'Paz, are you there?' Milt is saying.

'Yes,' she manages to say into the large black receiver, her voice choking. She so often doesn't understand what has been intended when it comes to other people. But this hadn't been only in her head. The writing felt so private it seemed to belong to her. She enters the belief of it with Romy. She feels a rush of happiness. The baby has started to cry upstairs as she hears Milt's voice in and out of her ears. *Close circumstantial case. Sloppy policework. Cut on his face. Nothing documented. No breathalyzer. Only one witness. Doorman's history of psychological problems. Inconsistent statements are the weakest form of evidence and need to be substantiated with the strongest of evidence.*

```
THERE IS NOT ENOUGH EVIDENCE TO PROVE BEYOND A
REASONABLE DOUBT THAT THE DEFENDANT IS GUILTY.
THE INDICTMENT AGAINST THE DEFENDANT IS THEREFORE
DISMISSED.
```

Paz says something to Milt, the sound of her own voice pricking through her like static. She hangs up the phone, a bit stunned, and breathes in and out very slowly. There is an icy feeling in her stomach, but she doesn't let her body move. She feels the weight of all the unspoken things between them. What she'd thought was the beginning of a long process is now closed. She didn't know that she hadn't been ready for that. There are too many feelings at once, and now she is sitting there full of sweat and dread and the awareness that something in her life is ending. Flea's cries pierce the heat. She's crying hard now, wailing, and Paz runs to her.

Friday
three weeks later

WHEN SHE ARRIVES, HIS ARM is resting on the metal gate. She feels herself swallow hard. She has thirty minutes inside the house and then she has to leave the key in a lockbox and decide. The house is set back from the road, with a wall of bougainvillea on the south side. Billy watches her twist the key in the lock, a ray of sun falling on her hand.

Inside it's spacious and bright with big windows. With the small bit of money that she got from the sale of Aunt May's house after the assisted-living payments, it could just work. They walk through the rooms not saying anything. Before, everything would have depended on what his reaction would be. If he didn't like it, it would not only affect how she liked it, it would mean that the possibility of something good would have died. There is a big glass door out to a back garden, but they stay inside, standing there facing each other. 'It's good to see you,' he says, reaching inside his jacket and pulling out a pack of cigarettes.

Paz opens doors and moves around while he smokes. She no longer knows how to be around him. She's not sure she knows what they are to one another. She is tired of trying to understand him. She is through trying to understand him. She has been trying to understand him since they met. She finally says, 'I wish you could have been honest with me. About women. About what happened the night Romy died.'

He takes a sharp inhalation of smoke. He seems surprised at her directness. 'I don't even know what happened. I still don't.'

'You drink too much,' Paz says, her throat beating.

Billy looks at her and then says in his low voice, with a bit of rasp in it, 'It's always too late when someone tells you that you drink too much.' He waits out a respectful pause. 'But now I see how hard it is for everyone around me. It's wrecking me. It's how I lost Romy.' He looks at her, a bit far away. 'I never used to like it when someone would say that they'd lost someone who'd died. It seemed so euphemistic,' he says. 'But, it's actually more accurate. That's exactly what it feels like — as though they are missing.'

Paz is silent. She'd never believed that all the time she spent thinking about Romy had anything to do with Billy. But the time he spends thinking about Romy feels, to her, like a personal affront.

He turns to her. 'I didn't want to mourn her because that would mean she was truly gone. I'd have to admit that, even trying to fill the gap, it remains something else. And that is what it should be. It's the only way to hold on to something that can't be let go.'

'And yet you had slept with — other women.'

He looks startled. 'It wasn't — it wasn't something that happened very often. Only if I had been drinking very heavily. I didn't even remember it the next day. Nothing ever would have happened sober.'

'So, I wouldn't have happened sober?' Paz asks.

He looks at her with such warmth, it floods her. 'Paz,' he says. She hears in his voice how undone he is from what happened and suddenly feels such emotion for him. And then she shakes her head. This is what he does — he's good at it. She's so disoriented trying to think of what to do next that she walks into the door, hitting her nose on the glass. She steps back, stunned, holding her hand over her face. 'You were both plotting your own disappearances,' she says, neutrally, though wanting a reaction.

'I know that you keep pieces of Romy's writing, and that you read her journals. I don't know why you do it, because all it seems to do is to depress you.' He pauses. 'Besides, they were ideas,' he says. 'You're too literal.'

'I'm truthful,' she says, unsettled that he's known this all along.

'Are you?' he asks, looking directly into her eyes. Something about them stops her. 'Before you went to the desert, you asked me if I thought I knew you. But I'm not sure you even know yourself. You seem to hold so much back — at the expense of who you are. At first, I thought it was because you are young, but I wonder if you would be like this at any age.'

She considers this. 'It seems wrong,' she says, 'if between us we can't find the truth.'

'Is it the truth you're looking for?'

Something shifts in the room, and she realizes the sky has darkened outside. Paz opens the door and they walk out into the backyard. There is a wind that sounds like sugar on the dried-out palms. Big black clouds move across the sky. After all the months without rain, it's the first sign of any weather. If only it would just rain. But even if it did, what would it matter? There is a drought in them too deep. She doesn't like standing out here with him, his overwhelming height, so tall looking down at her. She feels so small, so she sits down on the grass. He sits and then lies back on the grass, and she lies back beside him, their shoulders touching, looking up at the sky.

It's been three weeks since she's seen him. She needed distance after the indictment, she had told him, and he'd respected that. She's staying with Essa, who is looking after Flea so she could come here.

'I saw the photos at Ora's of what you did in the desert. *Light Transformation*. Is that what you are calling it?'

'Yes.' She waits for him to comment, but there is a long stretch of silence. She can hear a siren in the distance. Just when she can't believe he's not going to say anything, he turns to her. 'It ambushed my heart,' he says. 'In the way only something perfectly executed can do.'

He sees her now that her body has been filled with the gold light of the desert. Couldn't he see her before? He is offering her one last chance to change her mind, to continue as they always had. It makes her think of the line she once read — *Who is invisible enough to see you?* And she thinks that it was Romy who first saw her, even though she hadn't yet seen herself.

They lie there in all that wind, and she thinks she can feel a drop on her face. And then another.

'We need to talk about what happened,' he says.

The vibrating stopped in her body after she burned The Cielo down, but she is starting to drift. She wants to say, I don't know how to love myself enough to know who I am. But also, the realization that it's Romy and the baby, all along, that have held me to you. She knows in her heart that her understanding of Billy will never be settled again, no matter what he says or doesn't. She closes her eyes and feels the dry grass pricking her skin. She has made the work of her life, she has a metal finger, and he has been let go, found guilty of nothing. And still she is conflicted because being around him presents the same feeling she first got with the baby, something so powerful she believed she might die if she didn't see it through. It all completely narrowed down to love. But even love wasn't enough in the end. At least not this kind. Whatever decision she had made has been abandoned, if indeed she had ever decided anything. It could have been an illusion, like the rain falling on their skin.

A heavy silence hangs between them until finally he begins to speak. 'The thing is, I just don't know what happened that night.' She is suddenly very alert.

'I don't need to know what happened, but you need to know what happened, because you are going to have to actually deal with it at some point — whatever went on.'

Billy shakes his head. He says he just doesn't know. He just doesn't know. He covers his face with his hands. Her heart is beating wildly. A line of tears streams from under his fingers across his cheek, and she doesn't know why but she licks it. It tastes like salt. The rain begins to come down hard now, soaking them, but they just lie there, unmoving, their clothes stuck to their bodies.

She's always been the one so close to tears, but right now she is frozen. She takes a breath and opens her mouth, but the words aren't coming out, they're stuck in her. She feels she is slowly edging toward the center of herself, but she can't find any words. A car drives by, its tires sluicing sharply through rainwater.

She says, 'I want to live here.'

'Is that what you want?'

She thinks and then says it.

'I want to feel free.'

Edinburgh,
2018

YOU WALK UP THE HILL. The air is damp and the sky is dark with thick clouds. There is a hard, gray rain and you're already a bit drunk, alone in this new city. You waited too long to pay for vegan food, sodden and tasteless, and have struck up a conversation with a moon-faced teenager in a wheelchair named Demi, 'after Demi Moore'. [Too Wizard of Oz?]

Edinburgh Demi Moore says, 'Are you, em, here long?' She says 'em' instead of the American 'um', which endears her to you.

'Just till Friday.' Your phone pings and you see a text. CHANGED HOW? It's from your agent.

'Are you vegan?' Edinburgh Demi Moore asks.

'Sort of,' you say distractedly. 'If you don't count cheese.'

She sees you looking at her fingernails and holds them up. Each fingernail its own universe.

'It's the-novels-of-Nicholson-Baker nail art,' Edinburgh Demi Moore says.

'So it is,' you say, getting a closer look at the nail-sized book covers, a different one at the end of each finger.

You have a bit of a headache, but you don't want to go back to your hotel room yet, so you walk past the tourist shops selling eternal-expiration-date shortbread and made-in-China tartans, and find a bar up the road and order a Scotch.

The literary festival invited you for your recent novel. You are trying to explain to your agent what's happening to this next one, which was supposed to be a non-fiction book about 1970s feminist performance artists. IT'S A NOVEL! you type and then send it to your agent, though you wish you hadn't. At least not with an exclamation mark. After writing a lengthy follow-up about image-rights problems with certain estates, unanswered interview requests, people wanting money before they'd show you anything, cultural organizations seeming to have better things to do, you delete it. You want to say that the way it was going you could hardly stand writing it. It didn't at all honor the radical work these women were making. You could find almost nothing on most of the artists you wanted to research. It seemed like a falsified history of that era — only the works by men had been written about. The few small mentions of women were labeled 'feminist' or 'collective', as though none of them had their own talent or names.

IS IT PLOT-Y?

You are trying to figure out how to respond because you know what she's asking. You're thinking there's probably not a lot of —

DOES IT HAVE TO BE THE SEVENTIES?

You switch your phone to airplane mode, put it in your bag, and take out your notebook. You can barely see what you're writing in the dimly lit bar. The bartender, who is drying a glass with a towel, seems to notice and moves a candle over. 'Another Scotch?' he says. It's the first time you've felt warm since you arrived. You nod.

You reach in your bag for your pen, and the Tic Tacs you bought at the bodega before you got in the taxi to JFK rattle around. They feel like they're from another dimension, the inferno of New York August to a wet green autumn, though it is August here too.

It was raining this afternoon when you met the Scottish journalist who now writes for *The Guardian*. He interviewed you not for *The Guardian*, but for some BBC podcast about art and writing. You were his fourth interview that day. You were to meet on a street corner. It was raining. You thought Edinburgh was beautiful in the rain. It looked undersea with the rain-slicked stone and glistening bright moss. You'd told him you would be in a trench coat. When you apologized for being late, he said, 'Don't worry, I've just sat here leering at women in trench coats.' You looked around and realized everyone was in trench coats.

He asked if you wanted to see some of Edinburgh, but when you got in the car, he drove you out of the city. You rolled down the window and let the cool damp air in. You wanted to keep driving while he told you about the origins of Edinburgh that dated back to the Middle Ages.

'Where are you at with this next book?' he asked when you were sitting outside with milky coffees under some famous bridge. You could barely hear him, the wind was whipping so loudly. Does watching The Bionic Woman reruns count as research? you thought. You wondered if they got American TV shows like that in Scotland. Or maybe he was just too young. He must have been at least ten years younger than you. 'Research,' you sort of yelled.

A band of tourists filed aboard a Harry Potter tour bus below you. You turned to him. 'Do you think people who travel like that are unevolved?'

'Jesus, mate,' he laughed. 'I don't judge them.'

The photographer had shown up. He was quiet, in running shoes, a windbreaker zipped up.

'It was a confusing era.' You had to yell to be heard over the wind. You'd started to wonder about his location choice for recording a podcast.

'What era?' he asked.

'The seventies. I mean, Bertolucci's Last Tango in Paris came out at the same time Michael Landon was directing Little House on the Prairie. Janis Joplin and Jimi Hendrix had just died —'

'Every era has its contradictions. And its geniuses who die young.' And then he said, 'God, sorry.' He knew about your mother. Of course he did, he was interviewing you.

'It's okay,' you said.

'How is it? Going back to that time,' he asked.

You were still thinking of *Last Tango in Paris*, and how Bertolucci said that he and Marlon Brando came up with the butter as lubricant for the anal-rape scene off-screen. He didn't tell Maria Schneider about it because he wanted her 'to react as a girl, not as an actress. I wanted her to react humiliated'. And when Pauline Kael famously reviewed the film for *The New Yorker*, she compared it to Stravinsky's *The Rite of Spring*.

The bus of tourists lumbered up a hill in the distance, leaving the air thick with lingering exhaust.

'I also feel incapable of sprinkling in dialect that people used unironically, or slurs that everyone casually used. The women were basically treated as garbage. I mean, how did they bear it?'

'Drugs,' the photographer said out of nowhere.

'And sex,' the journalist said. 'They all seemed to be having way more sex than people do now. Even movies now have way more violence and way less sex than they did back then.'

The photographer said that the disintegration of love in Western society can be linked to the rise of consumer capitalism. Something about how the concentration and centralization of capital has profoundly altered our character structure and therefore our capacity to love. What we now have is some kind of pseudo-love based on projection and fantasy.

The conversation moved into quantum on the drive back to town. The photographer was talking about the event horizon — essentially the space around a black hole from which nothing, not even light, can escape. It turned out that the photographer was from London and was studying at Columbia, a doctorate in physics. You didn't get a chance to ask how that related to taking photos in Edinburgh. It was hard to hear anything, and turning around to face him in the back seat made you feel nauseated because of the traffic circles and winding road. He said something like, *We need to know the entire future space-time of the universe to determine the current location of the horizon, which is essentially impossible.* You could barely keep your eyes open.

You pay for the Scotch and walk back to your hotel to change. You've left the window open by accident and your room is damp, so you turn on the heating, cranking it high, and dump everything out of your suitcase onto the bed, looking for some combination of things warm enough to wear.

According to Google Maps, it's a thirty-four-minute walk to the theater in the old town. You know if you Uber there, you will fall asleep. Your publicist has invited you, and now he can't go. You almost stay in your hotel room, but you decide to go anyway. Your hair is snapping so wildly in the wind as you walk, you have to hold it back with your hand so that you can see where you are going. You are wearing very tight pants that you note did not used to be, and you wonder how much longer you can do that. As in, when will it no longer be age-appropriate. WHEN IT ISN'T, TAKE ME OUT TO THE BACKYARD AND SHOOT ME, your friend in Brooklyn texts back.

The opening act is a punk band with a young singer who for some reason strikes you as sweet. Screaming and jumping, it seems like a genuine pseudo-primitivist reaction to the powers that be. You like punk because you like it when someone takes something to an extreme. After her set, you see the singer walking through the crowd with her laddered stockings and skin-tight dress full of safety pins, carrying a baby. It makes you identify with the baby, and how you would have been dragged around by a mother making art too.

You are already feeling a bit lousy, and standing for so long isn't helping. When Pussy Riot finally comes on, you let the high-pitched Russian words being screamed angrily into the mic wash over you. The lead singer talks about how she risked her safety to travel here tonight by car from Russia, navigating checkpoints, risking imprisonment. It is translated into English with subtitles on a screen. The crowd blankly stares back, not comprehending what she is saying. All this audience seems to have known is freedom. At one point, a shirtless male bandmate in falling-apart shoes and pleather jeggings is suddenly jumping wildly on stage and spraying water all over you, literally throwing water on you and most of the crowd. You're soaked and annoyed at yourself for wearing your good boots.

When the lights come back up there is still a huge crowd in the theater. You step through the pools of water and clumps of wet bodies and make your way toward the door, drinking a beer from a red, non-recyclable plastic cup. You are almost outside when you see him.

'I wouldn't have pegged you for a fan,' he says.

You smile at him, water dripping from the ends of your hair.

The photographer is taller than you, which is tall, considering you are almost six feet. You hadn't noticed because he had been pretzeled into the back seat the whole ride back to town. You determine you are both going in the same direction, so you decide to walk together. He knows his way.

Walking down, standing at the top of the hill, the city looks like a dream — the winding dark river, the colored lights of the Ferris wheel below, the purple-black sky with big thick misty clouds.

'I've been reading about dark matter because it's what my mother was reading, before she died. I've been thinking about black holes and then you mentioned them in the car today.'

'What were you thinking about them?'

'I don't know. I've never really known what they are, or what they do. But they've come up a lot since I've been writing this book. And then you mentioned them. What is it you learn from studying them?'

'You can deduce the absolute limits of the outer edges of the information contained in an area of space.'

'Is this what you want to go into?' you ask. You wonder if you sound like an idiot. Can a person even 'go into' black holes?

'There is a physicist who once said that we need to understand how much information is required to describe the universe.' He stops in front of a building that faces a small park not far from your hotel. It must be where he is staying. He asks you if you want to come inside, and you find yourself saying yes.

It's beautiful, with very tall ceilings and wood floors and long windows that face a lovely private park lined with immense green trees. You know this because you sat in it earlier and tried to write on a bench, not knowing that these parks are private. No one kicked you out, but you figured it out after a while. The flat is a friend's who is in Ireland, he says. It's sparse, but the furniture that is there is very iconic, mid-century designer, which you didn't see until after awkwardly navigating his bike in the quasi-dark hallway, partially knocking it over.

'Would you like some Scotch?' he says.

'Sure.' You haven't slept for at least thirty-six hours and have already drunk more Scotch today than you have in your entire life. You were speaking in front of a crowd on a stage this morning at about 3.00 am your time, so you are finding it harder than usual to read him. You feel a bit shivery, maybe a fever or a cold coming on. He appears in the room with two glasses, and you both sit on the couch. He pours the Scotch, and he mentions his friend again and you find yourself trying to interpret if he had somehow feminized the word. Maybe this is your opening to ask, but you sip the Scotch instead. It's good. It hits your center and spreads warmth back into your body, making you aware of how chilled you are, your clothes still wet.

There are some loud bangs outside that startle you. It sounds like gunfire.

'Fireworks,' he says. 'They do it every night during the festival. They make you jump a bit. I like that.'

'Oh,' you laugh. 'Are you here long?' you say.

'I have to go back to London tomorrow and then to New York. I needed to get away for a while.' You are wondering if everything important in life happens by chance, which you think it does. Especially when you consider that just being born is a series of improbable chances. You don't ask him why he needs to get away — you are suddenly tired of talking, your voice is growing hoarse. You take a big sip of Scotch and rest your head on the back of the couch.

He gets up and puts music on. Something you don't recognize, though it sounds a little like a version of a song you used to like. You played it as a teenager, and it made you feel perversely alive. You tell him this. That listening to this music makes you realize that the music you enjoy the most is the music you listened to when you were sixteen.

'Maybe you like it because nothing else now could ever give you that same feeling. Of that excitement for things that haven't yet happened,' he says.

He sits back down beside you. You like his smell, like the air here, alive and green. 'Tell me about the information required to describe the universe,' you say.

'I am looking for a signal.'

You look at him, suddenly serious. 'What kind of signal?'

'Something that will show us the matter of the universe. All the stars and planets and people — we make up only about five per cent of the universe. Most of it is invisible. It drifts through the world, through us, like ghosts through a wall.'

'If it can't be seen, how do you know it exists?' you say, curious but trying very hard not to yawn.

'Because we can observe its effects on what we can see.' He says something about how black holes contain crucial clues to the basic quantum physics of gravity. A massive star that has run out of fuel can produce the kind of extreme density needed to create a mangled bit of world. *Mangled bit of world* — you like that. You want to write it down. You are trying to stay awake, the ideas sending electricity to your head. He asks about your book and you tell him a bit about the seventies performance artists, and how land art was a radical movement away from the commercialization of art, but the feminists made it very differently from the men, who seemed inclined to destroy the environment, a lot like their colonizing forefathers. He nods. You get excited telling him about the performance artists. *They made estrogen bombs! They cooked the horizon! They drove abortion caravans! They weren't afraid to call a cunt a cunt.* 'Cool,' he says in a way that makes you aware you're talking to a very tall feminist in a windbreaker.

You tell him you went on a tangent and read about Valerie Solanas, who long before that movement wrote *SCUM Manifesto* and ended up dying alone in a welfare hotel, described as a kind of hellscape last stop for dying whores and junkies with piss- and vomit-stained carpets. Her body was found four days after she died, kneeling by the bed, covered in maggots.

'God, that's grim.'

'That seems to be the prevailing message,' you say, taking another sip of Scotch.

You rest your head back on the couch again. 'I need to hear more about dark matter.' He pours more Scotch into your glass. Back at home, you are both in things you are trying to get out of. At least you think that's what you hear being said. But he also might have been talking about how basic geometry bends and ripples depending on the information in the black hole.

'I've got to go,' you say, suddenly standing up, putting your glass down.

'Really?' he says.

You stare at him for a moment — it might be a second or two, but it feels like a long time — and you put a thought out of your mind. It is ridiculous. You don't know him, and he doesn't know you.

'Thank you,' you say. 'For the drink.'

He gets you your trench coat, which is still very damp, off a hook in the front hall. He offers to walk you to your hotel, but you tell him you're fine. It's close. You can walk alone. In those few moments of silence in the half-dark, you think he feels what you do, and this thought is almost unbearable. You catch each other's eyes and then he stands in the doorway and watches as you put your coat on and leave.

In your hotel room, you peel off your wet clothes and have the longest hottest shower, and now you feel awake again. You put on a huge sweatshirt and drag your laptop into bed. If you can't sleep, you might as well work, so you begin transcribing your scrawled notes from the bar, which are almost indecipherable. You were under the impression you'd written something good. Instead, you can't even read your own writing. A man coming in bleeding from his face and elbows. A mother who is more violent and unpredictable than other mothers in the neighborhood. A couple who night after night for dinner eat nothing but Hershey bars.

You'd started a list of bad seventies men that quickly became modern:

A man who leaves the toilet seat up

A man who pushes a woman's head down

A man who lets a woman wash his wacked-off underwear

A man with an all-male Spotify playlist

Ditto for books

A slut-shamer

A gaslighter

A man who says 'mankind'

A mansplainer

A man who offers to go Dutch on an abortion

A man who says he 'doesn't believe in' things that clearly exist

You get up and pace around restlessly and realize that you are hungry. Really hungry. There is not enough minibar. You consider making tea and tear open a complimentary shortbread. The sugar packet has a quote from Keats. You see your reflection in the black window and it almost startles you. You could disappear, you could be anywhere, no one would know. Whenever you have lived or traveled far, you always feel laid bare, aware of the total randomness of being alive. Travel is a bit like death, a breach in continuity that detaches you from the details you've consented to as your life. You find yourself still thinking about the photographer.

Your head is now pounding, and your throat is sore. You walk over and stare out your window, and there is Karl Ove Knausgaard, staring back. He's wearing a jean jacket, his leonine hair tousled in his black-and-white portrait blown up for the festival. He is set to speak about his new book the day after you leave. You had begun one of his books, but after reading thirty pages of him trying to figure out how to smuggle beer out of his house in a plastic bag as a teenager, you found yourself thinking, *Hide them in a backpack, you idiot!*

You make tea in a mug with a flower design on it and bring it back to your bed, and open the e-mails you've been avoiding from home and from work. Suddenly, you feel as though you are being watched from above, and a little shiver goes through you. You turn your head very slowly, almost comically slow. Long legs crossed, dark men's pants and rolled-up sleeves, pale hair and intense shining blue eyes, tatty white tennis shoes. *Tennis shoes!* All the pictures of her were always cut off somewhere around the shin. You never knew what it was she wore on her feet.

She calls you Utopia, the fanciful hippie name they gave you, though you've never, ever, used it. Your mom always called you Flea, and then by your middle name, because growing up in the decade of second marriages, shoulder pads, and Reagan meant that you had to throw out any earnest idealism. The past had become completely embarrassing, as it does. Your name was a stark reminder of an idealized time light years from this one.

'Romy?' You don't even think of saying 'Mom'. Mom has always been Paz. You've thought about Romy your whole life — your mother, who is now sitting beside you, taller and younger than you. You both stare at each other for you don't know how long, and you lose all awareness of your body, and suddenly you are both crying.

'You — you cut your hair,' you finally say, and quickly feel ridiculous at such inane first words to the person you've thought of most in your whole life.

'Oh. I'd forgotten,' she says, running her hand up the back of her neck. It is messy, boyish, chopped as if she's cut it herself. 'I'm so glad you are here, and you are being celebrated for your work. That you're okay.'

'I'm fine,' you say, still crying, 'I'm fine.' You don't tell her that you are not *that* celebrated but it's okay. You are also a bit unwilling, or possibly incapable of playing the game. And you've not settled upon what side of art or commerce to come down on, though god knows you've been steeped in examining the arbitrariness of art careers lately — who got to speak and why, who died like dogs unless they compromised. There's so much you don't know about Romy, which strikes you with such intensity and surprise that you can't even begin to think of questions.

'How are you?'

'Angry,' she says, staring directly at you, which catches you off guard.

'And lonely,' she says, 'I'm so alone,' which makes you both cry. 'All this reeling around for eternity.' She takes your hands and you hold hers. She says yours feel very damp, and you see that you both have the exact same hands, which makes you cry again. You try to compose yourself.

'What is it like?' you ask.

'Like nothing the living should know about,' she says in a low voice, quickly switching the subject. 'I'm so confused.'

'About what?' you say.

'I don't know.' She flops back in her chair. 'I can't tell what's going on with anything. There is a lot of static from the living. I can't tell what it is. All these bodies on the radio.'

You are not sure what she is saying, something about inner circuitry all lit up. 'Are you talking about the internet?' you finally realize.

She looks at you blankly.

You find yourself talking about computers, Steve Jobs, and server farms in California. About scrolling through toneless empty data. About internet poisoning.

She is still looking at you blankly. 'I'm pretty primitive,' she reminds you. 'What were you doing earlier?'

You wonder if she saw something with the photographer, but you realize she means your computer.

'I was actually trying to compose an e-mail — an electronic letter — to a curator who said she was struggling around your bio for an upcoming exhibition. She explained that when they include a biography of a male artist in a show, they would not be worrying about mentioning his family at all, and she was wondering if it was even correct to bring in biographical information to an introductory reading of your work. It was something she was grappling with. Despite the work all the feminists did to make change for us, nothing seems to be able to alter the structures of how art is made, sold, and written about.'

'We used to send paper. That must seem funny to you now.'

'I don't know. Feelings get eroded over time. Journals and letters are proof that a person really felt something. They made the days permanent. After searching through archives these past two years, and re-reading your journals, I think that it's the written word that survives. On paper.'

'My journals?' she says, startled.

'You had a lot of them,' you say, not sure why she seems surprised.

'I'd — asked Billy to destroy them, if —'

'I didn't know that,' you say, a bit stung. They are the only thing you have of hers that is your own. You've clung to them. She'd put it all down. You are grateful for them because it's rare to get access to your mother as a person. Even her work you'd always had to share with everyone. You'd felt a surprising intimacy handling her notebooks, not just because of their private content, but knowing she'd once held them too.

'She had brought them out to burn at The Cielo, but at the last minute, Mom understood I might one day want them. She gave them all to me to read when I was old enough.'

'Mom,' she says stiffly.

'Paz.'

'Right,' she says. She's smoking again. Or is it still the same cigarette? 'She's been good to you,' she says, lowering her gaze to meet yours.

'Yes,' you say carefully. 'She has.'

There is a flicker of images on your computer and you can see she's interested. 'You chose the right path, working with light. There is no longer anything singular about video. Images are everywhere,' you tell her. 'But the light work still resonates.' She didn't live long enough for her works to get jaded. Instead, they look forever in a state of formation.

She watches you closely. As if she might be able to see that her daughter doesn't have what she did, all that life burning inside her that sometimes made her dark.

'You're getting a lot of it right,' she says after a moment.

'A lot of what right?' you ask.

'The novel,' she says. 'You also might be the only one who actually knows what my wearing suits meant.' She takes a drag off her cigarette. 'Would that be easier now?'

'Easier?' you repeat. 'Well, there are words for it, pronouns. And a hope that we're moving toward thinking that a person's biology isn't their destiny.'

'In the early days, I was so terrified of being a feminist in the sense that I longed for something outside of gendered identity through my work. Now I wish I'd done more.' She stops. 'But I want to hear about you.'

'You know you became known, and then even a bit famous, when a certain group of millennial feminists discovered you, which has helped your work find a more — mainstream audience. There are protests staged at his openings. They —' You're not sure how much to say. Her death has become a kind of parable of the relative power of women and men in the art world.

'God, what a horrific position for you.' She looks uncomfortable. 'What about you? What are you doing here?'

You tell her about talking to Ali Smith while you both piled samosas on your paper plates in the festival yurt, with its tribal rugs and heat lamps. And the entourage of Getty photographers out back. You tell her about being the non-famous writer on the bill with a famous one. 'I mean, I say "famous" loosely, because your average person wouldn't know her name either. Writing might be worse than art in that you invest so much of yourself to gain so little.'

'Nothing's changed,' she laughs. 'Fame was always for actors and athletes.'

Her wrist beeps and she looks distractedly down at it. 'It says I slept zero hours last night.'

'Wait, are you wearing a Fitbit?'

'A what? I don't know what this is.'

'How does it work? I mean, not that, but *this*,' you say, motioning to her.

'I don't know,' she says, looking genuinely bewildered. 'It's not that I haven't been here. I think I have always been here somewhere, but it was like something had been switched off.'

'I wish I knew what switched it on.'

'Anger,' she says again.

You want to talk about this, but first you look through the minibar and hold up a tiny bottle of vodka. 'Can you drink?'

'Not really.' She looks uncomfortable. 'I need to talk to you about something.'

'Anything.'

'Do you know what happened on the roof that night?' she asks.

It's not what you expected her to say. 'You don't' — you're not sure how to say this — 'remember?'

'I remember. But other than Billy, there were no witnesses.'

You're not sure if it would have mattered if there were. Famous writers sometimes shoot their wives' faces in crowded bars and kill them. Or stab them at parties and then go on to have several more wives. Other famous writers talk about these acts as quote unquote artistic metaphors. A woman, on the other hand, can write books and plays, a radical feminist manifesto, and the only thing she will be remembered for is shooting an artist in a silver wig.

'He doesn't remember anything,' you say, filling the kettle and plugging it in to make more tea. You had once asked your father about that night and he'd looked torn apart. It was never spoken of. You come over to her and sit at her feet and rest your head on her knees.

'I hadn't slept,' she says. 'You were only seven weeks old. I'd never had so much to drink.' Her voice grows quiet.

She strokes your hair. 'You are so damp,' she says for the second time, which makes you realize that it might be unpleasant to her, your human dampness.

'There was so little evidence, and everything seemed so — inconclusive.'

'It's okay,' she says. 'That's not actually what I meant.'

'There is a black hole where that night is for him,' you say slowly. You are both silent for a moment. How could you explain that he'd spent the rest of his life in a kind of irreparable despair. After a long silence you say carefully, 'What I feel is that he'd drunk so much that he doesn't remember anything, which makes him feel guilty. Because either way, he is responsible.' You lower your head. It's the first time you've ever admitted this to anyone. Romy reaches out and puts her hands on your shoulders. You start to shake again, feeling gutted. Your cheeks are dripping with tears. 'I'm so sorry,' you say.

'Please, shh,' she says. 'Don't be.' She stops. 'You should know, that night, I was so angry I wanted to break his teeth,' she says. 'And now, anger is like an alarm I can't turn off.' She takes a drag off her cigarette.

You feel heat radiate up from your face as you take inventory of everything she'd gone up against. When a person dies at twenty-nine, largely unrealized as an artist, in the middle of a messy marriage, she remains forever unrealized, forever fixed in that mess.

She sees the pain on your face. 'Please,' she says. 'Don't worry for me. Anger is information. Besides, the point of anger is to have less anger.'

'I have so many things I want to ask you,' you say, wiping the tears that slide down your face. 'I don't even know which one to ask.'

'I'm ready.'

'Okay,' you say, straightening, wanting to change the subject. 'What were the early falling works you mentioned, and the falling studies that were at The Cielo?'

'What?' The Fitbit beeps and she ignores it. 'How do you know about them?'

'There are a couple of references to them in your journals, and then there were the photos,' you say, eyeing her wrist. 'Listen, I know you don't know about this stuff, but you have to take that thing off. It's designed to co-opt human agency and free will. It's a kind of surveillance that takes away the part of a person that's private.'

'Photos?'

'Mom brought them back from The Cielo. They were falling studies you'd made near — near the end of your life.' You open up a notebook to find them, and one of the postcards from Fina falls out. 'Actually,' you say, picking them up, 'do you recognize these?'

Romy shakes her head. 'That's not my writing, if that's what you're asking,' she says, touching the Fitbit and pulling it off, and then turns one of the postcards over. 'But that moon sketch is mine —' She pauses. 'I gave some of those planetary drawings to Sam.' *Sam!* You should have known. You've seen his letters to her. They had the same writing. Your mom said he had never really accepted what happened to Romy. He always felt the case should have been re-opened. Maybe that's what he was trying to do.

'The falling works.' She grows quiet for a moment. You don't think she is going to say anything, but she says finally, 'It seemed like the only choice.' She pauses. 'The message to women artists was, *You can do anything you want, but it won't matter.* Early on I had been interested in making a series of images about falling. I had a camera, a really good Leica, and black-and-white film. I made nine images. But the people I showed only saw the body of a woman in the images. They commented on how I looked. They couldn't see them as art at all. Even though falling, oddly, is a kind of doubling. The person falling loses self-possession — they become an object. Billy was struggling with what his next work would be at that point. He was teaching and unhappy not getting to work. He didn't consider himself a teacher because that's not what he was. And it just happened naturally that I took the falling images of him instead. We had started to collaborate, but it was problematic — a young unknown artist with an older established male artist. I knew the images would never work with a woman in them. At least not in the same way, objectification, subtext, et cetera. When we first met, we often worked side by side. But he was twelve years older than me, and well known. He never granted interviews or talked to the press. All that silence,' she laughs. 'It actually made his reputation grow and gave him a kind of cult status. The falling work was credited to him and only him, and he never corrected that. For what it's worth, he didn't see it that way,' she says. 'We'd collaborated so much at the beginning, he remembered the falling pieces as more his idea.' She stops. 'I didn't know what was worse — having done it, or knowing that if I hadn't, if I'd presented the work as mine, nothing would have happened with it. And then they were bought by MoMA. It's what we argued about the night I —'

You feel bad getting her to talk about this.

'The falling images were good,' she continues, 'but he went on to make the pieces around masculinity, and those are the works that literally defined who he was as an artist, which seemed correct. That was his struggle. But his success was difficult for me. It forced me to develop my distance from him. To start again. I chose light. And then, when The Cielo sold, I guess I came full circle. I was ready to perform the falling pieces myself. I stopped telling him things. And when he drank, I began to see him as a lesser person, which was terrible for us. We had been so close, I was oblivious. It's possible to be so close to someone that you don't actually see them. When he drank, he became dishonest with women. I'm not sure if that's what happened with —' She pauses. 'Your mom.'

You're trying to figure out how to tell her that it wasn't entirely like that. Paz was the one who helped you research and protect Romy's archive of work. It occurs to you that Paz, by lighting The Cielo on fire, was the only one who had actually honored Romy's wishes around her work. After the desert piece, there was supposed to be an article in the *L. A. Times*, but nothing came of it. She made some more desert works and went back to academia, and is only now starting to get interest in her colored-smoke pieces thanks to a group of Twitter feminists. Billy moved to Rome. His third wife, only eight years older than you, is a former competitive swimmer who makes internet art that is, in your opinion, not very good. She told you she never once asked him about what happened with Romy, she trusted him completely.

Romy continues, 'I don't know. Now it all seems like such a luxury after all this deadness. I am a being that nothing can happen to, I don't eat or bleed. I'm a being who no longer creates anything.' After a moment, Romy breathes out and says, 'There's actually something else I need to tell you.' She looks at you and quickly clears her throat. 'I used to be anxious about how my memory wasn't that great. And then I realized nobody's is. But what does stay, what you hold on to, are feelings. I barely remember what happened on the roof. And the few weeks that led up to it. But I remember exactly how I felt — about my work, about you,' she says, blowing out smoke. She closes her eyes and then opens them, looking directly at you. 'He watched me fall.'

You feel the full weight of your body. For a few seconds you hear nothing, just distant muffled voices outside, a lone far-off dog barking, but nothing is landing, sound drifts over you.

'But it's not how you think,' she says. The moonlight has picked out Knausgaard's shining eyes. 'He didn't stop me,' she says slowly, 'because I made him promise he wouldn't.' You sit there not moving because there doesn't seem to be any movement right now that would be acceptable.

'When we were into the falling pieces, the first time I came to see him in Rome, I made him agree that when it came to my performance work, he couldn't intervene. He couldn't stop me. No matter what. Then I moved away from performances, working out at The Cielo. But when the building was bought, I fell into a very dark period. That was right when Billy's falling pieces were bought by the MoMA. I had this awful compulsion to compete with "male" artists, which is to say almost everyone. I saw I had nothing. The world, as far as I could see, was a zero-sum game for women — the survival of one, the complete destruction of the other. It asked who was most powerful, and the answer was always painfully clear.'

You feel hot, very hot suddenly, an extremely uncomfortable pricking sensation all over your skin. You'd read about the agreement but never understood it. Your mind is racing over her words. You also see how you should have been writing but were unable to. You need to go back and revise from the beginning, understanding how easy it is to write so much while leaving out the actual truth. You need to get it all down, every single thing, otherwise what will happen to all these atoms of experience?

'Once I'd devised the mental construct, the rules were set and that was that. I'd told myself to wait for a sign, something that would tell me to begin the piece. Something had crossed over in me and I couldn't go back. Only,' she continues, 'I knew he wouldn't be able to do it.' She stops. 'I saw it in his face, up on the roof, a look I hadn't seen for a long time. Oddly, I felt like we were on the edge of something honest. And yet, I found it impossible not to go toward the thing that would mean the end of me.

'I knew I couldn't set it up properly, and I accepted that as part of the piece. The failure of it. I realized I didn't need anything. He was the one who needed the outside world, I did not. My body felt like it was disappearing at the edges. I became theoretical,' she says. 'I remember asking myself, *Exactly what is the true nature of reality?* We spend our entire life refusing to believe that death is all any of us has waiting in the end. But there is not a single thing that can save us from it. Nothing. Not careers, not children, not art, not lovers, not family.' She sits back, blinking. 'But now what I see when I look at you' — her voice chokes — 'is everything I've missed.'

You feel her body cold against yours. She's shaking. Everyone has their own interpretation of what happened to her, even you. If her true intentions had been known, she would, as a mother, have surely been labeled a monster. But from the moment you die, you lose all rights to your own story. Nothing protects you. You have no privacy, no laws protecting you. Nothing belongs to you anymore, if it ever did. The key is having somone you trust agree to live longer. But even then. You have thought of her so much, and thought you had every part of her story figured out. Finally having your mother after wanting her your whole life, the feeling is intense, more total than you ever thought it would be. You can't move.

'I didn't have a death wish,' she says, her face very pale. 'It was the opposite.' She pauses, turning to look at you, her eyes welling. 'But I haven't been able to live with what this has meant for you.'

After what feels like a long time you say to her, 'If knowing someone makes them stay with you forever, not knowing someone can do the same thing.' Your whole life you have always tried to keep your emotions as still as possible, but everything is slipping out from under you. Her face is a few inches from yours, frozen in its beautiful youth. It's her eyes that have so much time in them. 'Your death didn't take you away,' you tell her, wiping the wet from your face. 'It only made you exist stronger in me.'

She hugs you. Both of you crying — you can't even see, your tears running hot and then cold. You are both quiet for so long. Some people never get what they want, you think. Or they get it but manage to keep it so briefly. You blink back tears and sit up facing her.

'I wonder how you could ever forgive me —' She is shaking, and her eyes are so large looking at you. 'I wonder if I had done it differently. If everything would have turned out better if —' she says, using her sleeve to wipe her face.

'Better how?'

You hear the elevator ding. Outside it's grown quiet. There are no shouts, no traffic, the street is deserted, though a short distance away are stars and wind and actors on stages still performing because the festival is twenty-four seven.

'I'm worried that time is running out,' you say, taking her hand. 'You can tell me anything you want in any order.'

'I could say the same to you.'

'Please,' you say.

'I'm so proud of you. I wish I hadn't used such crappy paper. I wish I'd been able to see my work through. I never made something that totally pleased me. As an artist you are lucky if you make one thing that sets you out in the sun.' She pauses. 'Every decision has its rewards, its costs. We agonize over the alternatives, because being human means to doubt.'

There is a beep from the Fitbit again.

'I've also come to realize that life is a complete joke if you don't serve the truth.' She pauses. 'No one really remembers work when you are gone. They only remember how you made them feel.' And then she says, looking directly at you, 'I would have given anything for five more minutes with you.'

Your eyes fill with tears. The kettle clicks off and you jump up to get it, wiping your eyes with your sleeve. You pour the boiling water and wrap the string of the teabag around the mug handle and add some sugar. More Keats. *Nothing ever becomes real till it is experienced.*

When you turn around, you are suddenly, utterly alone. The room is darker, damper than it had felt before. It seems to have less air. There is the thinnest scent — camphor, Noxzema maybe. Your stomach contracts to a sharp pain as though you might throw up, but you realize that you are crying, really sobbing, shaking with grief. You run around the room, frantically opening the closet and the bathroom doors. But there is no one there but you.

You don't know what to do. Your whole body is shaking. It's just you alone crying in your room, and you don't want to be alone. You are not sure what to do, so you turn on the TV. You flip through channels. Someone selling some old coin — 'a real showstopper' — on the shopping channel. Bronzed humans sweating and panting like athletes, which you realize after a moment is porn. *Mission: Impossible* is playing. Maybe you should watch it. It might calm you down. You like it when someone is really good at a task. You try to sip the tea, but it just tastes like shower water. You can't be in this room right now, so you throw the hotel robe over your sweatshirt and walk downstairs in the puffy white hotel slippers.

Outside the hotel, you are sitting on the steps, still shaking. You tighten the robe around you. The sky is inky and beautiful with thick low clouds, the Ferris wheel lights glittering in the distance. You hadn't even noticed him, but the night-desk receptionist says goodbye to a man who was vaping there in a black hoodie in the dark. Night Desk asks if you want a cigarette. Thank god people still smoke actual cigarettes. It's just you, Night Desk, and Karl Ove. You don't smoke but you say yes, calmly, trying not to give him any indication of basketcasery. You haven't smoked in years but are quickly getting the hang of it. You smoke two in a row.

Night Desk says finally, 'You in five-oh-four, then?'

You nod.

He ducks into the lobby and then comes back out onto the steps. 'Someone came round with this,' he says, handing you a quantum physics book with a note you will look at later. 'Tall bloke.' You place it in your pocket and look up at the sky. No stars, just beautiful blue-black air. You love a city night sky — it's so many colors at once.

'It's always darkest just before it goes totally black,' you say out loud.

Night Desk says, 'Who said that?'

'Me,' you say, blowing out smoke, 'and Chairman Mao. And Sylvia Plath. And season one, episode seven, of *The Bionic Woman*.'

There are some drunk Belarusians making a bit too much noise in the lobby, and he goes back inside.

You are thinking about your mother. All along you have thought about her, and she has always just been right there, in you. You feel what she felt. You are living what she didn't live. You want to write down the last thing she said, but you think you will remember it. You touch his book in your pocket.

I never did know when I had it good. I still don't.

Acknowledgments

Gratitude to the Canada Council for the Arts, and the Ontario Arts Council for generously supporting this work. To Carla Gilders, and endlessly to Sandra Webster for the writing space.

A thousand thank yous to all of the people who made this book possible, especially to Jane Finigan, for her early insights and support, and to Molly Slight and Deborah Sun De La Cruz — I am wildly grateful for your fierce brains, your faith, your brilliance.

To Emma McIntyre for early conversations. To Jill Connell and Claire Cameron for valuable feedback. Thank you to Claudia Dey for laser insights, and for everything on the page and off.

To Jason Pollan who I loved, who did not live long enough to draw every person in New York.

To Steve Sopinka, Amy Sopinka, Zoe McCready, and to Nick and Suzanne Sopinka for a lifetime of support.

Thank you to Lux, Soren, and Winter — true starlight. And forever, to JL.

To Ana Mendieta, Hannah Wilke, Ree Morton, Adrian Piper, Lee Lozano, Judy Chicago, Eleanor Antin, Carolee Schneemann, Valie Export, Martha Rosler, Suzy Lake, Miriam Schapiro, Helen Pashgian, Guerrilla Girls, Barbara Loden, Chantal Akerman, and Valerie Solanas — artists who worked outside the system to dismantle the system. This book is for them.